AIRSHIP 27 PRODUCTIONS

GUN GLORY
© 2015 R.A. Jones

Published by Airship 27 Productions
www.airship27.com
www.airship27hangar.com

Interior illustrations © 2015 Neil T. Foster
Cover illustration © 2015 Graham Hill

Editor: Ron Fortier
Associate Editor: Fred Adams Jr.
Marketing and Promotions Manager: Michael Vance
Production and design by Rob Davis.

ISBN-13: 978-0692370049 (Airship 27)
ISBN-10: 0692370048

Printed in the United States of America

10 9 8 7 6 5 4 3 2 1

R.A. Jones

CHAPTER 1

Jason Mankiller had no intention of taking another man's life that day. He'd only been in the town of Ft. Rogers, Texas, for a couple of hours. The only reason he was there, in this bustling community some forty miles to the west and north of Dallas, was because the farmer who'd given him a lift was headed there.

Like many others in America in this spring of 1874, Mankiller was without work. In the aftermath of the economic bust some were already calling the Panic of 1873, nearly one man in every three was in the same situation.

Actually, until a few days ago he had been employed, by a small rancher. Then the owner of the spread announced he'd gone belly up. The little he'd make from selling his land and cattle would cover most of his debts, but leave nothing to pay his few hands. So they were all cast adrift.

And in Mankiller's case, afoot as well; he hadn't owned either the horse or saddle he'd been using. He'd walked most of the distance to Ft. Rogers, until he accepted the charitable offer of a ride for the last ten miles.

Now he was slowly wandering down Front Street, known to the locals as Tiger Town, home to many of the town's ample number of saloons. As he came to each one, he'd paused long enough to glance inside, then moved on.

He now found himself in front of an establishment called the Last Stand. Stepping up to the batwing doors at its entrance, he again paused to scan the inside.

This time, he saw what he had been looking for.

He pushed smoothly through the swinging doors, only to quickly slide to one side as he did. This removed him from being backlit by sunshine in the doorway. He stayed pressed against the wall, allowing his eyes time to adjust to the dimmer light within.

Better to be wary than to be dead, he thought.

Mankiller was a tall and lean man; he'd stopped growing upward just north of six feet by the time he was sixteen, and his wiry frame was leathery muscle obtained by hard work when he could get it.

Luckily, he had no aversion to labor of all sorts. In his day he'd been a soldier, a bullwhacker, a stagecoach shotgun rider, muleskinner, a hunter for the Army and the railroad, even a store clerk.

Mostly, though, he'd worked cattle, both in the States and below the border, where he'd picked up a tolerable command of the Spanish language.

His grandmother on his mother's side had been a full-blood Kiowa Indian. The only overt signs of this part of his heritage came in the form of his thick black hair and high, prominent cheekbones. His skin was dark, but no more so than that of any man who spent more time in the sun than out.

His eyes, however, were a pale and icy blue, with an intensity that could seem to bore right through a man to peer into his very soul.

He wore a black felt hat with a flat crown and brim. A concho style hatband of tooled tin circled it. Around his neck was another indicator of his Native origins: a choker necklace made of bone and shell.

His light gray shirt was tucked into the waist of his black trousers. Equally black leather leggings ran from just below his knees nearly to the floor; each was tied around his leg at the top with leather thongs.

Being that as of late he had as often to walk as to ride, he wore low-heeled boots. His one nod to affectation came in the form of the large-roweled, silver Mexican styled spurs strapped to the boots.

He wore a well cared for .44 Colt pistol in a cross-draw holster that rested on his left thigh.

A sheath on the right side of the gunbelt held a razor sharp skinning knife with a six-inch blade. A few long strands of hair dangled from the bottom tip of the sheath. Among the legends that would grow around him was the one claiming this hair to be from the scalp he had taken from a Comanche war chief after killing him with his bare hands.

In truth, they were only decorative strands taken from the mane of a horse.

Not that he ever bothered to correct anybody who thought otherwise.

His eyes now grown accustomed to the dust-filtered light of the saloon, Mankiller made his way to the bar, which ran down most of one side of the place.

Behind the bar stood a heavyset man of middle years. With one finger he brushed at the edges of a drooping moustache. The other hand held a damp rag, with which he swiped at the bar's surface.

An easy smile lifted the corners of the moustache as he saw Mankiller sidle up to the bar, and he slid down to serve him.

"Howdy," he said by way of greeting. "I'm Sam Dobbins, and I run this place. What can I do for ya?"

Mankiller motioned toward the end of the bar farthest from the entrance. Next to it sat a small table. Set out atop it were various cuts of meat, sliced bread and onions. In a large glass jar, pickled eggs floated.

"What's a fella have to do to get a run at your lunch spread?" Mankiller asked.

"That's simple enough, friend. All you have to do is buy a beer and you can help yourself to the sandwich fixin's."

"And how much might a beer be?"

"A nickel a glass."

"That sounds fair," the drifter replied, fishing a nickel from his right pants pocket and sliding it toward the bartender.

He wasn't about to tell the man that this represented the totality of his monetary funds. He'd had a dollar earlier, but had felt obligated to give it to the farmer who had provided him with his transport into town.

Dobbins pocketed the proffered nickel without comment, then filled a short mug from the nearest keg. Swiping the brew's foamy head off with the practiced swipe of a small wooden paddle, he pushed it toward Mankiller.

As he walked toward the lunch table, the unemployed drifter took a small sip of his beer. It felt good going down; this saloon must have access to ice, he thought, for it was chilly on his throat rather than lukewarm.

He set the mug down on the table and picked up a chipped but clean plate, placing two slices of bread side by side on it. His stomach clenched like a fist and growled with anticipation; his tongue flicked across his lips as he peered over the spread.

Embarrassed lest anyone realize that he had eaten nothing in nearly three days, and then no more than a few strips of tough jerky, he restrained himself to one slice of beef and one of ham, and an egg he deftly fished out of its jar.

Retrieving his beer, he turned from the table, only to bump shoulders with a man who was walking brusquely toward the back of the saloon. A few drops of beer splattered out of Mankiller's mug.

"Beg pardon, mister," he said.

"Watch where yer goin'," the man snarled, turning toward him. He was older than Mankiller, not as tall but broader. He hadn't shaved in days and his mouth seemed to curl in a permanent sneer. His right hand hovered near the gun worn low on his hip.

"No offense intended," Mankiller said, the softness of his voice belying the menace a smarter man would have detected in it.

"Like hell!" the unshaven man barked. He slapped out with one hand, knocking both plate and glass out of Jason's hands.

Mankiller stared down at the floor. The plate had broken on contact, the components of the sandwich strewn about in puddles of beer, liquor, tobacco juice and everything the bar's patrons had brought in from outside on the bottoms of their boots. The food had been rendered totally inedible.

The solitary pickled egg rolled a ways across the floor before being flattened underfoot by an unnoticing passerby.

Mankiller raised his gaze to see the unshaven stranger was actually giggling softly, like a schoolboy, so pleased with himself was he.

The giggling stopped when the back of Mankiller's hand slapped him across the mouth hard enough to send him staggering back a few steps, though really more from surprise than from the force of the blow.

"No!" the bartender shouted, racing toward the end of the bar where the two men stood.

With no warning, the unshaven man went for his gun.

In the years to come, the number of men who would claim to have seen what happened next would grow to such that it would have taken several saloons the size of the Last Stand to have held them all.

The few who truly were there all agreed on the specifics. To them it seemed almost as if Jason Mankiller's Colt had simply disappeared from its holster, magically appearing the next second in his extended right hand, so fast had been his draw.

While pivoting into a sideways stance to limit his own profile as a target, he snapped off his first shot. Its heavy slug was boring through the center of the unshaved man's chest while his own pistol had barely cleared leather. The shock of the bullet's blow caused his entire body to tremble even as he struggled to raise his gun to take a shot of his own.

Taking a step forward, Mankiller cocked his pistol and coolly fired again. This time, the lead burrowed into the center of his opponent's head.

The man's eyes rolled upward. A finger twitched just enough to finally fire his own weapon, the slug digging harmlessly into the floor. His body stiffened as he pitched over backwards, and he was dead by the time he hit the boards.

Ignoring the dead man, Mankiller spun around and dropped into a slight crouch, cocking his Colt again. His eyes swiftly scanned the room to see if anyone else, possibly a friend of his victim, might be wanting to make a play against him. None did.

He swiveled toward the bartender who had yelled out before the gunplay began. Sam Dobbins was standing stock still, both hands up and open to show he was unarmed.

Reasonably sure the danger was passed, Mankiller walked over to kneel beside the corpse. He slid a bullet from the man's gunbelt; seeing that it too was a .44 caliber, he withdrew a second shell. Flipping open the loading gate of his own weapon, he ejected the two spent shells, replacing them with those taken from the dead man.

He then casually rifled through the man's pockets. From one, he withdrew a small wad of bills. He shoved them back into the pocket. From another, he extracted a few coins; removing one, he replaced the rest.

"Does anyone begrudge me this?" he asked, loud enough to be heard throughout the saloon. He was holding up a nickel.

No word being spoken against him, he turned and walked to the bar, where Sam Dobbins now stood with his hands palms down on its top.

"You have any problem with what just happened?" Jason asked him.

"Not a bit," Sam assured him. "One thing I do want ya to know, son. The only reason I yelled out was to try to warn you off, that's all. I thought sure you was about to get yourself killed."

"Why's that?"

"I guess you don't know it, but that fella you laid out is Zeb McClure. He's poison mean, tough as old boot leather and would steal the gold teeth from his own mamma's mouth. Not bad with a gun, either. He'd as soon kill ya as give ya the time of day. Till today, there's been few would brace him, and none who walked away if they did."

"There's always a first time."

"I reckon."

"I appreciate your concern, Mr. Dobbins."

"Call me Sam."

"Well, Sam," Mankiller said softly, setting the nickel down in front of the still shaken barkeep, "would it be acceptable to you if I was to take another *pasear* at your lunch table?"

Dobbins was almost too surprised to speak.

"Why, sure," he said at last. "But there's no need for you to pay again. It wasn't your fault, what happened to your first plate."

"It weren't your fault either. So I'd feel better if you took the money."

Dobbins nodded and pocketed the nickel.

"And do you reckon it'd be all right if I got a cup of coffee to go with my sandwich this time?"

"That'd be fine, son. I just brewed a fresh pot for myself. And, uh..." Dobbins leaned forward and lowered his voice. "I noticed you kinda skimped on yourself the first time around. That wasn't much of a sandwich you made. Load it up proper this time."

"I'll do that."

Mankiller returned to the lunch table and followed the barkeep's suggestion. This time, he stacked slices of beef, ham and chicken two inches thick on one slice of bread, then took the time to slather some mustard on the other.

There was a plate of sliced onions set out; they were a mite small and green, as early in the year as it was, but he still placed a good, thick slice of one on his sandwich. He scooped not one but three pickled eggs out of their jar.

He carried his more substantial meal to a table that was away from the doors and windows, one placed so he could sit with his back to the wall. By the time he took his seat, Sam Dobbins was already there to place a tin cup of coffee before him.

For years, Jason had not allowed himself to take up the use of either hard spirits or tobacco; he had seen too many times what the craving for either could do to a man. He could live just fine without coffee too, and had many a time, but he did enjoy a cup of the brew when the right occasion presented itself.

Before commencing to eat, he let his eyes again travel around the room. Even though there was a dead body still sprawled out on the floor, most of the men therein were ignoring both it and Jason, or at least pretending to. The excitement over, their interest had returned to their drinks.

Some ways off to his right, a lone man sat playing solitaire, and Mankiller's eyes lit on him. Young, with neatly trimmed, ash-blond hair, the man was dressed impeccably in a light gray suit, a blue tie around the starched collar of his bone white shirt. He had the look and bearing of a professional gambler.

His eyes met those of Mankiller, and he smiled warmly. He lifted a shot glass in a toasting motion directed at Jason, took a small sip of the golden liquor within, then returned his attention to his cards.

Only now did Mankiller feel it was safe to get on with his meal. He forced himself to take small bites and chew slowly, savoring the flavors and giving no sign of how strong was the urge to wolf the food down ravenously.

His pride was just strong enough to temper his appetite.

He stopped in mid-chew when he saw a new figure enter through the saloon's batwing doors. Mankiller had little doubt this man was what passed for the law in Ft. Rogers; he'd probably gotten word of the killing not long after the last shot was fired.

He was a man late in middle age, well-built but going to paunch around the middle. He'd probably been a regular ring-tailed bobcat in his day, but he'd left that behind.

Mankiller had seen his kind before; tired and cynical, marking time until he could reach an age when he could retire on whatever small pension the town could provide. Not a bad man, just too worn down and out to be overly good.

The marshal stopped at the bar to talk to Sam Dobbins, wordlessly and naturally accepting the free drink the barkeep slid toward him. When he finished the drink, he moved over to give the corpse a perfunctory examination.

Sighing and hitching up his belt slightly, he then turned and began to walk slowly toward the table where Mankiller sat. The drifter had already slid his right hand below the top of the table, resting it lightly on the butt of his pistol while continuing to eat using only his left hand.

He'd kept his head down slightly since the lawman entered the saloon, but his eyes were raised to see all that transpired. As the marshal drew closer, he lifted his head up so as to look the man in the eye.

"Sweet jeezus!" the marshal exclaimed aloud as he got his first clean look at the drifter's face. His eyes widened in recognition and he involuntarily recoiled at the sight.

"You're the man who cries *blood*!"

CHAPTER 2

"It is well that war is so terrible; we should grow too fond of it."
-Robert E. Lee-

The legend began to take shape on Thursday, July 2, of 1863, just a few miles south and east of the sleepy Pennsylvania town of Gettysburg.

General George Meade had replaced Major-General Joseph Hooker as commander of the Union Army of the Potomac just three days before having to face the full force of General Robert E. Lee's Confederate Army of Northern Virginia.

It was like being pulled out of Sunday school and thrown into hell.

Late in the afternoon of that Thursday, the second day of this pivotal confrontation, the Union's XII Army Corps under the command of Major-General Henry Slocum had arrived on site after marching up the Baltimore Pike.

Among Slocum's troops was a fresh-faced boy of eighteen named Jason Mankiller, about to face his first major action.

Part of XII Army's Second Division, led by Brigadier General John Geary, Mankiller was an infantryman in Company C of the First Brigade, under Colonel Charles Candy.

Just a few weeks earlier, the boy had been living on a farm in eastern Ohio.

Despite his youth, he and all his comrades were fully aware of the significance of this battle, which had already been raging for over twenty-four hours. The seat of the precarious Federal government, Washington D.C., lay only seventy-five miles to the southeast of the battlefield. A Confederate victory here would leave the way to Washington free and clear for Lee's army.

The previous day's fighting had resulted in combined casualties of some twelve-thousand men. The number of dead and wounded was fairly evenly divided between the opposing sides, but most rumors racing through the ranks said that Bobby Lee's Rebs had enjoyed the better of the encounter, forcing the Union troops to retreat before them up to Cemetery Hill.

The bulk of Slocum's XII Corps had been ordered up to form a right flank to the main Union forces, spreading out from Culp's Hill to just south of Spangler's Spring.

But the men of Company C were given a special assignment. Under the command of Captain Wallace Bedford, they were ordered to take up position on a promontory called Wolf's Hill, located just over a mile to the east of Slocum's main line. They were to use the height to enable them to scout the area and send back reports on enemy movements to Slocum.

They never got the chance.

The company of Union soldiers had barely reached the heights when a contingency of Confederate soldiers, the II Corps under Lieutenant-General Richard Ewell swung down from the north to engage Slocum's command. In doing so, the Rebels effectively cut off the men on Wolf's Hill from their main body.

Pressed flat to the ground, Private Mankiller still managed to snake forward enough to gaze down upon the nearby Confederate force. So close were they that he was able to spy General Ewell himself, riding up and down the line.

There was no mistaking the man, for Mankiller could see he had but one leg. His left one had been lost at the battle of Second Bull Run. Yet still he commanded, though he now had to be lifted up onto his horse by his men and strapped into the saddle.

A heavy hand fell on Mankiller's shoulder, and he turned to look into the weather-beaten face of Sergeant Peter Downing. The veteran noncom, who had fought in the war against the Mexicans, had taken a liking to young Mankiller, in part because the farm boy had sense enough to listen to him and follow his orders without complaint.

"Back away," he whispered to the private. "If you're spotted, we all become targets."

Mankiller nodded and slithered backwards silently. The many hunting trips he'd made with his father had taught him both the need and the ability to move with stealth.

Atop the hill, the men of Company C had been employed in a rough circle. Captain Bedford was down on one knee in the center of the circle and now spoke just loudly enough for all to hear him.

"Just keep your heads down, men, and everything should be fine. The Rebs have no idea we're here, and therefore have no reason to attack.

"We've just got to be patient. When the time comes, we'll find a way to get into the fight.

"Carry on."

Sergeant Downing grunted and shucked off his backpack. From it he removed a small trench tool and began to quietly dig at the earth.

"What're you doing, Sarge?" Mankiller asked.

"I don't have as much faith in Johnny Reb's ignorance as the captain does. There's not a whole lotta cover up here, so I'm making me some."

Mankiller nodded and, without further question, emulated his sergeant. As the two of them scratched at the dirt, a couple of soldiers nearby chuckled and shook their heads.

Both men ignored them and kept digging.

When they had excavated a shallow trench, they slid into it after piling some of the dirt in front of it like a short breastwork. Then, like all the others in the company, they simply waited.

Throughout the rest of the day, they could clearly hear the sounds of battle to the west: the roar of cannons, the incessant popping of firearms, even the occasional screams of men and horses.

"Bad as it sounds," Mankiller commented at one point, "I think I'd rather be out there than up here." He took a short sip from his canteen.

"I know what you mean, boy," the sergeant replied. "Sometimes, just sitting and waiting can be the hardest thing of all."

"To be honest, Sarge, I was thinking more like if you was in the middle of fighting, you wouldn't have time to think so much about being afraid."

The veteran noncom chuckled. "Ain't nuthin' wrong with being scared, private, nor nuthin' ta be ashamed of. Fear's one of the things helps keep ya alive, long as ya don't let it paralyze ya."

"How do you keep that from happening?"

"I'm not really sure. Not everybody can do it. I think you got plenty o' sand in ya, though; so when the time comes, you'll do just fine."

"I hope you're right, Sarge."

"I usually am, boy," Downing replied, smiling grimly.

As dusk at last approached, a lieutenant who'd been making his way around the circle of men stuck his head down into their trench.

"You men be ready," he said softly. "Captain Bedford's decided that, come full dark, we're getting off this hill.

"We'll descend on the far side, head south a ways, then west. See if we can't get around the Rebel lines and hook back up with the rest of the corps."

"We'll be ready, sir," Sergeant Downing replied. The noncom briefly left the shelter of the trench to pass along instructions to the other members of his squad. He then slid back into his shelter with Jason, and they waited.

As full dark at last blanketed the hill, young Mankiller felt the palms of his hands begin to sweat more profusely. He rubbed them briskly on the legs of his pants. Orders were being whispered in the dark, and he could hear men shuffling about. He and Sergeant Downing left their trench to join the others.

He had barely risen to his feet when another, unfamiliar sound came to his ear. It was an almost melodic hum that seemed to be growing louder.

"Back in the hole!" Sergeant Downing shouted, giving him a shove. "Everybody take cover!" he yelled loudly, before diving back into the trench beside Mankiller.

The next instant, a shell burst in the midst of the Union troops, lighting the night and emitting a great roar.

"What the hell is that, Sarge?" Mankiller almost screamed.

"A *Whistling Dick*," the noncom replied. "Reb cannon. Damned thing can throw an eighteen pound shell."

"But how'd they know to shell us?"

"Obviously, some of us wasn't as well hid as we thought. And now we got no place to go."

Again Jason heard the whistle, and again lightning was pulled from the sky. From that point, the explosive shells seemed to rain down upon them like hailstones.

As relatively exposed as they were, the small Union force was blasted to shreds. Mankiller pressed himself against one side of the trench. His knees were pulled up to his chest and he pressed his hands as tightly as possible over his ears; not so much because of the explosions but rather from a vain attempt to blot out the shrieks of his comrades-in-arms.

Screams louder than the whistles of the incoming shells pierced the night. Even from his hole he could see bodies, more often, merely pieces of bodies, flying in all directions, leaving sprays of blood and other matter in their wake.

Dirt, grass and debris thrown up by the explosions then drifted back down upon the hilltop. The hill shook as if a legion of giants was marching across it.

Not far from where young Mankiller cowered, a whistling shell struck a cottonwood tree square on, shattering its trunk and sending pieces of wood flying like shrapnel in all directions.

One such splinter slid along Mankiller's left eyebrow. Only a glancing blow, it still elicited a yelp from the private. There was more surprise than pain, though he could feel warm blood begin to trickle down the side of his face.

A low groan coming from the opposite side of the trench caught his attention and made him forget his own slight pain. Sergeant Downing was sitting with legs sprawled, staring down at his middle.

Mankiller followed the noncom's gaze. Bile rose in his throat as he saw a large piece of wood, thick as a man's wrist, protruding from Downing's stomach.

Scampering on hands and knees, Mankiller hurried across the trench. Part of his brain registered that the shelling had stopped for the moment, though his ears still rang.

Sergeant Downing began to slide over sideways. Mankiller caught him, holding him up by cradling him in his arms.

"What do I do, Sarge?" he pleaded. "Tell me what to do!"

He could barely see the sergeant's eyes, for his sockets appeared to be filling with dark red fluid. Downing tried to speak, but all that emerged from his mouth were bubbling gouts of blood. His legs jerked, then jerked again.

Then he died.

Hand trembling, Mankiller reached up and closed Downing's eyes. He gently laid the noncom over on his side.

The Rebel cannons were still silent, so Mankiller risked raising his head slightly over the rim of his trench, looking inward around the top of the hill.

"Is anybody there?" he hissed.

The only response he could hear were the groans of the wounded and the hellish screams of the soon to be dead.

Even in the darkness, he could see the hilltop had been largely stripped of its foliage. Craters pocked the ground. There hadn't been time yet for the bodies to start to stink, but still the air was pungent with the mixed odors of cordite, sweat and human waste.

And the whistling started again.

Crying out in fear, the young man dropped back into the trench. Fresh shells began to pound down on the hilltop. Lack of same was obviously not a problem for the Rebels.

Part of one wall of the trench caved in, partly burying Mankiller. He pulled loose from its grip before the dirt could fully settle.

He fell over, finding himself nearly face-to-face with the late Sergeant Downing. Acting in desperation, with no clear thought, he tugged at the body, rolling it over until it lay heavily atop him.

And still the shells poured down on Wolf's Hill, like the wrath of God. For hours that seemed like years the artillery barrage threatened to bring the entire hill crumbling down. Shock waves tore through even the earth, till the young private was certain his eardrums would surely burst.

The noise and the fear wouldn't stop. Lying petrified under the scant shelter of a corpse, Jason Mankiller's resolve was blown away and he screamed. He knew he screamed.

He just couldn't hear it.

And the shells kept falling.

CHAPTER 3

The sun had barely risen on the third day of Gettysburg when the Confederate infantrymen began to trudge cautiously up the western slop of Wolf's Hill.

The day was already humid and warm, on its way to nearly ninety degrees, but most of the sweat that beaded their brows came from fear. Each man clutched his musket tightly, anticipating possible attack from the heights above.

They were just over halfway up when they began to spot body parts.

An arm here. A leg there. A shoe with a foot still in it.

All in tatters of the blue uniform of the North.

But no shots greeted them, and slowly they began to relax.

"I tell ya, boys," said the lieutenant leading the way, "after ol' Whistling Dick got through with this here hill, I'd be surprised if we find a groundhog still alive up there."

A couple of his men chuckled nervously.

As they drew close to the top of the hill, they spied a nearly intact body lying facedown in their path. His tunic and the flesh beneath it had been shredded as if by the lashing of a bullwhip.

One of the Rebs knelt beside the body and rolled it over. He could see sergeant's stripes on one sleeve of the man's tunic. A large piece of wood, thick as a man's wrist, protruded from his belly.

Still alert, the gray-clad soldiers at last topped the rim of the hill.

It was as they expected. Shattered trees. Fallen limbs and branches. Craters of varying sizes and depth dotting the ground. Some of the debris had caught on fire, sending up lazy plumes of smoke that seemed even darker against the glow of the rising sun.

And bodies. And remnants of bodies.

None of them moving.

Even those veterans who had now been at war for two years were awed by the carnage. Those who had been farmers, who thought of the earth as a living thing, now knew that even the land could die.

Some had already turned to begin the trek back down Wolf's Hill when that land began to move.

From beneath what the Rebels had assumed was merely a loose pile of fallen tree branches, young Jason Mankiller, the only Union soldier still alive atop that mound of death, burst upward from the foxhole right in front of them.

He presented a most fearsome image. He screamed madly at the top of his lungs. The wound to his brow had long since stopped bleeding, but thin rivulets of rusty ochre that had coagulated and frozen in place on his left cheek were still visible, looking like tears of blood.

In each hand he held a pistol, taken from the uncomplaining bodies of slain officers. They were Colt's Model 1850, the one most favored among officers, in .44 caliber and holding six shells apiece.

The sudden appearance of this seemingly mad apparition rising from the pit froze the Reb soldiers in their tracks for the span of several heartbeats.

That was all the time Mankiller needed to start blasting away at them with both guns, laying down a withering fire. One of the first to fall was the lieutenant in charge of the gray line.

He was not the last; every bullet fired by Mankiller found its mark with unnatural accuracy, and gray-clad corpses began to pile up before him. Most never even had time to try to return fire.

When both pistols clicked on empty chambers, Jason tossed them aside. He had also filled his trench with all the workable muskets and rifles he had been able to retrieve after the shelling had stopped, and he now snatched up two of them: Springfield Model 1861 rifles.

He fired one with each hand, with the same ease and accuracy as he had the pistols. Flinging them away, he grabbed up two more, leaping now out of the trench and charging forward.

A minie ball tugged at his sleeve, but he ignored it, killing the man who had fired it with a shot to the head. He dropped the empty rifle, raised the other to his shoulder and fired pointblank at another Reb, throwing him over the rim of the hill and into those still standing below.

Mankiller swung the rifle like a club. Its metal barrel clanged dully as it met and shattered a Rebel skull.

The blue-clad killer had reached the body of the fallen Rebel lieutenant, and he knelt to snatch the officer's pistol from his lifeless fingers.

Some of the Confederates who lived to tell the tale of Wolf's Hill would go to their graves believing that it had not been a mere man they had encountered that day, but rather some demon their own cannons had summoned up from the depths of perdition, bringing with him fire and death.

Mankiller thumbed back the hammer of his purloined pistol and fired. Another soldier fell before him. Then another.

Leaderless, some already beginning to fear more for their immortal souls than for their lives, the remaining Rebels turned and began to flee back down the hill.

Even this didn't save some of them. To the crazed Jason Mankiller, there was no difference between an enemy's front and his back. He continued blasting away with his pistol. Soldiers fell and tumbled forward, their bodies speeding on the retreat of their comrades.

More than one would later swear they heard the raging killer atop the hill *laughing* as they fled for safety.

Reaching the bottom of the slope, a few of the Rebel lads dared to look back before continuing to race back toward their main line.

At the rim of Wolf's Hill, they could still see the wild man who cried blood. He waved a rifle above his head, continuing to scream wordlessly, seeming to challenge them to try again to scale the heights that he had claimed as his own.

The challenge would go unanswered.

CHAPTER 4

Brigadier General George Armstrong Custer had also been very busy on that final day at Gettysburg.

The most feared of the many able Confederate cavalry commanders, General J.E.B. Stuart, had started the action by launching an attack against Brigadier General David Gregg's cavalry division near the Union's right flank.

Fearing that his boys would not be able to stand alone against Stuart's assault, Gregg had requested reinforcements from a brigade of Michigan cavalry under the command of Custer.

Though not of Gregg's division, Custer eagerly accepted the challenge; he was unable to resist the urge to pit his men, and by extension himself, against the vaunted Stuart.

Leading the 7th Michigan and other Union forces against Confederate Brigadier Generals Fitzhugh Lee and Wade Hampton, Custer engaged in charge after charge, with little ground lost or gained by either side.

Finally, Stuart himself led one final surge, only to be met on three sides by Custer's 1st Michigan and elements of Gregg's division. This counterattack forced Stuart to concede the day and leave the field to the Union forces.

Flushed with victory, Custer rode down the front line of his troops, waving in acknowledgement to their cheers. At twenty-three years of age, barely out of West Point, Custer was the youngest brigadier general in the Army of the Potomac; some had taken to calling him "*the boy general.*"

He barely made it to this final battle, having nearly lost his life on the preceding day. During a battle fought at the village of Hunterstown, four miles from Gettysburg proper, the young officer's horse had been shot out from under him, its body pinning him to the ground.

Seeing the helpless Union officer, an eager Rebel soldier raced toward him, saber drawn and at the ready. At the last second, the attacker was himself shot and killed.

The boy general had been saved by a lowly private in his company. This would be perhaps the first, but not the last time men would speak of "Custer's luck."

By the time the war ground to a halt, Custer would have nearly a dozen horses shot from under him, while suffering only one wound himself.

With the battle against Stuart ended, Custer turned to the west, in search of more action. He and a contingent of the 1st Michigan emerged from a stand of trees to find themselves closer to Wolf's Hill.

He pulled up to survey the scene. A tight smile tugged at the corners of his mouth as he heard a trooper behind him retch. By this time, late on the final day of the battle, the bodies of thousands of men and hundreds of horses and farm animals had been lying exposed to the sun long enough to make the air smell like the foulest of charnel houses. It would grow worse in the days to come. Even Custer pulled the distinctive red neckerchief he liked to wear up to cover his nose and mouth. It did little good.

His eyes narrowed with curiosity. He could see a few Union soldiers dotting the slopes of Wolf's Hill, but even more were simply milling around at its base. Lightly putting the spurs to his mount's flanks, he trotted over to investigate.

Seeing his approach, a captain separated himself from his troops and moved to meet Custer. Though dirty and disheveled, clearly weary, he snapped a smart salute to his superior officer, and it was returned.

"What's going on here, Captain?" Custer inquired, pulling his kerchief down from over his mouth.

"There's the damnedest thing goin' on up top o' this hill, General," the captain replied. "If I hadn't seen it with my own eyes, I don't think I'd have believed it."

"Just what might that be, Captain?"

"Words can't do it justice, sir; at least, no words that I know. I swear, in all my born days, I never seen anything like it. You'd just have to see it for yourself."

"Then lead on," Custer ordered, motioning toward the top of the hill. "Let's see if I'm as easily impressed as you are."

The captain took hold of Custer's horse's bridle and set off up the slope. Some of the soldiers dotting the rise, upon seeing the general, jumped to their feet and came to attention. Most were too tired to bother, nor did Custer blame them. They'd all fought long and hard these last three days, and shouldn't be expected to stand on ceremony.

Guns could still be heard booming and popping off to the west, where

"What's going on here, Captain?"

the last elements of Pickett's doomed charges against the main Union lines were being repulsed in the action that would end this horrific battle.

By the time the smoke cleared from Gettysburg, the two sides would have seen nearly fifty-thousand men killed or wounded, and the tide of the war would have begun to turn inexorably against the Confederates.

No one knew that at the moment, least of all Custer. But as he now topped the rim of Wolf's Hill and laid eyes on what lay just beyond it, the full horror of the conflict pressed itself in upon him.

"Dear Lord," he muttered softly, the closest he usually came to actually swearing.

No action he ever had or ever would encounter could have compared to the sight now spread out before him.

Jason Mankiller was seated near the upper rim of Wolf's Hill, though not on the ground. He had taken the bodies of every dead Confederate soldier who had fallen before him, dragged them to one spot, then carefully arranged them in a pile that grotesquely resembled a throne of gray, streaked with red,

He was perched atop this obscene stack of corpses, staring straight ahead as if oblivious to the gaping Union soldiers standing nearby.

He held a pistol in each hand, with a third tucked into his belt. Loaded long guns leaned against his throne within easy reach.

Custer's horse snorted and jumped slightly at a muffled pop to one side. Custer turned to see the familiar cloud of smoke coming from a photographer's flash pan.

He likewise recognized the man taking the photograph. His name was Leslie Bellows, and he was one of several newsmen on hand to cover the battle.

His work appeared primarily in *Harper's Weekly*, though he freelanced for some newspapers as well, and he was known for the sensationalistic slant he gave his accounts. Still, the public was greatly fond of the words he put to paper; it was this popularity that often prompted even high-ranking officers to grant him exclusive interviews.

Custer himself was a favorite subject of the man, and frequently fed him stories. The resulting exposure, the general thought, could only abet the aims of an ambitious young officer.

The magazines and papers of the day lacked the technology to clearly reproduce photographs, but Bellows was also an accomplished artist and his battlefield sketches were widely disseminated.

The drawings sent with his dispatches from Gettysburg would bring him immediate pay and acclaim. But the photographs he took, especially *this* series of photographs, would make him close to famous and generate a substantial income for years to come as he continued to sell prints of them.

News publications were rapaciously eager to receive the fodder that was fed by his like, particularly as concerned a major battle such as this.

For the first time in American warfare, technological advances such as the telegraph and railroads allowed for news to be printed within a few hours of its happening.

By July 6, the *New York Herald* would fasten the banner headline "The Great Victory" over its coverage of Gettysburg.

So fierce was the competition for news that such niceties as truth were sometimes hedged if not completely discarded. The resulting stories sometimes read more like melodrama than journalism.

But they sold papers. And the works of Leslie Bellows sold more than most.

As Bellows now came out from under the black shroud at the back of his bulky camera, he spied Custer watching him.

"Evening, General," he called cheerfully, smiling and waving his free hand.

Custer nodded and brought a finger up to the brim of his hat in acknowledgment.

Slowly, so as not to provoke a violent reaction, Custer directed his horse forward, stopping directly in front of Mankiller. The private didn't move, didn't react to the officer's presence in any way. Up close like this, Custer could see the cracked and dried streaks of blood on the private's left cheek.

"Are you all right, son?" Custer asked in a soft, paternalistic tone, even though he was only a few years older than the enlisted man.

At this, Mankiller finally looked up at him.

"A sight better than these Rebs I'm sittin' on, General," Mankiller replied. He also gave Custer a sly wink, unseen by anyone else. Custer smiled.

"Say, General," Leslie Bellows said, rushing up to stand beside Custer. "Would you mind if I get a picture of you and this stalwart lad together?" The sharp newsman knew that the image-conscious boy general seldom if ever passed up the opportunity to be photographed.

"Is that all right with you?" Custer asked Mankiller.

The private gave him a curt nod. Custer dismounted, holding his horse's reins as he moved to stand close to Mankiller.

Bellows eagerly raced back to his camera. Sighting through the viewfinder of his camera, he couldn't suppress a smile. Even Custer's horse was media savvy, he thought; it stood perfectly still as if knowing this was required lest it appear blurred in the finished photo.

As soon as the flashing pop and puff of smoke from the camera indicated the photo had been taken, Custer again turned to Mankiller, saluting him.

"At ease, private," he said. "Your work is done for today."

Jason let both pistols drop from his hands, then returned the salute.

Leslie Bellows was hurrying upward with pencil and notebook in hand as Custer remounted and turned away from the scene. Near the rim of the hill, the captain who had escorted him up was still standing, waiting expectantly.

"Walk with me," Custer said to him, and the two of them made their way down to the base of Wolf's Hill.

Along the way, the captain gave Custer an account, as best he could, of what had happened atop the hill, including the babblings of Reb prisoners about a demon who cried blood and shot with deadly accuracy.

"Captain," Custer said, motioning back the way they had come, "when all this folderol is over, I want that man sent to my unit. I'll see to it that all the proper transfer papers and orders are completed."

"Are you sure about that, sir?" the captain said skeptically. "I mean… well, hell, sir…seems to me that boy up there's a mite touched in the head."

In response, Custer threw his head back and laughed.

"Captain, you give me a hundred men just as crazy as him…and I'll be celebrating Christmas in Richmond!"

CHAPTER 5

Jason Mankiller awoke with a jolt, bolting upright. Doing so sent a sharp crackle of pain leaping from one side of his skull to the other. He squeezed his eyes shut, pressing the palms of his hands against the sides of his head. He moaned as his belly churned, threatening to throw out its contents.

When the pain in his head subsided to a dull roar and the beast in his belly calmed, he again risked opening his eyes. He was in a small, unfamiliar room. The curtains were drawn over the single window, but enough light insinuated itself around the edges to tell him it was full day outside.

But his last memory was of nighttime. He'd somehow ended up in bed, though how and when he couldn't recall. Somehow, all of his clothes had been shed before he ended up between the sheets, but he neither knew precisely where he was nor how he got there.

The mattress rolled slightly under him, and he swiveled to the side to see that he was not the only occupant of the bed. A pretty girl with raspberry colored hair, as naked as was he, was lying belly down beside him, apparently still dead to the world. As he watched her, she moaned slightly and smiled contentedly.

He slowly lowered his head back on his pillow and lay staring up at the ceiling as memory of the previous evening's doings began to return unbidden.

It was only two weeks since the mayhem of Gettysburg. His new commander, General Custer, had granted his men a brief leave in Philadelphia. Several of Jason's new compatriots had taken it upon themselves to see to it that the farm boy enjoyed every pleasure that the city had to offer.

Mostly, that consisted of bar crawling from one end of Philly to the other.

Though he was young, Jason wasn't entirely a babe in the woods; he'd drunk his share of corn squeezin's along with his pa. But his newfound buddies had plied him with so many varieties of Who-Hit-John, in such copious quantities, that he was three sheets to the wind well before midnight.

At some point in the evening, the boisterous party had been joined by Leslie Bellows, the newspaperman who was trying his best to make Mankiller into a hero of epic proportions. He'd had no trouble at all selling stories of both the boy and General Custer to the *Philadelphia Inquirer*, which had headlined one of his stories coming out of Gettysburg: "Victory! Waterloo Eclipsed!"

Bellows' lurid and exaggerated account of what had transpired atop Wolf's Hill, mostly fabricated by himself, had fired the public imagination. He saw this evening as a possible opportunity to find even more fodder for his florid pen.

If Mankiller's fellow soldiers seemed at any point to be slowing down, Bellows would pick up the slack, buying Jason many a drink that night and matching him shot for shot.

Jason was blissfully ignorant at that point as to just how thoroughly Bellows had latched onto and milked the image of Mankiller as a man who cried blood. In the newsman's accounts, the boy literally shed tears of blood, and did so at the end of every battle, as if he embodied the sorrow of an entire country amidst the turmoil of a war that pitted brother against brother in a conflict that would determine the fate of a nation.

To hear Bellows tell it, the boy from Ohio had been touched by the hand of God Almighty. His eager readers ate it up as if he was feeding it to them by the bucketful.

Between Mankiller and the flamboyant General Custer, Bellows had used his pen to gain a fair amount of fame for himself and a bank account so hefty it would scarce notice the drain on it caused by the money he was throwing around at saloons and taverns that night.

It was at the doubtless sincerely patriotically inspired pub called The Spirits of '76 that Jason had met Rose, the young lady now blissfully slumbering beside him.

Nearly as young as he, this flower of womanhood was a "hostess" at the pub. She had taken a genuine liking to the boy even before being told by Bellows of his great acts of heroism at Gettysburg. At that point, Jason remembered still being sober enough to be embarrassed by all the fuss.

Nor was he the only one so bothered.

A local tough by the name of "German" Mike Lail was also in The Spirits of '76 that night, and also much in his cups. Add to that his proprietary feelings for the lovely Rose and trouble was sure to follow. When he saw the Rose plant herself squarely in Mankiller's lap, German Mike could stand no more.

Staggering only slightly, Mike made his way to the table where the hero of Gettysburg and his companions were sitting. Coming to a weaving halt beside Mankiller and Rose, he glared down at the pair.

"I don't think yer nuthin' special," he snarled, the words slurring out of his mouth.

Jason looked up to see a veritable hulk towering over him. German Mike had all the size and heft of a stevedore, which is what he was. From the wild tangle of his curly black hair and beard, little could be seen of his face save for his bared teeth and red-rimmed eyes.

"I agree with you, friend," Jason said, smiling up at him.

"Huh?" German Mike blinked. That wasn't the sort of response he had anticipated, and it threw him off balance. Then his grimace returned.

"And that's my woman," he declared loudly, pointing at Rose.

"I'm not any such thing, you big lummox!" she snapped.

"Last I heard, mister," Jason said calmly, "we're fighting a war to make sure people can't be owned by other people." He smiled again.

"Why don't you sit down and join us in a toast to the Union?"

"You go ta hell!" German Mike replied tersely. His hand flashed out, grabbed Rose by the wrist and roughly pulled her from her perch. Without a look back, he began to drag the protesting girl toward the bar.

"You gonna let that wooly beast brutalize that poor child, Jason?" Bellows asked.

"I reckon not," Mankiller said. It took him two tries to get out of his chair and onto his feet. Hitching up his trousers, he set out after German Mike.

"Go get him, boy!" Bellows egged him on.

The other soldiers seated at the table laughed and began to place bets on the outcome of the fight that was sure to follow. Most of the smart money was on German Mike to win.

Feeling no pain, either his own or that young Jason would soon have inflicted upon him, Leslie Bellows covered all bets, favoring Mankiller to be the victor.

German Mike had bellied up to the bar, one arm circled around the struggling Rose's waist and holding her close to his side. So engrossed was he in ordering drinks for the both of them that he barely felt the tap on his shoulder.

"The lady obviously doesn't care for your company, sir," Jason said stiffly. "So I think it'd be best if you let her go."

What German Mike did instead was swing his beer mug around savagely. With a loud clonk, the thick glass mug slammed into Mankiller's temple, sending him staggering to one side before he fell to his knees.

Seeing there yet remained a few precious drops of beer in the mug, German Mike lifted it to his lips. After draining it, he slammed the mug back down on the bar and prepared to finish the job it had started.

The soldier was still down on one knee, seemingly too dazed to rise. Laughing, German Mike reached out to grab him by the hair.

Before he could do so, Mankiller shot his right fist straight out and into his attacker's groin. This stopped him dead in his tracks, his hands going to his privates.

Mankiller pushed himself up off the floor, and in the same motion swung a booted foot up between German Mike's legs. The man's groan of pain as he felt his outtards being propelled up into his innards was matched by a collective cry of empathy from the men watching the brawl.

With his opponent bowed over before him, Mankiller hopped up into the air, using the momentum of his passage back down to increase the speed and force of his fist as it struck German Mike's jaw. When the stevedore stumbled backwards, Jason followed.

By so doing, he walked right into a smashing backhand blow delivered by the hulking German. A bludgeoning right and left combination caused Jason's arms to drop weakly to his sides.

German Mike, roaring like a bear with its foot caught in a trap, launched himself forward. He slammed into the dazed soldier, enveloping him with his arms in such a way so as to keep Mankiller's own arms pinned down. He lifted the soldier bodily off the floor and began to squeeze.

Jason tried to wriggle free, but lacked the leverage to do so. Yet he knew that if he didn't do so quickly he would either pass out or possibly even suffer a broken back.

He could hear the patrons of the pub shouting encouragement, though whether to him or to German Mike he couldn't tell. As if through a gauzy red curtain, he saw Rose looking on. She was horrified by the sight, and kohl-tinged tears were rolling down both cheeks.

He then looked down into the face of German Mike. His eyes were wide with bloodlust. Below his bulbous nose, his mouth was brutally curled with mirth.

Below that bulbous nose.

Jason quickly snaked his head down...and bit off the tip of German Mike's nose.

The stevedore released him, backpedaling in both astonishment and pain, his meaty hands clamping down over the bloody remnant of his nose.

Mankiller contemptuously spit out the rest of it, using his mouth to suck in great draughts of desperately needed air.

Leslie Bellows leaped forward and threw a mug of beer in his face. He sputtered, wiping beer and blood away with one hand.

"Don't stop now, m'boy," Bellows exhorted. "You've got him right where you want him!"

Jason looked at him like he was insane, but before he could make reply, a pair of hands shoved him from behind.

Going with it, Mankiller lowered his head and rammed into the dazed German Mike with one shoulder. Despite the stevedore's weight, the soldier lifted him just high enough to slam him back down atop the nearest table.

The legs of the table buckled under the stress and it and both men crashed heavily to the floor. Mankiller was the first back on his feet, and he swept up one of the broken table legs.

Wielding it like a truncheon, he brought it cracking down on the back of German Mike's head as the bullish thug was rising to his knees. He grunted heavily, but continued trying to rise.

He'd gotten one foot up under himself when Jason brought the table leg down on his curly pate again. Not waiting to see the result, the soldier drew the leg back and struck again.

This time the thick piece of wood broke in half. Mankiller raised what was left, prepared to strike yet again. He held himself in check when he saw that this time his opponent would not be getting back up.

German Mike rolled heavily onto his back, loudly passing wind as he did, then went limp as the last vestiges of his consciousness fled him.

Mankiller threw away the remnant of the table leg. He was almost knocked down again himself as Rose threw herself into his arms. Her own arms circled his neck as she rewarded her champion with a hard and lingering kiss. Her body pressed against his felt warm and inviting.

When the kiss ended, he smiled rather stupidly at her.

"Nobody move!"

Mankiller jerked his head around to see Leslie Bellows, amazingly, dragging his cumbersome camera equipment in through the front door of the pub. As he passed the table where he had been sitting with the soldiers, he paused long enough to scoop up his winnings from the fight and stuff them into a coat pocket.

"We've got to preserve this moment for posterity," he proclaimed as he set up his equipment. He then moved to pose his subjects.

He positioned Rose on Jason's right side, telling her to put her arms around the soldier. After placing Jason's right arm around the girl, Bellows then directed the soldier to lift his right foot and place it atop the supine and still slumbering German Mike, as if the stevedore was a prize big game animal brought down in a hunt.

Bellows bounced away a few feet to look at his posed tableau. He held both hands up before him, palms out, a few inches apart so he could look at his subject as through the camera. He frowned.

"Something's not quite right," he muttered.

Then a smile lit his face and he snapped his fingers with sudden inspiration. He dropped to his knees beside German Mike and began to gingerly inspect the stub that was all that remained of the unconscious stevedore's nose. As Bellows expected, dark blood was still oozing from the gaping wound.

Dipping one finger into the gore, Bellows stood and carefully traced a thin line of blood from the corner of Mankiller's left eye to halfway down his cheek.

"Perfect!" the newsman cackled, rubbing his hands together and trotting back to his camera. His head disappeared momentarily beneath the black shroud as he focused his shot, then popped back out.

"Kiss him again, darlin'," he directed Rose. "But only on the cheek this time. We don't want to hide that beautiful face!"

Giggling, Rose stretched up on her tiptoes and planted a kiss on Jason's cheek, holding it until the flash of the camera told her the picture had been taken. The pub erupted into cheers. One of Mankiller's fellow soldiers leaped to his feet.

"This calls for a drink!" he shouted loudly, before stumbling backwards and falling over his chair and onto the floor.

So it went. The locals fell all over themselves pressing drinks into Jason's hand, urged on by Rose.

And...that's when the memory again became no more than a blur. Head spinning, the young soldier vowed never again to partake of so much hard liquor.

Moving slowly so as not to awaken his bedmate, Jason slid from beneath the covers. Walking on legs like sticks in a gale, he made his way to a nearby bureau, atop which sat a porcelain basin and pitcher of water.

Filling the basin halfway, he dipped both hands into the water and brought it up to softly scrub his face. Doing so caused him to wince as he felt a sharper pain around his left eye. He raised his head to look into the bureau's mirror, expecting to find that his brawl with the burly German Mike had left him with a nice shiner as a memento.

What he saw instead caused him to cry out harshly.

He appeared to be bleeding from the corner of his eye! A single red teardrop could be seen in the middle of his cheek, at the end of a narrow trail it had left behind up to the eye.

Almost frantically, he dipped his right hand back into the water, then brought it across his face to wash away the blood. His heart sank as he looked again into the mirror and saw the trail of blood still there. He rubbed at it again, but again it was to no avail.

"Ain't no amount of scrubbin' gonna wash that away, sweetheart."

He turned at the sound of Rose's husky voice. She was now sitting upright against the headboard of the bed, smiling at him. It clearly didn't bother her in the least for him to see her unclothed, for she made no effort to cover up her nudity.

"What do you mean?" he asked.

"C'mere," she said, holding her arms out toward him. He numbly shuffled back over to the bed, sitting down on its edge. At the moment, he was so befuddled as to be equally oblivious to his own state of undress.

"Havin' a little trouble rememberin' what happened last night?" she asked, sliding over and draping her arms over his shoulders from behind.

"A little," he admitted. "About some things."

"I'm a little hazy myself," she told him. "I kinda lost track of where all we went after we left The Spirit. But I do remember at one of 'em we met the Peacock."

"Who?"

"The Peacock. Down around the piers, they call him that on account o' all the ink he sports."

"Ink?"

"Tattoos. They say he's covered from his chin to his ankles." Rose moved her arms, slipping them around his waist.

"The Peacock gives tattoos as well as receives 'em. So one of the boys, I think it was that fella what took our picture, decided *you* needed a tattoo. He even paid for it."

She didn't tell him that, afterwards, Bellows had taken several more photographs of the newly decorated soldier: alone, with his buddies, with Rose. These too would proved to be quite profitable for the newsman.

"You mean," Jason muttered, touching his painted cheek lightly, "I'll have this thing forever?"

"Only till ya die, baby," Rose crooned.

She was now kneeling on the bed behind him. She began to softly kiss his ear, his neck. Her hands expertly caressed him.

Mankiller turned, swinging his legs onto the bed. Taking the woman in his arms, he laid her down and pressed his mouth to hers.

As his own hands began to explore her ivory skin, she moaned just loudly enough for him to hear. Clearly, she approved of what he was doing. Their mutual passion began to quickly build.

At least this time, the young soldier thought as he covered her body with his own, he'd be able to fully remember what it was like to be with a woman.

After all, though male pride would not have allowed him to admit it either to her or to his buddies, Rose had been his first.

CHAPTER 6

Of course, young Mankiller and his fellow soldiers did not celebrate Christmas in Richmond that year; nor the next, either.

Although Robert E. Lee lost seventy percent of his officers during the three bloody days of Gettysburg, the Rebel army under his command would doggedly continue on with the fight.

Many battles had followed Gettysburg: Brandy Station, Yellow Tavern, Cold Harbor. Custer always kept Jason close to hand, as if he were a talisman, a good luck charm. Even when the general left the Michigan Brigade to assume command of the Union's Third Cavalry Division, he made sure Mankiller came with him.

Together, the boy general and the man who cried blood forged a dark and violent legend, with them at its center.

Being a mere enlisted man, Mankiller was never allowed to rise above the rank of sergeant. That was fine with him; he fought against accepting even this promotion.

Sergeant Mankiller stood right behind Custer outside the farmhouse at the village of Appomattox Court House, Virginia on that ninth day of April in 1865 when Lee finally and officially surrendered to General Ulysses S. Grant, ending the long national nightmare.

After the surrender, Jason Mankiller was glad to leave the service, though Custer personally tried to convince him to stay.

And now here he was, nine years later, penniless in a dusty town in Texas.

He coolly appraised the flustered lawman standing before him, who was now fighting to regain his composure.

"I'm Clayton Russell," he said, trying to look suitably official. "Marshal of this town. And you *are* Jason Mankiller, aren't you?"

"I am."

"Well, sir, near as I can tell, you were the aggrieved party in this little dust-up. I won't be pressing any charges against you."

"That's good to know."

That being said, Jason returned to eating his sandwich, having lost all interest in what had transpired earlier. Yet the marshal still eyed him suspiciously.

"I suppose you'll be wanting the *re-ward*?"

Mankiller stopped in mid chew, setting the sandwich back down on his plate.

"What reward?"

"You don't know?"

"Obviously not."

"Well, in case ya also didn't know, Zeb McClure over there was a thief, with a hundred dollar bounty on his head."

"Is that a fact?" Mankiller said, glancing over at where the body still lay. "But if he was a known outlaw, marshal…why hadn't you already arrested him?"

"Well…uh…well, as far as I know, ol' Zeb there hadn't broken no laws in this town. Anything that happens outside the city limits is none of my concern."

"Uh-huh."

Mankiller picked his sandwich back up, taking a bite as he eyed the lawman. He had the definite idea that Russell hadn't much *wanted* to take on the late Zeb McClure. Not because he was a coward, exactly; he looked tough enough. More likely it was just because he wasn't a young man anymore and at his age going up against a gunman he didn't need to just wasn't worth the effort or the risk to his life, such as it was.

"So what do I have to do to collect this reward, Marshal?"

"Nothin'. Just stick around for a while. I'll have to wire Austin to get authorization and a bank draft. The whole thing shouldn't take more than a week.

"But till then, and even after, you'd best tread lightly, boy."

"Why's that?" Jason asked, bristling at what he took to be a not-so-veiled threat.

"'Cause Zeb McClure has several kinfolk in these parts. Some of 'em are even meaner than he was, and none of 'em take kindly to having one of their own gunned down."

"I appreciate the warning," Jason replied. He lowered his head and resumed eating.

Thinking he'd been dismissed, and not sure how he felt about that, Marshal Russell spun on his heels. Before leaving the saloon, he drafted a couple of the locals on hand to pick up McClure's body and follow him down to the town's funeral parlor.

As the batwing doors flapped closed behind them, Sam Dobbins came around from behind the bar, carrying a bucket of water. He slung its dingy contents onto the bloodstained spot on the floor where the fallen gunman had lain. That would be all the cleaning he attempted until after closing.

Mankiller finished off the last bite of his final pickled egg, washing it down with the last of his coffee. His money problems would soon be alleviated, and for that he was glad. But he was still penniless today and knew this meal wouldn't hold him for a week.

He rose from the table and carried his empty cup and plate over to the bar, setting them down before Sam Dobbins.

"That was a mighty fine spread, Sam."

"Thank you. We aim to please."

Mankiller hesitated just a beat before speaking again.

"Would you happen to know if anyone in town is doing any hiring at the moment?"

The barkeep thought on it good and proper before answering.

"Boy, I tell ya, Ft. Rogers has been hit real hard by this here depression. Real hard. Was there any particular line o' work you was wantin' to pursue?"

"Don't much matter," Mankiller replied, "long as it's legal. I ain't no coffee boiler, neither, when it comes to work. I've never shied away from hard labor. I always aim to give a good day's work for my pay."

"I believe ya. But like I said, there just ain't much available 'round here."

"I understand. Thanks anyway." The drifter tipped his hat and turned to leave.

"Hold on," Dobbins called after him. He glanced at the back of the saloon before continuing on. "I may have a job for you right here, if it's to yer likin'."

"You need a swamper?"

"You'd do that?" Dobbins asked incredulously. He'd heard the exchange between the marshal and Mankiller, knew at least a little of the drifter's reputation. He was amazed such a man would consider a job as lowly as that of mopping floors in a saloon.

"I've done it before," Jason informed him. "There's no shame in it."

"No, no," Dobbins said quickly, not wanting to insult anyone as good with a gun as Mankiller. "'Course not. I just had sumthin' else in mind, that's all."

Coming around from behind the bar again, Dobbins motioned for Jason to follow him as he walked to the rear of the establishment. Against the back wall stood a square wooden platform, about four feet high. On one side, a short flight of steps was attached.

The two men climbed to the top of the platform. Sitting atop it was a small table and a ladder back chair.

Resting on top of the table was a double-barreled, 10-gauge shotgun.

"I assume you know what this is for?" Dobbins said.

Jason nodded. The platform was a fairly common fixture in saloons on the frontier.

From it, a man could sit and keep a lookout for trouble anywhere in the room. If needed, he would be expected to keep order in the place, both downstairs and upstairs, where soiled doves usually were on hand to ply their ancient trade.

"Last fella I had upped and got married a week ago Tuesday," Dobbins explained. "He's moving back East with his bride; gonna work in her family's business. The job's yers if ya want it, Jason."

"What are the particulars?"

"I'll need ya here from the time things start ta pick up in the evening… say, oh, about six o'clock or so. Stay until such time as the last dog dies and I decide to call it a night.

"In return, I'll pay ya two dollars a day, cash money, payable at the end of each night. All the free coffee ya want, and one run at the sandwich table."

Wanting to make this hire, and feeling he might need to sweeten the pot, Dobbins impulsively threw in an incentive he hoped would seal the deal.

"And if you want, you can enjoy a free poke with the girl of your choice, once a week."

Mankiller fought back a grin and thrust out one hand, which Dobbins grabbed and shook vigorously.

"You got yourself a man."

CHAPTER 7

With a few hours before his first shift would begin, Mankiller took a leisurely stroll around the town, beginning to learn its layout, its streets and alleys, especially those with dead ends. It was a habit for him to do so in any town in which he expected to be spending any length of time. Before long, he'd be able to find his way around like a native, day or night.

Coming to an open space between buildings near the edge of town, he paused to watch a group of Mexican laundresses going about their work. One in particular caught his eye: an older woman, struggling to tip over her large wash tub to empty it of dirty water.

"*Con permiso*," Jason said to her, coming over to grab one edge of the wooden tub. The *vieja* gave him a nearly toothless grin and stepped back.

Heaving upward, Mankiller easily tipped the tub up far enough to spill out its contents. He then snatched up a bucket sitting on the ground next to the tub. He carried it to a very large metal tub nearby, which had a low fire burning under it. He dipped the bucket into the warm water, filled it, then carried it back to pour into the old woman's empty wash tub. He repeated the process until her tub was sufficiently full.

"*Gracias,*" she said, reaching out and squeezing his hands. He could see that her own were twisted and swollen from arthritis.

"*Por nada,*" he replied.

He then asked her, in only slightly accented Spanish, if she might have a small remnant of soap he could have. From atop a nearby bench she scooped up a fragment of soap, no bigger than an infant's palm, and pressed it into his hand.

Walking a short distance to the north from the outdoor laundry, Mankiller came to the banks of a narrow, shallow stream. Turning, he followed its shore westward for about a mile.

Picking a likely looking spot, he pushed his way through bushes and down to the edge of the little waterway.

Sitting on its grassy bank, he pulled a worn handkerchief from his pocket. He used the cloth to wipe away as much dust as he could from his hat. He next pulled off his boots and buffed them with the same cloth, lightly dampened; the same for his leather leggings.

Standing and looking carefully around on all sides, he then stripped naked. Kneeling beside the stream and using the soap the old laundress had given him, he thoroughly washed his shirt, pants, kerchief and socks. After rinsing the suds out of them, he carefully laid the wet clothes atop bushes that would catch enough sunlight to dry them.

Finally, he waded out into the stream till the water was at about knee high depth, sat down and used the small piece of lye soap remaining to scrub himself.

Being less delicate than his clothes, and probably in even greater need of cleaning, he rubbed himself so hard with the harsh soap that even the darkest parts of his skin were starting to take on a pink glow.

Throughout, his pistol lay on the bank within easy reach.

When he felt he'd done all the damage he could, and the nubbin of soap wasn't much bigger than his thumbnail, he laid back and let the water cover him completely, its cool current washing away both suds and grime from his skin and hair.

Returning to shore, he crawled into the midst of some of the bushes, out of sight from all but the most prying of eyes, and laid himself down.

Time and circumstances had taught Mankiller the importance of sleeping where and when you can, even if only for short periods. On occasion, he had even slept in the saddle.

He almost always fell asleep quickly and easily, and had found he didn't require large amounts of rest. He slept soundly enough, yet at the same time very lightly; even asleep he was instinctively aware of everything around him, tuned to any untoward sound. More than once, this instinct for survival had saved his life.

Aided by his gun, of course, which he held in his hand even as he slumbered.

A few hours later, he awoke fully alert. The position of the sun told him he had plenty of time to make it back to the Last Stand at the appointed hour. He confirmed this by consulting the old, battered but still accurate pocket watch that was the only tangible legacy he had from his father.

As expected, his clothes were sufficiently dry, and he dressed quickly, using the flat of his hands to smooth out as many wrinkles as he could.

He knew he was a bit rumpled, but at least now he wouldn't look like a tin-towner nor smell like a wet horse blanket when he reported for his first day on the job.

He'd been at his post in the saloon for about an hour when he saw a young woman coming toward him from the area of the bar, carrying a steaming coffee cup in both hands.

One look told him she was a painted cat; one of several prostitutes who plied their trade in the Last Stand. Her green dress was cut high on the bottom and low on the top, to amply display her greatest assets. Her hair hung down in tight blonde ringlets, and her face was probably rather cute under all the rouge and powder. Her curves looked full and soft.

Only her eyes were hard.

He nodded his thanks to her as he bent at the waist to take the cup she held out to him.

"My name's Dixie," she chirped.

Sure it was, he thought.

"Nice to meet you, Dixie. I'm Jason."

"Oh, I know who you are," she said. "Why, pert near everybody in town has heard about you by now."

He didn't reply to that, or even look at her. Instead, his eyes had resumed sweeping back and forth across the room.

"But I hope to get to know you even better," she said suggestively. He nodded, but still didn't look at her.

"Oh, hell," she snapped. "I'll never get to know you if you won't even look at me!"

"Darlin'," he said firmly, "you really shouldn't try distracting me while I'm working. You could get me or somebody else killed."

"Oh."

"Now, when I'm *not* working, though," he said by way of softening the blow, "I'll be happy to spend time with all you girls."

He finally spared her another glance and she could see there was no anger in his eyes.

"Maybe you can even tell me about that pretty little mole on your right shoulder."

Dixie's face brightened, assured now that his attention to his job had not prevented him from noticing and appreciating her charms. That was enough to satisfy her vanity for the moment.

She gave him a mock curtsy, then turned to find someone able and willing to pay for her attentions.

"Dixie?" Jason called to her.

"Yes?" she said eagerly.

"Would you do me a favor before you set about your own labors?"

"Anything!"

"Ask Sam if he has a spare *bung starter* I can have."

The girl's face twisted in puzzlement, but she merely shrugged and set out to do as he'd asked.

Mankiller smiled as the soiled dove flounced away. He'd been with his share of women since that first night with his Rose of Philadelphia. All shapes and sizes, all colors and breeds; he remembered with great fondness a little porcelain-skinned Celestial gal up Denver way.

Professional girls and otherwise, none had ever proven to be any more than a temporary distraction: welcomed patches of beauty in a world more filled with ugliness.

He couldn't claim to understand the fair sex exactly, so he settled for simply appreciating it.

As Mankiller's eyes scanned back and forth across the saloon, they lit on the dapper-dressed gambler who had saluted him after his shootout with Zeb McClure. After studying him for a while, even from a distance, he determined the gambler was at least *mostly* playing fair and square with his marks. Like most professionals, he seldom needed to do otherwise.

The first night of the job was fairly uneventful. Late in the evening, one drunken patron did get a bit rambunctious, but a rap on the head with the bung starter, a thin wooden mallet normally used to open kegs, put him down like a lamb. Jason dragged him out to the alley to sleep it off, then returned to his perch.

It was about three o'clock in the morning when the place emptied out and the doors were closed and locked.

"You did real good tonight, Jason," Sam told him, handing him two crisp dollar bills. "Hope it wasn't too boring for you."

"Not at all," Mankiller said, shoving the bills into his front pocket. "I actually kinda enjoy watching people. You can learn a lot that way."

"I s'pose so."

"Could I make one suggestion, though?"

"Sure. What is it?"

"Your shotgun. You might want to think about taking it to a good gunsmith and having him saw off part of the barrel and the stock."

"Why's that?"

"Its length could make it cumbersome in a place crowded like this one can be. The shorter length would make it easier to maneuver, more effective as a tool. Just a thought."

He then said goodnight as Sam let him out and locked the doors back behind him. Taking a slightly circuitous route and making sure no one was following him, he again made his way to the river outside town.

Finding a different spot this time, he again crawled out of sight into the midst of a stand of bushes. Lying down and placing his hat over his face, he was asleep within minutes.

This time, and for the first time in a while, he allowed himself to sleep until he awoke naturally, well rested and pleased to have greenbacks in his pocket.

After washing up a bit in the stream, he drifted back into town. He'd been in cities larger and smaller than Ft. Rogers: this was about the size he liked. It had a variety of commerce and didn't seem to rely primarily on just one. This boded well for its continued existence; towns that sprang up virtually overnight in response to something like a gold strike had a tendency to boom today and blow away tomorrow.

He again meandered up and down the streets, further familiarizing himself with its layout. He even engaged in a bit of window-shopping.

As it got to be mid-afternoon, he entered a likely looking restaurant. For thirty cents, he was able to enjoy his first full meal in nigh on a week: a thick steak, cooked medium well, fried potatoes and turnips. For dessert, a slice of pie made from dried apples. All washed down with hot, dark coffee.

He felt content as he later headed toward the Last Stand to begin his work shift. Even before stepping up onto the sidewalk outside the saloon, he saw the gambler leisurely sitting on a curved back chair next to the entrance. Today he was wearing a dark blue suit.

"Could I have a word before you go in?" the card sharp said. This was the first time Jason had actually heard his voice, and he discovered the man had the sort of Southern drawl that seems to creep out of the mouth like slow moving molasses.

"Sure. What can I do you for?"

"I'm actually hoping to do something for you, Mr. Mankiller. There's a gentleman inside, a local tough by the name of Farley Meadows."

"Never heard of him."

"I'm not surprised; he's a man of no true accomplishment. What he is, however, a cousin to the scoundrel you sent to his reward yesterday."

"Ah."

"And the light shines down. Young Farley has been drinking and bragging in equal parts for over an hour. He says he means to kill you."

"Sounds to me like a man with too much mustard," Jason said dismissively.

"Maybe so. But he also has a reputation for being a man of violence; one who prefers his target to be looking away from him, if you catch my meaning. If he does decide to make a move, he'll give you no warning."

"Unless he's changed locations since I stepped outside, he'll be on your right as you go in."

"That's good to know. But why are you bothering to tell me this? What's your stake in any of this?"

"I have none," the gambler confessed. "But I cannot abide a backshooter. And I also have great admiration for any man who is as good at his profession as you are."

"What profession might that be?" Jason asked. "I've had lots of 'em: everything from cowhand to bullwhacker."

"Pfft," the gambler exhaled. "Those are merely *jobs*. No. You, my friend…you are a killer of men."

Jason was taken aback, not sure if he should be offended or worried that this man was right in his assessment.

"That doesn't sound like somethin' a fella should be overly proud of," he said at last.

He meandered up and down the streets...

"Perhaps it's best not to be. After all, 'pride goeth before the fall'."

"Sounds to me like you're describing a plain old murderer."

"Not at all. Any coward can be a murderer, given the right circumstances. There's one of them waiting for you inside.

"What you are, sir, is far more pure. Far more deadly."

Mankiller simply grunted in reply. "Regardless. I appreciate the warning. May I ask your name?"

"How rude of me not to have already given it," the gambler replied, smiling slyly. "My name is Cash Carpenter. Late of New Orleans."

The way he said it sounded more like "nawlins."

Now Jason smiled.

"I take it that is an assumed name."

"Not at all. I assure you, it's quite real. My dear old daddy gave it to me in hopes it would bring me wealth."

"Has it?"

"Sometimes."

Jason turned away, then looked back at the gambler. "What makes you so sure I'm a killer?"

"I saw the whole thing yesterday, remember?"

"I didn't start that trouble."

"No, but you ended it. Most efficiently. And with no more thought or emotion than if he'd been a rabid dog you had to put down."

"Now you make me sound like a monster."

"No such thing. A monster would have *enjoyed* the killing." Carpenter again smiled. "You were a soldier, isn't that right?"

"I was one of many participants in the recent unpleasantness, yes. Were you?"

"No, not me. I was a shade too young to take part in Mr. Lincoln's war. Plus, I lived in New Orleans; the Federals took that card out of play fairly early in the game."

"And what does the war have to do with what happened yesterday?"

"Maybe nothing. Maybe everything. Men who have to stare into the face of Hell react in many different ways. Some crumble at the sight. Some learn to block it out of their minds and their memories. Some leap into its maw and come out the other side as devils themselves.

"And for a very few, the hellfire forges them into steel. Cold, hard steel."

"And that's what you think I've become?"

"You'd better hope it is, Jason, given the way you appear to attract trouble."

"Hmm. Well, thanks again for the warning."

Mankiller again turned away, but he made no move to enter the saloon. He just stood there, facing the door.

The gambler leaned back in his chair and looked up, noticing that Jason had his right eye closed. A minute later, he stepped through the batwing doors and into the dimmer light of the Last Stand.

Mankiller's right eye snapped open, instantly detecting motion on that side. He swiveled, and saw a grinning idiot coming toward him. Farley Meadows already had his gun drawn, though he had not yet raised it to fire.

The idiotic smile was replaced by a look of fear as he realized his intended victim had not been taken by surprise, could see perfectly well, and was already raising and leveling his own firearm.

The gun barked and bucked in Jason's hand. The slug hit Meadows in the throat with a loud, wet splat. He was sent stumbling backwards into some of the men he had been bragging to minutes earlier, clutching at the bubbling wound in his neck.

As though fearing contamination, they pushed him away. He fell awkwardly to the floor, flopping helplessly on the boards for several seconds before expiring.

Mankiller didn't spare him a second look, though his eyes again swept the saloon for any sign of further trouble. Seeing none, he calmly holstered his Colt and strolled over to the bar, where Sam Dobbins was staring in open-jawed amazement.

"Evenin', Sam," Jason said as he walked past the barkeep. "I'll be at my post when the marshal comes to call."

Dobbins silently watched his back as Mankiller casually strode away. His eyes then darted back to the dead man on the floor, and from there over to the front door.

Cash Carpenter, still outside but looking in as he held his hands atop the batwing doors, was also eyeing the dead man.

When he looked up, his eyes met Sam Dobbins gaze and he shrugged.

As he climbed atop the platform from where he kept watch, Mankiller smiled tightly. Sitting on the table was his shotgun converted to his specifications.

The barrels had been sawed down and were no more than fourteen inches in length. The stock had been carved and sanded down into a semblance of a pistol grip.

Hefting it in one hand to get a feel for its new balance, he held it up and nodded an acknowledgment to Sam.

A few minutes later, Marshal Russell pushed his way into the room. Eyeing Mankiller warily, he stepped over to examine the drifter's latest victim. Satisfying himself that it had been yet another righteous killing, he again directed some of the onlookers to cart the body away.

Russell jumped back as Sam Dobbins seemingly appeared from nowhere to again sling a bucket of water on the mess, some of it nearly splashing on the lawman's boots. He gave the barkeep a warning wag of one finger before heading back to speak with Mankiller.

"You're just getting' richer by the day, aintcha, gun hand?" he said in icy tones.

"How so, marshal?"

"Why, you've just earned yourself another bounty. Ol' Farley there had a hundred dollars ridin' on his head, too."

"And I suppose *he* hadn't done anything to warrant your legal attention either, had he?"

"No, he had not," the lawman replied curtly. The right side of his lips then curled up slightly in a sneer.

"You're turning into quite the bounty hunter, Mankiller."

"A much maligned but alas all too often necessary profession," Cash Carpenter remarked, passing by on his way to his card table, emphasizing the last word.

Marshal Russell glared at the smiling card sharp, while Jason tried to ignore both men. But the lawman wasn't quite through with him yet.

"You plannin' on killin' anyone else while yer here, boy?"

"Marshal, I hadn't *planned* on ever killin' anybody at all, at least not since the day after Appomattox."

"Well, I would appreciate it if you wouldn't start makin' a habit of it now."

"That's not entirely up to me, now is it?"

The marshal squirmed uneasily under the icy glare of the drifter's pale blue eyes, then turned without another word and left.

The rest of the night was peaceful; word was already starting to spread that the Last Stand was not a healthy place to go looking for trouble.

After collecting his two dollars from Sam and exiting the saloon, Mankiller again set out for the nearby stream; he had decided to spend at least one more night sleeping there before investing any money in a room with a real bed.

The following afternoon found him kneeling beside the slowly flowing stream, naked from the waist up. After giving himself a quick rinse, he plunged his head into the water, enjoying its cool embrace before raising his head back up and combing his fingers through his hair.

The sound of a horse crashing through the underbrush brought him leaping to his feet, drawing his pistol in the same motion. The sight that met his eyes was most unexpected.

A frisky black gelding broke through the bushes and into the open. Riding the horse, pulling him to a stop with a firm yet not unkind yank of the reins, was a woman.

Dressed entirely in black herself, boots and what could have been a man's pants and shirt, she seemed almost to be one with the horse beneath her, so easily did she sit astride it.

One look and Jason allowed that she might well be the most strikingly beautiful woman he had ever seen. She had more of the look of an Indian about her than did he: with deep, dark reflecting pools for eyes and raven hair that hung straight and loose behind her nearly to her waist.

The woman was just as boldly and openly appreciating him. Her large eyes didn't pause at his distinctive tattoo, but continued to flow down like the water across his bare torso. The multiple scars standing out whitely against the darker flesh around them caught her attention as much as did the smooth flatness of his abdomen.

Then her gaze fell on the drawn pistol in his hand. Aimed at her.

Her head lifted to lock her gaze on his. One eyebrow arched, as if silently asking if he truly found her to be any sort of threat.

Somewhat embarrassed, he smiled tightly. Though usually not given to exhibitionism, he now gave his gun several fancy twirls, the last carrying it naturally and smoothly back into its holster.

Now it was her turn to smile, as she nodded her head graciously. Without a word, she pulled her horse's reins to the left, tapped it in the ribs with her heels and galloped away.

Chuckling softly and shaking his head as if he had just seen a pleasing mirage, Mankiller finished dressing and headed back to town.

CHAPTER 8

After stopping at a mercantile store, Mankiller returned to the place where the women were doing laundry. Finding the old one who had given him the piece of soap when he first arrived, he walked over and presented her with a full, new cake of soap.

"You're a good boy," she told him, again taking both his hands in hers but this time pulling them up and kissing them.

"Not so good, mother," he replied, bending down and lightly kissing her wrinkled forehead. "But I try to pay my debts."

Having started to get the growlies a bit, he left her to go in search of a meal. He chose a different hash house than the one he had eaten at the previous day.

Partly, this was done because he meant eventually to try all the different eating establishments in town before settling on any favorites. Mostly, though, he did it because he didn't want to form any sort of habitual behavior that an enemy could use against him.

At the diner he chose today, he devoured half a fried chicken with a plate of black-eyed peas. He also put away several large biscuits, sopping them in a bowl of "Texas butter": gravy made from flour, hot water and fried steak grease. For a welcome change, he accompanied the meal with a large glass of cool buttermilk.

That evening, not long after he had assumed his position atop the platform at the Last Stand, Mankiller spied Sam Dobbins heading his way personally, bringing a cup of coffee. Alongside Sam walked Cash Carpenter, the gambler.

This couldn't be good.

Yet both men smiled and greeted him cordially. They even engaged in a little idle chit-chat, with Dobbins noting that the place was already starting to fill up nicely. Jason took a sip of coffee, then set it down on the table, in a spot that would not impede his reach for the sawed-off shotgun.

"Y'know, Sam," he said easily, "if you keep beating around the bush much longer, there won't be any bush left."

The barkeep looked at Cash, reached back to scratch the back of his head, then looked up at Mankiller.

"Here's the thing, Jason," he said at last. "I think maybe Marshal Russell was right."

"About what?"

"Two hundred dollars is a lot of money. It'd get a frugal fella a mighty long way."

"I suppose."

"Why, sure. So..." Dobbins now seemed to be having trouble maintaining eye contact. "So after you collect your rewards...maybe you oughtta think real serious about getting' outta town."

Mankiller leaned back in his chair, almost enjoying the barkeep's discomfort.

"Are you unhappy with my work, Sam?" he asked at last.

"Oh, hell, you know that ain't it, son."

Glancing up, Dobbins saw Mankiller was smiling at him. Relaxing somewhat, his words were still in earnest.

"I'm just gonna tell ya how the cow ate the cabbage, Jason."

"I wish you would."

"That no-good Zeb McClure; you done the world a favor by plowin' him under. But he's got an older brother, Squire McClure. And Squire's got three growed sons. Ever'one of 'em's mean as rattlesnakes, even worse than Zeb.

"All of 'em have considerably stiffer bounties on their heads, and justifiably so. So far, no one's been stupid enough ta try ta claim 'em."

"What's your point, Sam?"

"My point's this. Once they get word you've dispatched not just one but two of their kinfolk, they're bound to come lookin' for ya."

"Sam's right, Jason," Cash chimed in. "No one would blame you if you chose the better part of valor and took off for friendlier climes. It's the only..."

Carpenter stopped in mid-sentence as something caught his eye. Gazing upward, a broad smile lit his face as he saw a familiar figure descending from upstairs.

Mankiller turned to follow the gambler's eyes, and his breath caught in his throat. Coming down the stairs was the woman who had come upon him near the stream earlier in the day.

She cut a somewhat different figure now. Her dark hair had been pulled up into a tight chignon at the base of her long, tapered neck. A necklace sparkling with small diamonds nestled against her throat. She wore an elegant black dress whose cut emphasized her thin waist; it's bodice was cut enticingly low, to expose and accentuate the upper swell of her breasts.

Mankiller was puzzled by her presence in a saloon; she had not at all the look or air of a soiled dove.

Joining the men and gracing each with a smile, she came to stand next to Carpenter, sliding an arm through one of his before kissing him lightly on the lips. It was no reach for her to do so, for she was nearly the same height as the gambler. Seeing the obvious look of bewilderment on Mankiller's face, she smiled even wider.

"Allow me," Cash said. "Jason, this is my partner and companion, Jane Starr."

"Mr. Mankiller and I have already met," the woman said. "After a fashion."

She and Jason exchanged smiles and knowing looks, so now it was Cash who was puzzled.

Mankiller already knew that, in exchange for a prime location at which to conduct his nightly poker games, Carpenter kicked back a percentage of his winnings to Sam Dobbins. Now he learned that Jane had a similar arrangement and would be set up at a table of her own. The only difference was that her game of chance was faro.

"If you get the chance, Mr. Mankiller," she said, "you'll have to stop by my table and play a hand or two."

"I'd be happy to stop and pay my respects, Miz Starr," he assured her, "but I won't be playing any faro."

"Oh? Why not?"

"I'll tell ya. I tried to buck the tiger a time or two in my misspent youth, and all I ever had to show for it was empty pockets. Same for poker, blackjack, roulette, chuck-a-luck. You name it, I'm bad at it."

She chuckled lightly.

"So I been cured of the urge to gamble. It's too much like throwing your money into the wind and hoping even more of it will blow back to you. It might...but it ain't likely."

"And yet you'll sit on this perch every night and gamble with your life," she stated, looking suddenly rather pensive. He tried to shrug it off.

"The difference is, if I lose my life, I won't go hungry."

The woman didn't know how to respond to that, so she simply smiled at him before turning and retreating to her faro table.

Not far away, near the end of the bar, the soiled dove named Dixie was trying to pretend to be interested in the cowhand who was pawing her. But her eyes drilled to the back of the room. She saw the smiles, faintly heard the light laughter. It didn't make her happy.

Apparently, Jason Mankiller was not opposed to *all* distractions.

The rest of the night was again uneventful, which was fine with Mankiller. Upon leaving at the end of the evening, the frugal side of his nature again asserted itself and he once more made his bed out of doors near the stream.

He didn't fall asleep quite so quickly as normal, though, and when he did his dreams were filled with raven-haired women astride coal-black horses.

The next afternoon found him as usual exploring the streets of Ft. Rogers, after enjoying one of the best meals of which he had partaken in quite some time. Following the advice and directions of the old laundress, he had sought out a certain cantina in the Mexican quarter of the town.

Tortillas slathered with goat's milk butter, chicken enchiladas, frijoles and rice, mixed with a bottle of cold *cerveza* had left him full and satisfied.

He'd barely left that part of town when a small boy of maybe ten years approached him, carrying a small armload of newspapers.

"Paper, mister?" the boy asked, holding up a copy of what Jason could see was bannered as being the *Ft. Rogers Diligence.*

"Maybe," he replied. "How much is it?"

"Two cents."

"Is it any good?"

"Best newspaper in town. Guaranteed."

Jason smiled. "Uh-huh. Now, it wouldn't just happen to be the *only* newspaper in town, would it?"

The boy simply smiled back.

"I'll take one," the drifter said. He made the boy's day by paying for the paper with a nickel and telling him he could keep the change.

Mankiller headed for the Last Stand, even though he still had plenty of time before his shift was to begin. Stepping up on the sidewalk, he planted himself in one of the chairs near the saloon's entrance and began a leisurely read of the newspaper.

A few minutes later, when he lowered the paper to turn the page, he was surprised to see Jane Starr sitting on the opposite side of the doorway.

She was scribbling with a pencil in a small notebook resting on her lap. Her classic features, along with the velveteen dress she wore today, so darkly red as to appear nearly black, elevated the appearance of the dusty sidewalk considerably, he thought.

"Good afternoon, Miz Starr," he said easily. "I didn't see you come out."

"Probably because you were so engrossed in your newspaper, Mr. Mankiller."

He frowned.

"Tell me, does hearing me call you 'Miz Starr' sound as odd to you as hearing you call me 'Mr. Mankiller' does to me?"

She chuckled. "You employ a unique turn of phrase...but in this case, I believe you're right."

"Then what say from now on we're just plain old 'Jane' and 'Jason'?"

"I'd like that," she replied. "But I don't want to keep you from your paper."

"Not a problem," he assured her, laying the paper down on his lap. "I mean to read every last word of it, and I've got at least the rest of the week to do so."

"You enjoy the news, do you?"

He shrugged. "Every time I hit a town, even if I'm just passing through, I make an effort to buy at least one edition of the local newspaper.

"There's been many a time on the trail when such has been the only company I had. I've been known to read the same edition several times, often by the light of a campfire.

"I've always had a general curiosity about the world, and I try to keep up with what's going on in it."

"Do you read well?"

"Well enough," he said. "I never had no formal schooling, but my momma, God rest her soul, always set great store by book learning. She made sure I knew how to read and write. I do tolerably well at ciphering, too, though I never liked it much."

"Do you read anything beside newspapers?"

"When I have the chance. Fenimore Cooper's all right, if a bit silly. Washington Irving spins a good yarn. I've read the more exciting parts of the Bible.

"I tried my hand at Shakespeare a time or two, but gave it up as a lost cause. I figure he wasn't meant to be read, anyway. Plays should be seen and heard, not read."

"I agree," Jane replied. "Have you ever seen one of his plays performed on stage?"

"A couple, actually. I prefer a good minstrel show or burlesque, but the plays have their appeal, too. I even saw Edwin Booth in one of 'em; *Hamlet*, I think it was.

"What about you, Jane? Do you like to read?"

"I love it!" she replied enthusiastically. "When I was a girl, books were the only way I got to travel, in my mind. Even today, I carry a valise full of books with me wherever I go. It drives Cash crazy! And I like to write, too."

Jason cocked his head toward the journal in her lap. "So I see. Is that your diary?"

"No, though I do write down what I see and hear. Mostly I work on ideas for stories I hope to write."

"What kind's that? Poems? Romances?"

"Oh, no," she scoffed. "I'll leave those to the proper English ladies. To be honest, I like a little more blood and guts in my reading material." She looked around a bit conspiratorially, leaned sideways toward him.

"I want to write for the *dime novels!*"

"You don't say."

"I do. Is that awful?"

"No, no. Not at all. Sounds like a crackerjack idea to me. Take me, for instance. I'm a sucker for penny dreadfuls about Davy Crockett."

"Me, too!"

"I mean, the poor soul's been dead for nigh on to forty years and he still leads a more exciting life than most people I know."

She laughed at this, a sweet, bubbling sound like river water breaking through the winter ice in the first spring thaw.

"Have you had anything published yet?" he asked.

She shook her head slowly. "No. I've only worked up the nerve to submit a couple of stories, but I don't think the editors back East took me very seriously."

"You think that's 'cause you're a woman?"

"I think so, yes. I think they worry that boys and men won't buy an adventure story written by a woman.

"But I'm not sure. I don't want to make excuses. Maybe I'm just not good enough."

"Oh, I imagine you're plenty good enough, Jane. Have you ever tried using a phony name on one of your stories?"

"You mean pretend I'm a man?"

"Why not? If nothing else, it might show you whether it's your writing or your sex that's the problem."

"Hmm. I just might do that."

"Then I'd best not keep you from it any longer." He started to return to his newspaper.

"Oh, no," she protested. "I don't often encounter a fellow bibliophile."

"A what?"

"Book lover."

"Oh."

"Besides, I'm enjoying talking with you, Jason."

"Me, too. With you, I mean."

"So, what brought you to Texas?" she prompted.

"Actually, I was born here."

"Really? But you fought for the Union side during the war, didn't you?"

"I did."

"How did that happen?"

"I guess you'd have to start with my daddy," Mankiller said, leaning back in his chair.

"He traveled a lot in his younger days. He used to say home is just what we call the place where we rest our heads at night.

"Way back in the '20s and '30s, he was a hunter and trapper. As such, he rubbed shoulders with the likes of Jim Bridger and the Bent brothers.

"One year, after the spring Rendezvous, he traveled to Texas at the invite of an older trapper he'd become friends with. That trapper had taken a Kiowa woman to wife, all legal like.

"The two of 'em had a daughter, name o' Willow. A lovely girl."

"Your mother?" Jane asked softly.

"The same." He smiled wistfully. "I came along in 1845 and spent the first ten years of my life here in Texas. I even spent some time with my grandma's people."

"Are your parents still alive?"

"No. The smallpox took my momma. She contracted it from some of those she was tryin' to help nurse. She was good that way.

"Anyhow…as much to get away from painful memories as anything else, my daddy packed me up and moved us to his own birthplace, up Ohio way.

"He never remarried, but he tried the best he could to raise me right. We worked a little farm together."

"Living there: is that why you fought for the North?" Jane asked.

"Not entirely. Oh, I thought theirs was the right side, all things considered. But I think it was just the thrill of adventure that mostly grabbed hold of me.

"I wanted to run off and join up right after First Manassas, but Daddy said I was still between hay and grass."

"What's that?"

"Too young. Neither still a boy nor yet a man. Only half grown."

"But you did join eventually?"

"Yeah. A couple years later. But even then it wasn't for no noble or heroic reason." He paused, obviously a little uncertain of what to say next.

"What was it?" Jane prompted.

"I was *paid* to go to war," he said in a rush of words.

"What does that mean? I don't understand."

"Me and Daddy had a couple of bad years on the farm. Too little rain, too many locusts. He didn't have enough money left to buy seed. It looked like he was gonna lose the place.

"Then, one evening, we was visited by a Mr. Delmar Hendrickson. He ran the grain and feed store in the nearest town, and had done right well for himself.

"He also had a grown boy, a fella who was worthless as teats on a boar hog, from what I heard. But his poppa loved him, and was upset that his boy was about to get conscripted into the Army.

"You may not know this, but in those days a man could *buy* his way out of service, either outright or by enticing someone else to take his place.

"That was one of the biggest disparities in the war. I'm told that something like ninety percent of all Southern men served in the Confederate military, while less than fifty percent of Northern men did likewise. And even with that, we had nearly twice as many men as the Rebs did. A lot of conscripted men bought their way out."

"And this man wanted you to take his son's place?"

"Yeah. He knew I wanted to go to the war, and he knew the pickle my pa was in. So Mr. Hendrickson offered me three hundred dollars, the going rate, and promised to give Daddy enough seed for the next planting, free gratis. That way, my pa would have seed and money to live on.

"It was a deal I thought we all could live with."

"Or die with," Jane said somberly.

"Aw, hell," Mankiller scoffed. "When you're that young, you don't think you're ever gonna die."

"What about now?" she asked. "I saw you kill that Meadows man the other day. I was watching from upstairs. You seemed calm as a summer breeze, both during and after." She fixed him with a hard stare.

"Doesn't it bother you to kill another man?"

"Not near as much as it would bother me to *be* killed."

"Does even that not really bother you? Do you have no fear at all of dying?"

"No more or less than most men have, I reckon." He gazed out straight ahead.

"Sometimes...sometimes I feel like the best part of me probably already died, a long time ago."

"No. It didn't."

His head snapped around at her words, but she was bent over her journal, scribbling away with her pencil. He started to resume reading his newspaper.

"I'd already heard lots of stories about you," she said abruptly. "Even before I met you."

"Oh?"

"Are they true?"

"Which ones?"

"Any of them."

"Hard for me to say, not knowing what all you heard. And I do know people tend to exaggerate." He exhaled softly.

"But I suspect a fair amount of what you heard is true."

"Even about what happened at Gettysburg?"

"Even that."

Now it was she who stared off silently into space for a short time. Then, straightening in her seat, she turned back toward him.

"Do you ever feel guilty?" she asked.

"Beg pardon?"

"Do you ever feel guilty?"

"About what?"

"About what happened that day."

"I don't know what you mean. None of that was my fault."

"I know. But I've read that sometimes sole survivors feel guilty because they didn't die when everyone else around them did."

"Hmm." He seemed baffled, as if the very thought had never occurred to him. "No. At the time, I was too glad to be alive to feel bad about not being dead. I still feel that way."

He smiled sadly. "It's funny, though."

"What's that?"

"You're not the first person to ask me that question; a couple of others have. But in all these years, ain't nobody ever asked me once if I felt guilty about killin' all them poor Johnny Rebs that day."

He turned to look at Jane.

"I reckon they all wanted to go on living just as much as us Union boys did."

"So I'll ask you," she said. "Do you feel guilty for killing them?"

"Not one damn bit," he replied without hesitation.

Her eyes locked with his for a long moment, as if trying to read what was in his mind and his heart.

Did he just wink at her?

And if so, what did it mean? Was he telling her a yarn? Was he trying to say that his seemingly ruthless indifference to life, his own or others, was at least partly merely a device meant to...do what? Enhance his already considerable reputation? Make others think twice before crossing him? Give himself an edge over them?

Or was it a barricade to protect himself from both the ugliness he witnessed and that he perpetrated?

Almost fearing to discover the truth, she dropped her eyes back down to her lap and resumed her scribbling.

"What about you?" Mankiller asked.

"What?"

"Here I've been babbling on and on about myself, enough to talk a donkey's hind leg off, but I don't know a thing about you. What's your story, Jane?"

She sat her pencil and pad down on her lap, folded her hands together atop them and took a deep breath.

"There's really not much to tell. Certainly nothing as exciting as what's happened to you in your life.

"I was born in St. Louis and don't you dare ask how long ago!" They both smiled.

"My mother died when I was five, and I was placed in a county home for orphans."

"What about your daddy?"

Her mouth tightened. "Apparently, he believed his obligation to me ended about a week after I came into the world."

"I'm sorry."

"So was I. But he died a horrible, lingering, torturously painful death… in my mind. Many times."

"So, in a way, you started weaving stories at an early age."

"I guess you could say that."

"How long were you in the home, before you were adopted?"

"I never was."

"Really? I find that hard to believe."

"Why's that?"

"I'd think anybody would be happy to have such a pretty and high-spirited girl."

She smiled wistfully.

"Not as much as they want a boy with a strong back. Not that the folks at the home didn't get plenty of work out of me. When they weren't laying the rod to me."

"Sounds horrible," Mankiller said. "How'd you get outta there?"

"Cash took me out."

"How'd that happen? Don't tell me he adopted you?"

"Oh, no," she chuckled. "He was in town working the gambling parlors down on the riverfront; he'd come up the Mississippi when he first left New Orleans.

"He was in a clothing store one day, buying new ties, when Mrs. Wickersham, the woman who ran the orphanage, came in with a few of us in tow. She always brought some of us with her when she went shopping, to carry her packages.

"As usual, we kids were practically dressed in rags, but the old biddy wanted new for herself.

"I was still not much more than a child, but Cash told me later that something about me just seemed to draw his attention. While Mrs. Wickersham was busy trying on new dresses, he struck up a conversation with me.

"She put a stop to that, once she saw what was going on. But Cash found ways to visit with me from time to time.

"Then he told me he was leaving St. Louis and offered to take me with him. I leaped at the chance. That was five years ago." Jane closed her eyes.

"He saved my life," she declared flatly, opening her eyes to look at Jason.

"And you've been together ever since."

"Mostly."

She saw Mankiller's eyebrows arch and smiled. "Sometimes, Cash feels the need to go off alone for a while. But he always comes back, or sends word for me to join him."

"What does he think about your writing?"

"I don't know; he's never read any of it. I'm afraid to ask him to, for fear he'll tell me what he really thinks of it.

"He did take the time to teach me to be one hell of a faro dealer, though." Both she and Mankiller again laughed lightly.

"I'd like to read your work someday," he said.

"Maybe," she replied. "Someday."

"Someday would be fine."

"You've traveled around a lot, haven't you, Jason?" she asked, none too smoothly changing the subject.

"A fair amount, yeah. I guess you could say I've seen the elephant."

"I haven't seen nearly enough to suit me," she said. "Mostly just the towns on the gambling circuit we follow.

"But I'd like to see New York City. Maybe even London and Paris."

"Well, then, you need to get that shiftless man of yours to take you to those places," Jason jested.

She smiled. "Unless there's a card game involved, I imagine I'd have a hard time getting Cash to ever go east of the Mississippi."

"Then just maybe I'll take you someday."

"Someday would be fine," she replied softly.

She smiled wistfully.

CHAPTER 9

At about the same time the next day, Mankiller was again seated in front of the Last Stand with his newspaper. Since this meant repeating his behavior, this time he put the paper down frequently to scan the area around him. Nothing was amiss.

"Looking for me?" a cheerful voice said from behind and to one side of him. A smiling Jane Starr was standing just inside the saloon's batwing doors.

"Of course," he replied lightly. "Won't you join me?"

She nodded and pushed her way out through the doors. As she took her seat on the opposite side of the entranceway, he noticed she again had pencil and notebook in hand.

"What shall we talk about today?" he asked.

"Actually," she replied, "I had some more questions about you I wanted to ask. Do you mind?"

"Not at all," he said, hoping she hadn't noticed his hesitancy before replying.

"What did you do after the war ended?" she asked, moving in quickly.

"I went back home, intending to do nothing more than settle down and help Pa run his farm. He needed the help; he'd worn himself to a frazzle trying to work the farm alone.

"But I guess after two years of war, the quiet life of a farm just didn't seem to hold much appeal for me."

"I noticed you called it 'his' farm and not 'our' farm."

"That's the way I thought of it. Now, I didn't complain none; I never would have. But I think Pa could see the signs. He'd felt the same way when he was young and had the wanderlust in him.

"So one day, he just upped and announced that he planned to sell the farm and make one last trek west, back to the mountains. I think it's really what he wanted, too. As he put it, we weren't either one of us really cut out to be a plow chaser.

"The man who bought Daddy's farm from him was Delmar Hendrickson; the same fella who'd paid me to take his son's place in the Army.

"Mr. Hendrickson was honest enough to tell me that it might have been a waste of his money and my life, as his son Peter seemed to have made it his life's work to consume as much alcohol from as many different saloons as was humanly possible.

"He also said he hoped I bore no grudge against him for having to go to war."

"Did you?" Jane asked. She was leaning toward him, eyes wide with interest in the telling of Jason's story.

"Not at all; and I told Mr. Hendrickson as much. I think he still felt a sense of obligation, though, as he paid Pa full market value for his farm, and a little above. Since the money was going to my daddy, I raised no objection."

"Tell me more about the war," Jane urged. "How did serving in the Army affect you and all the other men?"

"Maybe you oughtta ask Cash about that," Mankiller replied with tongue in cheek. "He seems to know more about war than I do."

"Would you rather not talk about it?"

"Naw. I don't mind," he lied, having already spoken more of it to her than he had to all others in nearly a decade. He sat collecting his thoughts for several moments without speaking further. Jane just sat and watched him, not pressing.

"It was like most wars, I guess," he said at last. "Started by the few, but paid for by the many. And what a price we all paid.

"Both sides took boys and near-boys, by the hundreds of thousands, and trained them all to be killers. Then those who survived the unpleasantness were just cut loose, without so much as a fare-thee-well.

"Most of 'em, 'specially the Rebs, had nothing to go back to, so they came here to the West.

"Far too many of 'em are still what they became during the war: animals that thieve and kill, rape and plunder."

"That's not what you became," Jane said.

"I was luckier'n most, I guess. I came from good stock and was taught to blame no one but myself for my faults and mistakes. Was taught to be strong enough to make my own way, instead of taking from the weak. Was taught that being poor in pocket doesn't mean you have to be poor in spirit.

"Most of all, I was taught that in hard times, you gotta just cowboy up and keep goin'."

"What about women?" she threw at him, her grin carrying a hint of the devil.

"What about 'em?"

"How do you feel about them? In general."

"I got sense enough to be scared to death of 'em," he replied, now sharing her smile. "But not enough to stay away from 'em."

"So there have been women in your life?"

"A few."

"Maybe more than a few? I've seen how the girls in the Last Stand react to you…and how you react to them."

He tried to shrug this off. "What can I say, Jane? You are creatures of endless fascination."

"Have you ever met one who was fascinating enough to settle down with?"

"More like I never met one who had the fortitude to put up with me long enough for that to happen."

"I think you judge yourself too harshly, Jason."

"If I'm like most folks, not harshly enough. How 'bout you and Cash? You're not married, are you?"

"No. We have something different."

"How so?"

"Like I said, he saved my life. I truly believe that. And he's been real good to me."

"So you're happy?"

"Happy enough."

He sensed she'd prefer he delve no deeper into this subject, so he didn't. Instead, he opened his newspaper back up.

"It's a strange world we live in, isn't it?" he said, apropos of nothing. "Listen to this. Says here that a local farmer, one Otis Smoot, has a sow that recently gave birth to a piglet with two heads." He set the paper back down and looked over at her.

"Have you ever heard of such a thing?"

Jane smiled and shook her head. "After your daddy sold his farm, did he make that trip out west?"

"We made it together, leaving the Old States behind us and never lookin' back. Spent nigh on to three years up in the Rockies.

"We hunted, fished, trapped. Broke bread with some of the savages, barely escaped with our hair from others. It was the happiest I'd seen Daddy since before Ma died.

"Guess that's why I didn't feel too bad when he passed over himself. He was content."

"What did you do after he died?"

"Oh, I've mostly just drifted ever since, wanting to see as many different places as I can. I've held more jobs along the way than Carter's got pills, to support myself."

"Have you ever worn a badge?"

He snorted. "Naw. Had one offered to me once, but I turned it down. I've been 'deputized' a time or two, to ride along with a posse. Helped string up a couple of rustlers once, but that's about it."

"How'd you get to be so good with a gun?"

"Mostly, that just seemed to come natural. Wasn't anything I planned or sought, though it's a skill I worked to hone once I realized I had it."

"Cash tells me you've had to make use of that 'skill' fairly regularly." Jane saw his jaw clench almost imperceptibly; the comment had obviously bothered him.

"I didn't mean to offend, Jason."

"You didn't."

"But you have had to use your gun more than a few times, yes?"

"Yeah."

"It's the tattoo, isn't it?" she said, noting that his hand moved up to touch it. "It makes you a target."

"Maybe. When a man pulls a gun or a knife on me, I don't bother to ask him why.

"That's one of the reasons I kinda like it down Mexico way; there are fewer men around who carry grudges from the war or who are seeking to build a reputation." His lips curled wolfishly.

"Plus, there's a fair number of Mexicans who are superstitious. They're kinda afraid of the man who cries blood."

"Have you ever considered trying to cover up the tattoo somehow?"

"Nope."

She dropped it there and bent to make some notes in her journal. He returned to his newspaper.

But, as if by unspoken agreement and arrangement, the two of them began to spend part of each afternoon sitting together and exchanging conversation. Always, Jane would be writing in her journal, even as they spoke.

Mankiller was amazed at how much the woman was able to get him to tell about himself and his life; this was something he was not prone to do. On the other hand, he was never able to coax her into telling him nearly so much about herself.

That seemed to be the way she wanted it.

CHAPTER 10

It started out as a fairly typical evening, with Mankiller stationed atop his perch in the Last Stand.

As his eyes scanned the room, he was performing a little slight of hand. Using the fingers of his left hand, he was slowly flipping a silver dollar back and forth across the top of the hand, purely by touch.

This was one of several exercises he routinely performed, in an effort to make himself as nearly ambidextrous as possible, on the slight chance that his right hand should ever be rendered useless. After years of practice, he could shoot as accurately with his off-hand as most men could normally.

He smiled as he saw the girl Dixie coming his way, steaming cup of coffee in hand. As he bent to take it from her, he noticed her war paint was even more heavily applied than usual, doubtless in a misguided belief that this made her look better.

"May I say, Miz Dixie, that you look especially lovely this evening." The lie had the intended effect; her face lit up in a way that actually did let some of her natural beauty shine through the covering coat of lust and loneliness.

"Thank you, kind sir," she replied. She then winked at him. "Y'know, Jason, you've been here for several days now, and you still haven't graced any of us girls with your presence after hours. We're beginning to think you don't like us."

"Just the opposite, sweetheart," he said to her, though she noticed his eyes had left her to again roam around the room.

"Faced with such a feast of beauty as you ladies present, I'm having a hard time deciding which dish to sample first."

He said the right words, but there was no passion behind them. The smile on Dixie's face evaporated, and she turned to head back to the bar. As she did, she cast a baleful look at the statuesque woman dealing faro.

Mankiller's eyes were increasingly drawn to the faro table as well, but not for the reason Dixie would have thought. It was one of the players at the table who was commanding his attention.

He'd seen the man once before, though only at the bar. He was a loudmouthed lout named Cyrus Goodell. According to Sam Dobbins, he was widely suspected of being a fellow who cast a wide loop, though he'd not yet actually been caught in the act of rustling cattle.

Jason figured he must be better at rustling than he was at gambling, for he'd been consistently losing to Jane Starr.

Early on, Goodell had merely groused about his bad luck. As the evening progressed, though, and his losses mounted, he began to darkly and loudly insinuate that the game was rigged. Jane simply smiled at him in reply. Mankiller laid his hand on his shotgun.

"You're a goddam cheat, woman!" Goodell fairly shrieked as he came up a loser again.

"I assure you I'm not," she replied, still smiling sweetly.

Neither noticed that Mankiller had left his perch.

"Yer lyin', witch!" Goodell growled, pushing up to his feet and going for the pistol stuck in his belt.

That's when he felt the barrels of a shotgun press up against his spine at the small of his back. This was followed by the ominous sound of one of its hammers being cocked.

Mankiller was curious, though. He had seen Goodell begin to stiffen even *before* he would have felt the shotgun at his back. He now looked over the rustler's shoulder and down at Jane.

To his surprise, he saw that the lady had produced a gun of her own; from where, he couldn't imagine.

It was a small, .22 caliber "knuckle duster" pepperbox pistol. Not terribly powerful, but at close range still capable of doing real damage. And she had it aimed squarely at Goodell's chest.

She now looked up at Jason, and they exchanged strained smiles.

Mankiller quickly cast his eyes to the left, to the nearby table where Cash Carpenter had been playing poker. There was no surprise this time; though he had not bothered to rise from the table, the gambler had pulled a .38 caliber Navy Colt pocket gun with a three and a half inch barrel from a shoulder holster. It too was pointed at Goodell.

Jason nodded to Carpenter. He had noticed the slight bulge of the gun beneath the breast of Cash's coat the first day they had spoken, and he had no doubt the gambler knew how to use it.

Cash tipped his head to Jason, then smoothly slid his gun back into its holster. He picked his cards back up, prepared to continue the game as if nothing had happened.

But even against such odds, Goodell was still tempted to go for his gun; Mankiller could tell from the way his body tensed.

"Go ahead," he hissed in the rustler's ear, pressing the barrels of the shotgun more firmly against his back. "You pull that thumbuster, mister. But if you do, I'll blow a hole in you they could drive the Union Pacific railroad through."

Though quivering with helpless anger, Goodell dropped his hand away from his pistol.

"That's better," Mankiller said. "Now just pull your horns in and turn around."

The rustler did as directed. Mankiller moved in unison with him, so as to remain behind him. He gave the man a soft jab with the shotgun to get him moving forward.

"Now get on outta here," he ordered. "And if you ever set foot in here again, I'll clean your plow."

He escorted the man most of the way to the exit, then gave him a shove to speed him on the rest of the way. Goodell risked one hate-filled glare over his shoulder at Jason, then continued on.

The entire room had gone silent with expectation, but as Goodell pushed his way through the batwing doors, everyone went back to what they'd been doing.

Everyone except Jason Mankiller.

He didn't turn away from the doorway to go back to his perch. Instead, he dropped down to one knee. He propped the butt of his shotgun against the spot where his upper leg and waist met, barrel pointing forward at an upward angle.

No one but Jane seemed to notice this, and she stared at him quizzically.

Barely had Mankiller assumed this position than the batwing doors of the saloon slammed open inward. Bellowing in rage, Cyrus Goodell came barreling back into the saloon, pistol drawn and cocked.

Eyes wide, he tried too late to skid to a halt as he spied Mankiller crouched just a few feet in front of him.

Jason tripped the trigger on his sawed-off shotgun.

A tight pattern of buckshot hit Goodell just below the sternum with explosive force. The blast lifted him clear of the floor and through the still-flapping batwing doors.

In no hurry at all, Mankiller rose to his feet and walked to the doorway. He could see that Goodell had flown across the sidewalk and tumbled down the steps. He lay unmoving, his limbs all at awkward angles, face down in the dusty street outside.

It was clear the rustler was dead, so Mankiller spared him no further attention. He turned and headed back to his perch, there to await the inevitable arrival of the marshal.

His path took him past the faro table. He could feel Jane's eyes on him as he walked by, but he didn't turn his head to look at her.

Back at his post, he broke open the shotgun to remove and replace the spent shell. Seeming to be totally removed from the stares and whispers around him, he set the shotgun back down on the table and resumed his watchful vigilance.

There'd be no more trouble that night.

CHAPTER 11

The next day, Mankiller was summoned to the marshal's office.

It was not a particularly impressive or imposing place, though better kept than many such. The floor was clean and swept. A pot-bellied stove stood in one corner.

The marshal was seated behind a sturdy oak desk, motioning for him to step inside. On the wall behind the marshal was a gun rack holding four rifles and a shotgun. To one side was the door Mankiller presumed led into the cell area.

"You wanted to see me, marshal?"

"More like I had to." Marshal Russell pushed back away from the desk, folding his hands in his lap.

"You've shown yourself to be quite the curly wolf, Mankiller. You've only been in this town a week, and you've already beefed three men.

"What are you trying to do, fill up our bone orchard all by your lonesome?"

"I'm just trying to get by, marshal."

Russell grunted, then opened a drawer in his desk. Mankiller noticed a stack of papers pushed to one side of the desktop: wanted posters, by the look of them. He wondered if the lawman ever bothered to look at them. His eyes slid back to the marshal as he saw him remove a slip of paper from the drawer.

"This here's your blood money, boy. A bank draft in the amount of two hundred dollars. Two killin's, paid in full. Sorry to say, there don't seem to be any money comin' to ya for Goodell." The lawman's voice was dripping with sarcasm. "Guess you just killed him for free."

Mankiller made no reply. He reached for the bank draft, but the marshal pulled it back.

"Once you get this cashed, boy...feel free to head on outta town, ya hear?"

Again, Mankiller chose not to reply. He snatched the bank note from the marshal's hand, tipped his hat to him and left.

Only when he was outside did he actually look at the note. He whistled softly. He hadn't held so much money in his hand at one time since Mr. Hendrickson had paid him to go off to war; and he hadn't really thought of that as his money but rather his pa's.

He had to admit to himself that he wasn't really sure exactly what to do with such a windfall, so he took a seat outside the mercantile to give it some thought.

After cogitating on the matter for close to an hour, he walked down the street to the First Cattlemen's Bank of Ft. Rogers.

He'd never been in a bank before, and was therefore uncertain as to what he should do after he entered its doors; so he just stood in the middle of the floor looking around.

Two tellers were working behind a nearby counter, but they ignored him in favor of others waiting for assistance. Farther back, he saw a couple of other fellows seated at large, shiny desks. They weren't assisting anyone, but showed no inclination to help him either.

Then he noticed a slender young man seated at a tiny desk way back in one corner of the room. He seemed to be watching Jason intently. Finally, tentatively, the man rose from his desk and approached the drifter.

"Excuse me," the clerk said. "Are you being helped?"

"If so, I can't tell it."

"Do you need some assistance?"

"Can you give any?"

The young man smiled. "Let's find out. Won't you come with me?"

He led Jason back to his tiny desk and offered him a seat, then took his own on the opposite side.

"My name is Byron Longfellow. I've only been working here a month and they mostly just give me simple bookkeeping chores; but I assure you I can handle whatever's required.

"So what can I do to help you, Mr. Mankiller?"

Jason cocked his head. "You know me?"

The clerk smiled again and tapped his left cheek with one finger, a clear reference to Mankiller's tattoo. "Ft. Rogers isn't that big. Pretty much everyone knows who you are."

Jason nodded. He then pulled the folded bank draft out of his shirt pocket and slid it across the desk. Longfellow gave it a look.

"All right. Did you just want to cash this, or did you want to do something more with it?"

"Well, I don't really need that much money all at once, but I'm not really sure what to do with it."

"Might I suggest you simply start a savings account with us?"

Longfellow went on to explain how Mankiller could make deposits and withdrawals, how interest would accrue on his money, even how he could use other banks and the telegraph service to make transactions from other locations.

The young man impressed Jason with his straightforward manner. He talked in plain and simple terms while never giving the impression he thought the drifter was stupid. Mankiller liked him and decided to follow his advice.

Within twenty minutes the two of them were shaking hands at the conclusion of their business. Mankiller prepared to leave the bank with thirty dollars in his pocket and a small deposit book in hand.

Before leaving, though, he took a slight detour in the direction of one of the older men seated at one of the larger desks. The fat, sweaty man seemed to be doing nothing more than shifting papers from one side of the desk to the other.

"Excuse me," Jason said as he drew near.

"Yes?" the man said impatiently, barely looking up. "What do you want, cowboy?"

Annoyed by the man's needlessly brusque tone of voice, Jason controlled his anger, even doffing his hat and holding it in both hands.

"I won't take but a minute of your time," he said. "Are you one of the owners of this here bank?"

"Hardly," the fat man sniffed.

Then he actually looked at Jason for the first time. At the sight of the distinctive teardrop tattoo, he skin blanched and he began to sweat even more profusely.

"I am the manager, though, sir," he stammered.

"Good enough," Mankiller replied. "I just wanted to tell you that you should keep a close eye on that young fella back there." With his hat, he motioned toward Byron Longfellow, who was already busily resuming his bookkeeping duties.

"Why?" the fat man said in a rush. "What did he do wrong?"

"Not a thing. I just wanted to tell you that he strikes me as being a real hard working go-getter. I think if you let him, he'll go far with this outfit. You'll be glad you did." Jason paused, thinking if there was anything more to be said.

"That's all."

He returned his hat to his head and exited the bank. The fat man watched him go, feeling his breathing begin to return to normal.

Then he turned to appraise young Longfellow with new eyes.

Outside the Last Stand saloon, Mankiller saw Sam Dobbins looking over some wooden boxes sitting on the sidewalk, checking an invoice to make sure he'd received all the liquor he had ordered. Jason drifted over and without being asked began to help Sam carry the boxes into the saloon's storeroom.

"Sam," he asked, "you wouldn't happen to have another room upstairs that I could rent out, would you?"

"Actually, I got a couple o' rooms ta spare." His eyebrows raised slightly. "Where have you been stayin' till now?"

"Oh, here and there."

The barkeep pushed it no further. "I can let ya have a nice, clean room for three dollars a week," he said. "Same deal I give Cash and Jane."

"Sounds fair," Jason replied. "Just one thing. Uh…you think you could give me a room that's not too close to theirs?"

"I gotcha," Sam said, giving him a leering smile. "Ya don't want any loud noises disturbin' yer sleep!"

"Yeah. Somethin' like that," Jason replied.

Mankiller was already at his post in the saloon that evening when Jane Starr descended from her upstairs quarters. His financial dealings that day had kept him from his usual afternoon conversation with her, which he figured she'd make mention of now.

To his dismay, she instead walked by him without saying a word or even looking in his direction. Then, halfway to her faro table, she stopped. Spinning around, she came back to his perch and glared at him with eyes that seemed to have grown even darker with anger.

"Look, Jason," she said, "I'm sorry if I somehow made you think less of me last night, but I don't think it's right if you do."

He blinked, confused.

"What the hell are you talking about, Jane?"

"I wasn't cheating that man."

"I never thought you were."

"Then, was it because you found out I carry a gun? I only use it for protection, same as you."

"I got no problem with that, either. Or with you. I think you're a fine piece o' calico, Jane. Fine as cream gravy."

"Then what is it?" she demanded. "Why wouldn't you even look at me after what happened?"

He stared down at his callused hands, struggling to find the right words.

"I didn't look at you...I didn't look at you because I didn't want to see how you might be looking at me."

"Now I don't understand," she said.

"Don't you?" he asked; but clearly she didn't.

"It's like this. I'd just blown a man to kingdom come in front o' God and ever'body; did it cool as you please. It didn't bother me at all. But if I'd looked over at you and seen fear or revulsion in your eyes...I don't think I coulda stood that."

Only now did he look up at her. She still seemed aggravated, but her features had softened considerably.

"Of all the...Did it ever occur to you that what you might have seen would be sympathy and concern?"

"No. It didn't."

"Well, next time, Mr. Mankiller," she said, with what he knew to be only mock severity, "give me the benefit of the doubt. All right?"

"All right."

She gave him a soft smile and walked away. He saw her pass by Cash Carpenter's table, pausing to rub his shoulder and give him a quick kiss before moving on to her faro layout.

The rest of the evening passed uneventfully. As it was winding down, Mankiller saw Dixie heading his way. Something seemed wrong. She was carrying the usual cup of coffee on a small plate and looked tense, almost fearful.

She set the cup and saucer down on his table but said not a word to him; she didn't even meet his eyes with hers before turning and hurrying away and out through the batwing doors of the saloon.

Pondering the soiled dove's odd behavior, Mankiller lifted the cup to take a sip. As he did, he noticed a folded slip of paper that had been sitting beneath it. Making sure no one was looking his way, he unfolded the paper. A short note was written on it:

Come to my crib after closing.
Urgent.

He slipped the note into his pocket and mentioned it to no one. When the last patron left in the early morning hours, he told Sam he was taking a walk before calling it a night.

A block north of the saloon, in a narrow lot that ran east and west, stood a row of cribs: small, poorly constructed one-room shacks in which many of the working girls lived and occasionally entertained when they weren't doing so in the saloons.

Dixie had told Mankiller on an earlier occasion which one was her residence, and he found it now easily. He stood across the street from it for awhile, satisfying himself that no shady figures were lurking about. He walked up to her crib's narrow door and tapped lightly.

"Dixie?" he said softly. "It's me." Silence.

"Come in," a tense voice called from inside at last.

He pushed the door open and stepped inside. The light was dim within, supplied by a single candle. It was enough for him to see the bed against one wall. Dixie was crouched atop it, pressed into a corner. Her face showed fear and tears rolled down her cheeks.

"What's wrong?" he asked, stepping farther into the room.

The next instant, someone who had been hiding behind the door slammed into his back. Arms wrapped around him, pinning his own arms to his sides and preventing him from reaching gun or knife.

The weight of the attacker carried them both to the floor. Mankiller struggled to get his knees under him, trying to buck free of his assailant.

Before he could do so, something metallic crashed against the back of his head.

His eyes rolled to the tops of their sockets, and his body went limp.

CHAPTER 12

Even when Mankiller awoke he was in the dark. His senses swam and his skull throbbed as if it was still being pounded upon. His eyes opened but saw nothing. His stomach was churning, as his body seemed to rise and fall up and down.

He felt coarse cloth rub against the skin of his face and realized at last that a burlap bag covered his head and was tied loosely in place by a cord around his neck.

He could barely move, and came to the realization that he had been thrown belly-down across the saddle of a moving horse. A rope stretched under the horse's belly was tied around his wrists and ankles, holding him helplessly in place.

The splitting pain in his head, coupled with the rocking motion of the horse as he hung upside down made him violently ill. His stomach roiled and bile spewed out of his mouth and into the confines of the burlap bag.

"Aw, hell," a raspy voice said. "He's done puked!"

Mankiller heard a second voice, though he couldn't make out the words. His horse came to a halt. Moments later, he could feel the rope binding his arms and legs together go slack as it was cut. A pair of hands dragged him roughly off the horse.

With the flow of blood to his feet having been cut off, he was unable to stand and flopped to the ground. His wrists were still bound together, but he tried to reach up and remove the suffocating bag from his head. For his efforts, he was rewarded with a rap across his knuckles by the barrel of a gun.

"You can't leave me to drown in my own vomit!" he shouted, assuming that if his captors wanted him dead he would never have awakened.

The two voices held a whispered conference.

"Keep yer hands in yer lap," one of the captors snapped. Mankiller did as he was told.

He felt the cord around his throat being loosened. The bag wasn't removed, but was pulled open enough to empty out most of its contents, which spilled down the front of Mankiller's shirt.

The spout of a canteen was pressed against his lips and he eagerly sucked in water that cleared his throat. Too soon it was snatched away and the bag was lowered and tied back around his neck. The smell of it almost made him puke again.

Two pairs of hands lifted him up and helped him into the saddle of the horse that had been carrying him. His hands were still tied at the wrists; his vision was obscured and his breathing labored. But at least now he was upright in the saddle.

For the rest of that day, as they rode along, Mankiller tried occasionally to engage his captors in talk, to no avail. He decided it might be wiser to shut up and listen instead, in hopes of learning something that might aid in his escape.

Before long it became evident that there was just the two of them holding him captive. Their names were Hector and Luke, and while it seemed to him that neither was smart enough to pour piss out of a boot, it also became clear that Hector was the dominant of the two.

When they stopped and made camp for the night, they tied their prisoner to a tree. He was given a small strip of stringy jerky to eat and an equally small sip of water to drink. In the morning, he was allowed another sip of water before they resumed traveling.

Except for the occasional unprovoked cuff to the side of his head or kick to the ribs, they were not especially cruel to him. But the routine of their journey never varied. Mind-numbing hours in the saddle. The bare minimum of nourishment was the only physical comfort he was allowed. He was even forced to soil himself, for no other allowances were made for bodily functions. So unchanging was the trek that Mankiller lost track of how many days had passed.

Finally, it ended.

Mankiller was grabbed and pulled from the saddle. After being dragged a short distance away, he was released from their grip. He heard footsteps moving away from him, the creaking of leather as men mounted horses.

Taking the chance, he reached up with his bound hands and loosened the cord around his neck. When no one made a move to stop him, he pulled the burlap bag off his head.

Fresh pain lanced into his skull as the full light of day hit his unprepared eyes. His hands flashed up to protect them, then slowly lowered as he adapted to the glare.

Blinking rapidly, he at last saw his two captors, sitting their mounts about twenty feet in front of him. One was heavily built, with eyes dull and devoid of humanity. Mankiller's hat sat atop his head of greasy brown hair and his gunbelt circled the man's waist.

The second man was taller but leaner of build. Even with his mouth closed he seemed almost to be grinning, for a raw scar pulled up one side of his lips. Mankiller's spurred boots now graced his feet.

"Look, Hector," the scar-mouthed man exclaimed. "He's seen us!"

"So what?" the bigger man replied smoothly. "We're a hundred miles from nowhere. Seeing our faces won't do him any good."

"It's hot as a whorehouse on nickel night out here. Without food or water, he'll be dead inside four days!"

"If you want me dead, big man," Mankiller said defiantly, "why not just shoot me now and be done with it?"

"Yeah, Hector," Luke said, his vulture-like head bobbing up and down. "Why don't we just shoot him now?"

"'Cause you and me ain't got no law papers on us yet, Luke, and I'd just as soon keep it that way."

"Why, hell, no one'd ever know we done 'im."

"Maybe. Maybe not. But remember what we was told when we was hired? 'Make him disappear.' That's what we're doin'. And since he was alive when we left 'im, they can't say we killed him."

Jason didn't say a word; Hector's literal interpretation of their orders meant their captive would get to live, at least for now. Meanwhile, he was intently studying his two captors, memorizing every feature of their faces for what he firmly believed would be his eventual day of reckoning.

"It's been a pleasure doin' business with ya, Mankiller," Hector gloated in oily tones.

"C'mon, Luke. Let's go spend us some of this money!"

Putting the spurs to their mounts, they galloped away, leading the horse that had carried Mankiller. In response, Jason simply took a seat on the hard, sun-baked ground.

About a quarter mile out, the pair slowed their horses to a less tiring walk. Mankiller watched them impassively, wanting to let them get farther out of sight before he began following.

He doubted they'd risk going back to Ft. Rogers right away. But, stupid and lazy as he judged them to be, confident that he would soon be dead, he figured they would head for the nearest settlement or outpost where they could gamble, drink and whore away their ill-gotten gains.

Since he had no clear idea where he was, it seemed doubly wise to follow them; they would lead him to a town. Then he would exact his revenge.

When the pair was nearly out of sight, Mankiller pulled off his socks and stuffed them into a pants pocket. They would offer his feet no real protection, so there was no point in ruining a perfectly good pair of socks.

Plus, the soles of his feet were heavily callused and nearly as tough as leather; he'd never even worn a pair of shoes until he was twelve. As long as he watched where he was stepping, he should be all right.

He was philosophical about the straits he was in. This was not the first time he'd had to ride shank's mare, travel afoot, nor, he was sure, would it be the last.

CHAPTER 12

Mankiller knelt to study the tracks left by his fleeing captors. There were three sets, of course, with one being lighter because that horse didn't have to bear the weight of a rider. One of the other horses seemed to have slipped a nail.

Judging by the approximate time they had ridden that day before abandoning Jason, and by the position of the sun, he judged they were

"...why not just shoot me now..."

headed nearly due west. The land here was flat and barren, but he thought he could just make out the shape of hills on the far horizon.

He set out along their trail, walking at a slow but steady pace. He seldom stopped, and then only briefly, eating up the miles. He continued on even after sundown, stopping for the day only when it became too dark to see their tracks.

About that time, he spied a small outcropping of rock thrusting up from the floor of the prairie; one that would offer him at least a little shelter.

Stepping gingerly so as to avoid stone bruises, he headed toward a particular section of the outcropping. It was a small, thin ridge, much like a fish's fin.

Sitting down with his legs astraddle this ridge, he began to rub the ropes still binding his wrists together back and forth along it, laboriously sawing at its cords. He didn't care how long it took; he had to have his hands free.

After what was probably an hour of sawing, strands of the rope began to part. When they were frayed enough, he was able with effort to break them apart.

It took him nearly as long to get all the blood and feeling back into his aching hands. The two strands of broken rope were probably too short to do him any real good, but he slipped them under his trouser belt anyway.

Then he curled up in the shadow of the rocks and went to sleep, ignoring the rumblings in his stomach.

He awoke at the first gray whisper of dawn. He was hungry and thirsty, but there was as yet nothing much that could be done about either, so he forced the thought from his mind.

Finding a small, smooth pebble, he popped it into his mouth to suck on and thus allay his thirst a little. Even in the faint light he easily picked up the trail of Hector and Luke and resumed following it.

Having had neither food nor water to fuel his strength for better than twenty four hours, by midday he was finding it harder to lift his feet and continue moving forward. Still, he allowed himself no more rest stops than he had the day before.

He pulled up at the sight of bleached bones lying to one side of the trail he was following. In life, it had been a mule, but that was long enough ago that predators and the elements had stripped it of anything resembling flesh.

Still, he dropped to his knees to pick through the bones, hoping to find something that might be of use to him. His fingers closed around the small end of one of the animal's jawbones, lifting it to stare at its stark whiteness. His sun-cracked lips curled upward.

If such a weapon was good enough for the biblical Samson, he figured, then it was good enough for him.

As the sun sank lower on this second day, the lack of water that had left him severely dehydrated and the long period of being malnourished began to take an even heavier toll on the man.

A low growl ahead and to the left of him dispelled his malaise and brought him instantly alert and dropping into a crouch from which he could spring in any direction.

The cause of the noise was hidden from his view by a solitary boulder rising some ten feet above the level of the ground. Mankiller softly padded over to it, pressed his back against its rough, uneven surface.

He slowly slid his way around the boulder till it began to curve away from him. Cautiously peering around the far side of it, he saw the source of the growls. Three coyotes, so emaciated he could clearly see the bones of their ribcages, were savagely gnawing and ripping at the carcass of a small deer.

Had the man's mouth still been capable of producing spit, he would have salivated at the very thought of this potential meal. He quickly removed his shirt, wrapping it several times around his left forearm.

Then, holding his jawbone weapon high, he ran toward the coyotes, emitting what he hoped at least approximated a blood-curdling scream.

At the unexpected sight and sound of this two-legged beast, the coyotes beat a hasty retreat, as he had hoped and expected they would.

But they didn't go far before they stopped. Shaggy heads low to the ground, they began to skulk back toward the abandoned carcass. They bared their fangs and growled out a warning to he who sought to rob them of their supper.

Mankiller had not anticipated this kind of reaction from such normally skittish and cowardly scavengers. They too must be suffering from a powerful hunger that they would be so willing to challenge him.

He barely had time to brace himself before they sprang to the attack. As one of them left its feet in a leap, Mankiller raced forward to meet it. His arm arced, the jawbone cracked against the coyote's head and caused it to fall to the ground.

He thrust his left arm into the gapping mouth of a second coyote. Its jaws closed down, but its fangs failed to penetrate the material of the shirt he had wrapped around the arm.

With the coyote still clinging to his limb, Mankiller spun and kicked the third scavenger in the ribs, eliciting a loud yelp. The coyote hanging on his arm succeeded in raking the man's side with the claws of its front feet. Mankiller spun faster and the animal released its grip, flying through the air until it slammed against the nearby boulder.

The coyote he'd kicked lunged forward again. He brought the jawbone down on its back. Leery of further pain, it and the other two coyotes loped away.

Still, Mankiller was sure they would return again, and soon. He'd have only moments to rip away a piece of the carcass for himself and beat his own retreat.

But when he dropped to his knees beside the dead deer, the rancid smell that washed over him made him reflexively gag and dry heave. Only now, up close, could he see that this was no fresh kill. The deer's rotting flesh seemed almost alive, covered as it was with wriggling hordes of maggots.

The coyotes might be able to stomach such rancid fare but he couldn't risk it, risk the sapping sickness it could visit on him, out here alone in the wilderness.

He staggered away, leaving the deer to the scavengers. As he passed through the descending veil of night, he could hear them snapping and tearing at the desiccated carcass.

Mankiller raised his makeshift weapon, staring at it in the fading light. It had done a good job, but he thought it wise to inspect it for damage. It seemed intact, and its leading edge reflected the pale light darkly, stained as it was with the blood of the coyotes.

He pulled it close to his face to make sure he was seeing clearly. Yes, it was wet with blood, flecked with tiny bits of flesh.

He popped the jawbone into his mouth like it was an ear of corn, sucking and licking away the blood and gore. It wasn't much and would do little to revive him, but it was the closest thing to food and drink he had had in two days, and he savored every drop of it.

Still, when at last he stopped for the night and curled up on the ground, he did not fall asleep so much as pass out.

CHAPTER 13

Even when his eyes opened the next morning, Mankiller didn't feel as if he were awake.

The world seemed less real, more like in a dream. Colors were less vivid; images were blurred by a heavy aura around them.

He was dying.

"I can't die if I'm moving," he said aloud, as if the sound itself could make it so.

He rolled onto his belly and pushed himself to his knees. Then to his feet. Sheer will power made those feet move.

He traveled neither far nor fast, but he refused to stand still. As the hours of the day slowly passed, he no longer looked down to make sure he was following the trail left by Hector and Luke on a true line. He stared straight ahead, focusing on a tall hill on the far horizon and using it as his guidepost.

That's why he didn't notice when the ground suddenly dipped beneath his feet.

Thrown off balance, too weak to compensate as his weight shifted, he fell flat on his face hard, sliding downward. As luck had it, he didn't have far to fall before the ground again leveled out on a flat.

The easiest thing would have been just to lie there. He couldn't do that. Not because he was afraid to die if he didn't get up, but because he knew that would allow his killers to get away free and clear. That he would not allow. This thought alone was sufficient to make him rise.

It was when he did that he saw the little house.

It was a solitary dwelling, a bit on the small side and made of simple adobe with a thatch roof. Near the house was an equally small, crude corral, with an attached lean-to. A few goats were leisurely grazing within the corral. In the yard, three or four chickens scratched and pecked their way around the hut. Beyond the dwelling could be seen tiny plots of ground devoted to crops: mostly corn and beans.

And in front of the hut was a *well*.

A sound like a laugh mixed with a groan crawled from his parched throat. He wanted nothing more than to race to it and throw himself into its watery embrace. But he resisted the urge, stumbling past the well to stand nearer the front of the hut.

"Hello, the house," he croaked. "Is anybody to home?"

He squinted, staring at the front door. Long seconds later, it opened just a crack.

"Go away!" a woman's voice cried from within.

Realizing he was still carrying his jawbone weapon, Mankiller dropped it in the dust and held his empty hands out to his sides.

"I'm unarmed, ma'am," he said. "And I mean no harm to you or yours."

No response, but at last the door slowly opened wider. A Mexican woman, no older than him, stepped out of the hut. Her long, dark hair hung in a manner that covered half her face. She wore a white peasant blouse tucked into the waist of a green skirt that fell all the way down to the top of her bare feet. He didn't blame the woman for fearing and mistrusting him; his current disheveled, unbathed self must have presented a most discomfiting sight.

Mostly, though, he noticed the weapon held in her hands. It looked to be an ancient blunderbuss. If she was to fire it, it might do as much harm to her as to her target. Still, he wanted to give her no excuse to use it.

From behind her, a little girl of no more than four years of age tried to push her way around the woman to look at the stranger. Her mother harshly scolded her in Spanish, to no avail, then glared back at Jason.

"What do you want?" she demanded.

"A couple of good, long drinks from your well would be a life saver, ma'am," he told her. "And maybe a bite to eat, if you've any food to spare."

"I don't."

He nodded. "I understand. These are hard times. Then, if you don't mind, I'll just get that drink and be on my way." He started to turn away, still moving slowly.

"What are you doing way out here, all alone?" she asked.

"It wasn't my idea, ma'am, I assure you. I was robbed and dumped out yonder by a couple o' real ne'er-do-wells."

At those words, the woman's left hand flashed up to her face. This pushed her long hair back enough to reveal two things about her. She was a comely woman, and she had a black eye. The latter was clearly recently acquired.

"They were here, weren't they?" he asked, describing Hector and Luke to her. The woman hesitated, then nodded.

Jason's face took on a new, pained expression, knowing that such worthless scum as those two had doubtless done far more than simply hit the woman. Then his eyes dropped to the child.

"The little one," he gasped. "They didn't...?"

"No." She looked down at her daughter sternly. "Unlike now, she listened to me when the others showed up and I told her to hide under the bed.

"But she saw..." The woman's voice cracked and she pulled the little girl closer to her.

Jason dropped his head, then raised it to see she was staring at him sadly.

"And your husband?" he asked.

"Gone six months now. Dysentery."

Mankiller winced, shaking his head. He'd seen the effects of dysentery during the late war, had dug many a grave as the result of its ravages. As many as a hundred thousand men on the two sides combined had succumbed to it.

But then, battlefield cleanliness was poor, virtually nonexistent, and diseases of all sorts had been rampant. Small wonder, in an atmosphere where thousands of men lived together in tight quarters and where latrines were nothing more than hastily dug ditches.

Pneumonia, measles, influenza and other communicable diseases were common and could reduce a brigade to nearly nothing in a matter of days.

With infections killing more men than muskets and cannons did, wounded soldiers feared the mere sight of a field hospital. In his mind's eye, Jason could still see amputated limbs piled in stacks taller than a man.

The lucky ones had the benefit of anesthesia during operations. Others were simply given a shot of whiskey and held down by sheer force while the doctors sawed away at them. Mankiller had performed such service more times than he cared to think.

He remembered that on occasion General Custer would order members of the regimental band to stand outside the surgical tent and play as loudly as possible in an effort to drown out the wails of the boys being virtually butchered within.

"I am truly sorry for all you've suffered, ma'am," Mankiller said with unquestionable sincerity. In a sense, he felt responsible for having brought some of that sorrow down upon her.

"I'll not trouble you any further," he said, turning to leave.

"Wait," the woman abruptly called after him.

He turned back to face her. She swayed back and forth, as if silently struggling with herself.

"Do you know how to chop firewood?" she asked him.

"I've broke a rick or two in my time, yes'm."

"You'll find an ax and a pile of wood on the far side of the lean-to," she said. "Cut an armload into firewood for me…and I'll feed you."

He nodded and turned away again. Before starting to work, he went to the well. He dropped the empty bucket resting on its stone rim down the shaft, then used the rope attached to it to pull it back up.

He lifted the bucket to his lips, restraining himself to a series of small sips, letting the blessed cool water swish around in his parched mouth before swallowing it. When he was sure he wouldn't make himself sick, he took a much longer, deeper drink.

He then raised the bucket higher. Tilting it, he poured the rest of the water over the top of his head.

A high-pitched but lilting giggle drew his attention back to the hut. The woman and child were still standing in the doorway watching him. Peeking out from behind her mother's skirt, the little girl giggled again.

Mankiller gave her a warm smile in return, then shook his head vigorously, like a wet dog, sending droplets of water spraying out in all directions.

The child broke out into peals of laughter at the sight of this. Then her mother shooed her back into the house, following her and firmly closing the door behind them. Even across the yard, Jason could hear the sound of a bar being thrown across it. He didn't blame her.

Lowering the bucket again, he drew more water and again drank deeply. After pouring more water down the back of his neck, he set out for the lean-to.

Calling the tool he found there an ax seemed a mite charitable to him. The lower third of its handle had been broken off. The nicked blade on its head was wobbly and barely sharper than a butter knife, and there was no sign of any sort of grindstone he could take to it.

Still, he set out to work as best he could.

An hour later, the woman heard a soft knock at the door. After first looking out the front window, she unbarred and opened the door and slipped outside.

To her right, against the side of her hut, sat stacked what was far more than a mere armload of firewood.

Mankiller, after knocking on the door, had retreated a good twenty paces away from the house and was now sitting cross-legged on the ground.

"If you'd like, ma'am," he said, "you can just set my food down outside the door and I'll come get it once you're safely back inside."

She stood with her hands on her hips, intently studying this most unusual man. She turned at last to retreat inside, then spun back on her heels to again face him.

"You come inside," she said. "Eat at the table."

"The ground'll be just fine, ma'am."

"No." She jerked her head toward the house. "You'll come inside."

"Only if you're sure."

"I'm sure." There was no hesitation in her voice.

Mankiller rose from the ground and slowly walked to the house, still focused on making no sudden or remotely threatening moves.

The woman turned in the doorway to let him pass. She thought it odd that all his clothing appeared to be soaking wet.

She didn't know that, after he finished cutting her firewood, the drifter had carried a bucket of water out of sight of the house and tried as best he could to wash the worst of the accumulated filth from both his body and his apparel.

He paused to take a look around the hut. It was nearly bare of furnishings, but everything was neat and clean as a whistle. The little girl was seated at one side of a small table, and he dropped into a chair on the opposite side.

"My name is Rosario Mendoza," she said.

"Pleasure to make your acquaintance, ma'am," he replied. "I'm Jason Mankiller."

Rosario nodded before moving to her stove and starting to fill a plate. "My giggling little monkey is Anita."

"Are you *really* a monkey?" Mankiller whispered across the table.

This brought a fresh wave of giggles from the girl.

Rosario set a plate down in front of him. It held a fried egg, a dollop of beans and a couple of tortillas. From a pitcher, she poured him a glass of goat's milk.

In his present state of hunger, it looked to him like a feast fit for the gods.

Snatching up a spoon, he prepared to dig in. Before he could get the first helping up to his mouth, though, he saw both mother and child close their eyes and cross themselves, preparing to say grace.

Mankiller laid his spoon down, placed his hands in his lap and bowed his head respectfully. To him, and given all that had happened to her, the fact that this woman could still find it in her to be thankful for anything spoke volumes about her character.

Famished though he was, he held himself in check, eating no faster than did Rosario. After finally finishing every crumb on his plate, he pushed it away from him.

"Would you like more food?" Rosario asked.

"Oh, no, ma'am," he said, patting his stomach and pretending to be full. "I'm fit to bust now."

She sighed and rolled her eyes before reaching out and snatching his empty plate. She moved to the stove and returned with a few more beans and tortillas for him.

"Eat," she ordered. "I don't trust a man who doesn't have a good appetite."

He eagerly took the plate offered him, quickly proving he was quite trustworthy.

Afterwards, Rosario rose and started to collect the empty plates and silverware. Mankiller also rose, and took them from her before she knew what was happening.

"You did the cookin', ma'am," he said. "And real good it was, too. So it's only fair that I do the cleanin'."

"That's not necessary," she objected. "You're our guest."

"An intruder's what I am," he replied. She opened her mouth to protest, but he'd have none of it.

"It's true and you know it," he said. "So just sit yourself back down and leave this little chore to me."

She did as he insisted, closing her mouth and taking her seat. He carried the dirty dishes to a metal tub sitting on a counter, beneath the spout of a small water pump. He filled the tub, then turned back toward the table.

"You wanna help me do the dishes, chickabiddy?" he asked the child.

"Really?" she said, her eyes lighting up.

"Sure," he replied. "I'll wash, and you can dry."

Anita hopped from her chair and ran over to the sink. She held her arms up to Jason and he lifted her up and set her down on the counter. Grabbing a clean dishtowel, she set to work.

"You're one of the best dish dryers I ever did see," Jason complimented her, knowing he would have to go in behind her and really dry the dishes. As usual, she giggled.

"What's that?" she asked, reaching out and touching his tattooed cheek.

"Anita Maria!" her mother scolded.

"It's all right, ma'am," Jason told her. "It's natural for little ones to be curious." He swiveled his gaze toward Anita.

"It's kinda like a picture somebody painted on me," he explained.

"It looks like a tear."

"Uh-huh."

"Were you sad when they painted you?"

"Sort of."

Rosario cringed at her child's prying.

"You're bigger than my daddy," Anita abruptly said, leaping to a new subject, as children will do.

"Well, we can't help what size we are, sweet pea," he told her. "I bet he was a real good daddy, though, wasn't he?"

"Uh-huh. One time, he made me my very own dolly, out of corn husks."

"Ya don't say? I'd like to see that dolly."

"You can't."

"Oh? Why not?"

"'Cause one of the goats ate her," she said matter-of-factly.

"Oh."

Rosario, who had been sitting and watching their interaction with great interest, now rose and came over to the counter.

"It's time for you to go to bed," she announced, scooping little Anita up in her arms.

"Do I have to?"

"Go on, little one," Jason said. "Maybe you'll have a dream about your daddy." She smiled at him.

As her mother was tucking her under the covers, Anita held out her arms for a hug, then whispered in her mother's ear, "I like him, Mommy."

Rosario kissed her on both cheeks before turning away from the bed. As she did, she noticed the man was no longer at the sink, but rather was standing by the door.

"It's getting late," he said as she approached him. "And I'm plumb tuckered out. Would it be all right if I spent the night in your lean-to before I go?"

She studied his face again before responding.

"I can put some blankets on the floor," she told him. "Make you a pallet."

"Thank you, ma'am, but the straw in the lean-to will suit me just fine." He reached for the door handle, then glanced back, looking almost confused.

"Can I ask you," he started, then paused. "You don't...you don't seem to be quite as, uh, scared of me as you was before. Why's that?"

"It's because now I know you are a good man," she replied confidently. He blinked at her response.

"How could you know that?"

"Because *she* knows," Rosario answered, nodding toward Anita, who had already fallen asleep.

"The whole time those animals were here," she continued, crossing herself, "she could see them from hiding." She closed her eyes tightly, as if doing so would also shut off the memory.

"She saw what they did to her mother."

Jason winced at the very thought.

"So now she knows about bad men," Rosario said. "And if she thinks you're not like them...I believe her."

The drifter smiled gratefully.

"So you can stay here if you want."

"Thank you, little lady. I appreciate that. But I know the nights have to be real bad for you, what with all that's come crashin' down on you of late.

"You wouldn't want a stranger around; it would just make things worse." He opened the door to go.

"The lean-to will do me fine. And come first light, I'll be gone."

True to his word, he arose the next day while the sky was still gray, after a deep and restorative sleep. Another long drink from the well and he was ready to go.

To his surprise, he turned from the well to see Rosario also up and standing in the yard, obviously looking for him. She was holding a small sack in one hand, a sombrero in the other.

She handed him the sombrero, which had no doubt belonged to her late husband, and he planted it on his head. From the sack, she pulled a pair of worn sandals.

He sat on the ground to put them on. They were a bit small, but they'd do to protect his feet in the short haul.

When he stood, she offered him a short machete, then handed him the sack.

"There's a gourd of water in it," she explained, "and a little food."

At this he shook his head.

"No. I'll take the rest, and be most grateful for it. But not your food. I don't want to create a hardship for you and the young'n."

"Take it," she insisted. "It isn't much; just a few beans wrapped in some tortillas."

He smiled and accepted the gift.

"Just one more thing. Did you happen to see the direction those two went when they left here?"

She nodded and pointed to the southwest.

"Is there a town anywhere in that general direction that you know of?"

"Si. San Ramon."

"And how far would that be?"

Now she pointed at the large hill that lay straight ahead from her humble home.

"If you could climb straight over the rocks," she said, "it's probably no more than fifteen miles from here as the crow flies.

"But everybody takes the road, of course. It meanders back and forth with the lay of the land so much that the journey to San Ramon becomes more like forty miles."

"And how long ago were they here?" he asked, studying the face of the formidable hill.

"Just the day before you arrived."

Mankiller grunted in satisfaction. Even afoot, he had clearly begun to catch up with them.

"Thank you for everything, ma'am," he said. "Tell Anita I said goodbye." Rosario smiled tightly.

"And I want you to know I'll find a way to repay you for all your kindness."

"That's not necessary, Senor Jason. You helped us, too."

"I think otherwise. And I will find a way to show my gratitude." Nodding a farewell, he walked away from her, then stopped and looked back over one shoulder.

"I don't know if this will help you any with what you've had to endure, Rosario, but I *will* find the two bastards."

"They are not so far ahead of you," she replied, hanging her head in shame, "because when they were here…they took their time."

His jaw tightened.

"That's one more reason why, when I do find 'em…I mean to kill 'em."

"Good," the woman said softly, then turned to walk back to her hut.

CHAPTER 14

Having rested and regained some of his strength, with food and water in his belly and shoes on his feet, Mankiller quickened his pace. Even after the sun went down, and for much of the night, he kept on.

He could no longer see his prey's tracks in the dark, but he gambled that they would indeed be heading for San Ramon. He chose to ignore their winding trail for now and instead set a straight course toward the town, over smaller hills and through gullies. Only when the moon was high in the night sky did he lie down for a few hours sleep.

Shortly after awakening and setting out the next day, he found himself standing on a dusty road that passed by the base of the final and largest obstacle between him and San Ramon.

Catching his breath before making the final climb, he also bent to look for sign on the road. Though the byway did not appear to bear particularly heavy traffic, it still took him several minutes to spot the three sets of hoof prints that told him the men he sought had indeed passed this way.

He knelt to pick up some of the droppings their horses had left behind. The dung was soft and moist, even faintly warm.

They were on this road, not far ahead, heading to the east in a way that would allow them to skirt around the steep hill.

Mankiller made no such allowances, and set his course straight up the face of the hill. No horse could ever make it up this way, nor was it easy for a man afoot. But he was determined to prove it was doable.

"Thank you, Rosario," he muttered to himself. If not for the simple sandals he now wore, even feet as toughened as his might have been cut and torn to disabling shreds by the rocky escarpment.

At one point, the palm of his left hand did get shredded, when a foothold gave way beneath him and he had to grab the nearest outcropping to stop his fall.

Upon finding a narrow ledge, he stopped to rest and pick pieces of gravel out of the wounds in his palm. He pulled one of the socks out of his pocket and wrapped it around the hand, to stanch the flow of blood and make sure its wetness was absorbed and wouldn't impede his ability to climb.

Looking upward, he saw a crack in the rock face above, seemingly running the rest of the way up to the top of the hill. He made for it and wedged himself between its two sides.

With his feet pressed against one wall of the crack and his back against the other, he slowly crabbed his way upward. He heard and felt the cloth of his shirt tearing, felt stone scraping away skin from his back.

He ignored the pain and kept climbing.

When his head popped up above the rim of the crack, he saw that, as hoped, he was at the pinnacle of the hill. Pulling himself up, and lying on his belly, only then did he look back down the way he had come. Clearly, the hill was tall enough that a fall from its heights would have proven fatal.

A few scrubby trees had found purchase in the poor soil of the hilltop, and he sought the shade of one while he got his second wind. While he did so, he allowed himself a few well-earned sips of water and swallowed a cold tortilla.

The far side of the hill was sloped more gently than was the face he had just ascended, and he made good time on his way down.

From the heights, he had been able to see the ribbon of the road that Hector and Luke would be traveling if San Ramon was their destination. Skidding the last few feet to the bottom of the hill, he stepped onto the roadway and again searched it for sign.

This time, no matter how closely he looked, he saw no sign of the two outlaws having passed this way yet. A smile threatened to curl his lips. It was possible, he knew, that this simply meant they had left the trail at some point and headed out in another direction. But he believed them to be of the sort to always pick the path of least resistance.

Scouting the trail, he found a place where it made a short, curving loop so as to bypass a small stand of trees. Mankiller walked among the trees, peering about intently until he spotted what he needed.

Using the machete Rosario had given him, he chopped a relatively straight limb off one of the trees, one that was approximately five inches around and some six feet long.

He stripped the limb of all its branches and leaves, then used the machete to sharpen one end of it to a long, thin point. He now had a weapon with some reach.

Finding a spot where he could watch the road without being seen, he sat down to wait, munching slowly on his last tortilla.

Less than two hours later, his vigilance was rewarded. Two riders appeared from the east, from around the concealing swell of the hill. One of them was leading a third, riderless horse.

Eyes squinting, he could only make out their general sizes, but not their features. That was enough. He silently slithered from under the trees, scooting over to the other side of the road and secreting himself in some concealing undergrowth.

As the two riders drew closer, Mankiller at last clearly saw that they were his former captors.

He was pleased that his initial assessment of their respective identities had also proven to be correct. The one who would pass closest to his hidden position was Hector. With both hands free, and possessing a slightly higher intellect than his partner, it was he who posed the greatest potential threat and therefore he who needed to be eliminated first.

Mankiller slowly rose to a crouch, remaining silent and concealed, tightly gripping his makeshift spear in both hands. He held his breath as the two riders drew closer and closer, now only yards away.

He burst explosively out of his concealment, screaming at the top of his lungs as he charged forward.

At the sound and commotion, Hector's mount reared in fright, its front hooves leaving the road. Thrusting up from below it, Mankiller rammed home the point of his spear, driving it deeply into the horse's soft underbelly.

With all his might behind him, feet churning, Mankiller kept pushing forward. Screaming in pain, the horse pitched over and to one side, carrying its stunned rider with it.

Quickly noting that the fallen horse had pinned Hector beneath it, Mankiller released his hold on the spear and turned his attention to the second outlaw.

Luke was trying to deal with both the frightened horse he was astride and the one he was leading. Running in a crouch, dodging and weaving so as to avoid flailing hooves, Mankiller made his way to the left side of the outlaw's panicked mount.

Leaping up, he grabbed a handful of the outlaw's shirt. Luke's eyes widened in astonishment as he saw the face of his former captive, now apparently risen from the presumed grave. Then he felt himself being pulled out of the saddle and dragged to the ground.

The will to live overcame his fear and he lashed out at Mankiller, catching him on the jaw. Jason struck back, knocking Luke into his steed; both it and the other riderless horse bolted away.

Dazed by the blow from Mankiller, Luke shot out a left fist. Mankiller blocked it with his right arm and threw a short left into the outlaw's ribs, nearly doubling him over.

A second quick left followed the first and Luke began to fold. Seeing an opening, Mankiller unleashed a sweeping overhead right that caught the outlaw in the temple and put him down on the ground.

Luke hit the road belly down, then attempted to roll over. As he did, Mankiller raised his right leg and brought his sandaled foot down with crushing force on the outlaw's stomach, driving the air out of his lungs and eliciting a loud cry of pain.

As Luke lay gasping desperately for air, Mankiller bent and snatched the outlaw's pistol from its holster.

Now ignoring the fallen outlaw for the moment, Jason sprinted back to the other side of the road. Hector's impaled horse had slid off and down the side of the byway. The spear still protruding from its breast did not move, for the animal had mercifully expired.

Hector's right leg remained pinned under the horse's body, and he was fiercely trying to pull himself free, using his left foot to try to push the dead weight off him.

Too late he noticed the grim Mankiller walking toward him. His efforts to pull free of the horse were forgotten as instead he frantically clawed at his holstered pistol.

"Far enough, Hector!" Mankiller barked, jumping down to stand over the outlaw, gun cocked and pointed at his head. Seeing the futility of resistance, Hector dropped back down, propped up only on his elbows.

"What now?" he asked.

"Now we see whether you can buy your life," Jason said. "All you have to do is tell me who hired you to take me out."

"Go to hell!" Hector snarled defiantly.

"You first," Mankiller replied calmly, firing a single shot.

Hector's head snapped back sharply, sprouting a red flower of blood. His back arched once and then he was dead.

Casually, in no real hurry, Mankiller strolled back to the other side of the road. Luke was still writhing on the ground, clutching his belly with both hands, struggling to regain his breath. His eyes bulged as he looked up to see Mankiller standing over him.

"Yer supposed ta be dead!" he gasped.

"Maybe I am, boy," Mankiller replied, grinning wickedly. He raised his pistol and cocked it.

"I asked your partner a simple question, Luke. He chose not to answer. You heard what I did to him.

"So now I'm askin' you, and I'm only askin' once. Who paid you to do this?"

"Don't shoot, mister!" Luke whined breathlessly, "Hector made this deal, not me."

"Made a deal with who?"

"It was one of the McClure boys. The youngest one. Tyrone, I think's his name."

"That's good to know," Jason said.

"So you'll let me go?"

"One more question, tough man. Whose idea was it to abuse that poor little Mex gal?"

"Who?"

Mankiller moved his pistol even closer to Luke's head.

"No! Don't shoot! That was Hector's idea, too. I didn't want anything to do with it!"

"Of course you didn't."

"I told you all I know, mister. Told ya true. So you'll let me go now, right?"

"Sure I will, Luke. I'll let you go right where Hector went."

Again, a single shot to the head did the trick.

When the last of the gun smoke had curled from its barrel, Jason slipped the pistol into his belt, turning his attention to the two horses that remained alive.

Having been badly spooked, they had still only cantered off a short distance, and now stood to one side of the road, heads lowered as they cropped grass.

Mankiller walked slowly toward them, speaking to them in soft and soothing tones. Neither objected as he took their reins in hand, led them to a nearby tree and tied them up.

Patting each a few more times to keep them calm, he then left them to return to Luke's body. The first thing he did was pull his stolen boots off the dead outlaw's body and return them to his own feet.

He unbuckled Luke's gunbelt, removing it and sliding the pistol out of his belt and back into its holster. He then went through the man's pockets; this time, he felt no compunction at all about stripping the dead.

He found a hundred dollars folded in one pocket: probably Luke's share of the fee for eliminating Mankiller. A second pocket yielded a few more dollars.

Crossing the road yet again, he retrieved his hat, gun, knife and holster from Hector, and likewise rifled his pockets. He'd obviously kept more of the blood money for himself than he had given to Luke, for Jason found one hundred and fifty dollars stuffed in his back pocket, plus a few dollars more elsewhere on his person. Included in that was the thirty dollars they had stolen from Mankiller along with his treasured pocket watch.

Grabbing the dead outlaw under his arms and straining mightily, Mankiller managed to pull him free from under the slain horse. He dragged the body well away from the road before dumping it in some bushes.

It took even more effort to pull the saddle, saddlebags and bridle off the dead horse, and Mankiller was sweating and panting heavily by the time the chore was accomplished.

He yanked his makeshift spear free of the animal's carcass and flung it away. There was no way he could move the horse's body, but he figured scavengers would quickly do their work sufficiently to hide the fact that the steed had not died of accident or natural causes.

He similarly dragged Luke's corpse off the beaten path before unceremoniously dumping it. The two outlaws had admitted to him that they had no bounties on their heads, so they were of no further use or interest to him.

Taking a seat on the side of the road, he next went through each man's

...and returned them to his own feet.

saddlebags. Anything that could be helpful to him he set aside; all else he tossed away in the woods.

Among the things he kept was a wrinkled shirt that he donned to replace his own tattered and torn garment. Everything else he kept amounted to enough to fill one saddlebag; the now empty one he strapped back on Luke's saddle.

The drifter closely examined the two surviving horses, his first priority was determining that neither carried a brand. He decided the dun they had used to carry him was the slightly better of the two: deeper of chest, with long, powerful legs. This one he would make his own.

He pulled the saddle off it, though, replacing it with the one from Hector's dead horse. The canteens each outlaw had been carrying were still more than half full; he poured the contents of one into the other to fill it up, drank what remained of the first before throwing it away.

Both captors had carried a rifle with them, in saddle scabbards, and he gave each a thorough exam. Not surprising, it was again Hector who had the better weapon: a Winchester .44-40 lever action. This he slid into the saddle scabbard of the dun he now considered his.

He slung the spare saddle atop that on Luke's horse, securing it in place; this horse would also carry the extra weapons he was appropriating.

Mounting his steed and grabbing the reins of the second horse, he set off at a walk down the road, in the direction where San Ramon should lie.

He didn't travel far, nor had he meant to; he simply wanted to put some distance between himself and the site of his bloody encounter with the two outlaws.

No more than three miles along, he began to weave in his saddle. His respite at Rosario's had been a true godsend, but he was still suffering from the effects of too little food, water and sleep.

It had taken every ounce of what strength he had regained to catch up with Hector and Luke and eliminate them. All he was going on now was determination, and that was fading fast.

He turned off the road and rode half a mile or so into a flat area dotted with boulders. Finding a spot shielded from the wind and preying eyes, he slid from his saddle.

Now finding a use for the strands of rope that had earlier bound his wrists together, he hobbled the horses' front legs with them to keep the animals from wandering off. He unsaddled and rubbed down both horses, gave them some water, tending to their needs before seeing to his own.

Matches filched from Luke's breast pocket enabled him to easily start a small fire. The two outlaws had been carrying at least meager supplies in their saddlebags, and he used them to heat up a plate of beans and salt pork. In a small pot he brewed some coffee, savoring its taste and its warmth.

As soon as he finished eating and cleaning his utensils, he scooped dirt onto the fire to extinguish it. Pulling a blanket over himself, he quickly fell asleep.

It was after noon on the following day when he rode into the hamlet of San Ramon. It was a bit more than a wide spot in the road; big enough, he hoped, to have what he needed.

Within minutes he spied the large front of a livery stable. He walked both horses through its open double doors. By the time he dismounted, a bow-legged, bantam rooster of a man with a bushy gray beard had come bustling out of a nearby stall.

"Can I he'p ya?" he asked, eyeing Mankiller warily, taking special note of his teardrop tattoo.

"I got one horse I want to stable for two, maybe three days," the drifter answered, "and one that I'd like to sell."

Without a word, the old liveryman walked around the lead horse, lifting each of its legs in turn to check for flaws. After a thorough inspection, he came back full circle to face Jason.

"I tell ya," he said, "I am in a generous mood today. I'll give ya thirty dollars for the old plug."

Mankiller just looked at him, amused.

"Does this pissant little town o' yours have a lawman?" he asked.

"O' course it does," the liveryman replied suspiciously. "What for ya wanna know?"

"I just wanted to ask him if he and the citizens of this fine town know they got a highway robber living in their midst."

The old timer turned his head and spit. Most of the tobacco juice hit the ground; the rest dribbled down to join that which already stained the front of his wiry beard.

"What number was you thinkin' fer the critter?" he asked, squinting with one eye.

"I was hoping for seventy-five dollars."

The liveryman just cackled.

"Well, sir," he said, "I'll tell ya what. You can wish in one hand and spit in t'other. Guess which one'll fill up first?"

Mankiller allowed himself a slight smile, shaking his head. "I'm too hungry and tired to haggle all day, you old turd. How's this: sixty dollars for the horse, both saddles and all the fixin's?"

The liveryman pretended to think long and hard on the offer, then thrust out a wrinkled hand.

"Done!"

Mankiller shook hands vigorously. Next he pulled the saddlebag off his own horse and removed the rifle and holstered pistols from the one he had just sold.

"Is there a gunsmith around here I could maybe sell these weapons to?" he asked.

"How come ya ta have so many firearms on ya?"

"I took 'em off the bodies of old farts who asked too many questions."

The liveryman giggled and ran a finger back and forth under his nose as if scratching an itch. "Fair 'nuff. Yeah, there's a gunsmith close to hand. Just across the street and down about two blocks. He'll treat ya right."

"As good as you?"

The old man slapped his left thigh two or three times. "Hell, son, ain't nobody else *that* good!"

Mankiller nodded knowingly, then reached out to stroke his horse's neck. "Treat him right, sir. And do you think you can give him some oats every day along with hay?"

"Sure. It'll cost ya an extry ten cents a day, though."

"Money well spent." He handed the reins to the liveryman. "I'm also looking for a decent place to eat and a clean spot to rest my head on." It had been nearly a month now since he'd lain between sheets, and the thought of sleep was calling to him as loudly as was food.

"The best hotel in town just so happens ta also sport the best restaurant," the old man told him. "That'd be the Tucker House Hotel. Right straight behind the gunsmith's shop, on the next block over.

"It don't come cheap, though," he warned. "Rooms are a dollar a night."

"I think I can afford that," Mankiller replied. "Thanks to your generosity."

The old man let loose with another cackle and spit out a fresh stream of tobacco juice. "I like you, boy. Almost makes me regret havin' cheated ya!" He started to turn away, but Jason halted him.

"Just one more question."

"Yeah?"

"Can you give me directions for the best way to get from here to Ft. Rogers?"

CHAPTER 15

Anita Mendoza was beginning to worry about her mother.
The little girl had just gotten dressed when her mother left the house to fetch firewood with which to cook them breakfast. Now, at least in her tiny mind, she'd been sitting at the table an awful long time and was getting really hungry.

So why hadn't her mama returned?

The child pushed back from the table and hopped down off her chair. Crossing the room, she opened the front door and stepped outside. Turning to her right, she froze in her tracks.

Near the corner of their hut her mother, Rosario, was kneeling on the ground. Her head was bowed and she was loudly sobbing. Anita fearfully ran to her.

"What's wrong, Mama?"

Rosario looked up at the child. Oddly, she was smiling even as tears continued to flow freely down both cheeks. She reached out with one arm, pulling Anita close to her.

"Nothing, little one. Nothing is wrong."

Anita turned her head to see what her mother had found when she came for firewood. In front of them stood not the dwindling pile of wood that had been leaning against the wall of the house when they went to bed the night before.

In its place now stood a large stack of freshly cut firewood. Leaning against the pile was a brand new ax.

On the ground in front of the woodpile rested the sombrero, sandals and machete that had belonged to Rosario's late husband.

Also sitting on the ground were two large burlap bags. From the larger of the two, Rosario had already extracted a sack of flour. She now pulled out corn meal, beans, salt, lard, molasses, canned goods of various kinds, salt pork and bacon, even some beef.

The second burlap bag yielded a sack of sugar, a small bolt of blue cloth and some sewing goods and a bundle of licorice twists. Rosario blushed when her hand brought out a lovely lady's hair comb made of polished walnut.

Her eyes widened as she pulled out a leather pouch that emitted clinking sounds. Opening it, she poured part of its contents into the palm of her left hand.

The pouch was filled with coins: gold and silver, of various sizes. Her breath caught in her throat. There must be hundreds of dollars here, she realized.

She would learn it was two hundred, fifty dollars to be exact. The same price that had been set as the worth of Jason Mankiller's life.

Had the drifter been there, the woman would have argued that this was far too much money for the small amount of aid and comfort she had given him.

To his mind, though, it was still far too little to compensate for the pain and sorrow he felt he had brought down upon the heads of this innocent woman and child.

Clutching the coin sack to her bosom, Rosario reached into the larger bag and pulled out one last item. Smiling, she showed it to her daughter.

It was a small rag doll, dressed in an equally tiny gingham dress.

"Aaah!" Anita cooed. "It's *beautiful*, Mama!" She turned her eyes to her mother. "Is it for *me*?"

"Yes, Anita *mia*," Rosario said, handing the doll to her child. "From our friend, Senor Jason."

Delighted, little Anita hugged the doll as tightly as she could, then jumped up and ran into the house to show her new friend where she would be living from now on.

Rosario remained behind, still on her knees, fresh tears welling up in her eyes.

She lifted her face to heaven, thanking God for sending the man with the tear of blood into their lives.

CHAPTER 16

Sometimes towns, like men, simply wither away and die.

After having left San Ramon and making his brief and stealthy visit back to Rosario Mendoza's little farm, Jason Mankiller had set his course for the straightest way back to Ft. Rogers. Once there, he meant to confront the man who'd engineered his kidnapping, which in turn had led to the degradations suffered by Rosario and her child.

That road to vengeance brought him to this place, which a sign on its outskirts identified as Angelus.

It wasn't quite a ghost town, though it clearly had one foot deep in the proverbial grave. Most of its buildings were empty, abandoned. There were no horses, no people on its wide main street, even though it was early afternoon.

Since he had no real or urgent reason to stop here, Jason intended to ride straight through.

"Sergeant Mankiller?" a strained voice from behind him called.

Mankiller spun in his saddle, right hand flashing across his body to the grip of his pistol.

To one side he saw a single man standing up on the sidewalk, his face and upper body obscured by the overhang of the building's awning. When the man moved forward and stepped off the sidewalk, Jason could see he was carrying a rifle.

It was an old, breech-loaded Springfield from the looks of it, probably of war vintage. The man held it upright by the barrel with one hand, clearly not meaning to use it.

He walked with a highly visible limp; his right leg being stiff and unbending. Mankiller relaxed and his eyes moved up to the man's face.

"Theo?" he said. "Theo Hutton?"

The man smiled awkwardly. His mouth was partially hidden by a bushy moustache; his hair hung long on the back of his neck. He was slender but not bony; the long sleeves of his white shirt were partly rolled up. Over the shirt was an unbuttoned black vest and he wore trousers of a matching color. His shoes were well worn but freshly polished.

"I'm glad you remember me, sergeant," he said.

Mankiller frowned; not from any negative feelings he held toward Theo Hutton, but rather from the memory his appearance here had called up, unsummoned and unwanted.

Nearly a full year had passed since that bloody day atop Wolf's Hill at Gettysburg. The days since had been just as grim, just as deadly. The dreadful war of attrition had begun to sap up the last measure of vigor from the Confederate army.

A new commander was in charge of all the Union forces: General Ulysses S. Grant. This hard-drinking, hard-fighting veteran of the war against Mexico more than a dozen years earlier, written off by many as a failure, now directed the course of the conflict.

He and his most trusted subordinates, William Tecumseh Sherman and Phil Sheridan, brought with them the concept of total warfare. No person who faced them would be considered a non-combatant; no house, barn, warehouse or out building would necessarily be spared the touch of the torch.

Within the next four months, Sherman would offer up to Abraham Lincoln the smoldering pile of ash that had once been the proud city of Atlanta, virtually assuring Lincoln's re-election to a second term as president.

While Sherman marched inexorably from the west, Sheridan would carve a path of destruction from the south, through the fertile corridor of the Shenandoah Valley.

It was up to Grant to sweep down from the north. The ultimate goal was for the three pincers to converge on one spot: Richmond, the still-beating heart of the staggering Confederacy. Only the ever-shrinking forces of Robert E. Lee could stop them from reaching that goal.

His once proud and mighty Army of Northern Virginia was on its last legs; defeats and Pyrrhic victories had whittled its numbers down to barely sixty thousand men, while Grant had nearly twice its number to throw against them in wave after pounding wave.

But there was no surrender in the Rebels: not yet. This would be savagely proven in the quagmire known simply as the Wilderness, just south of the Rapidan River in Virginia.

If an enormous bramble briar and a treacherous swamp were ever to mate, the offspring of that unholy union would be the Wilderness.

Sergeant Jason Mankiller found himself deep within that tangled forest on the day of May 6, 1864. With no officer to spare, his superiors had placed him in charge of an undermanned cavalry platoon whose mission was to serve as support for a company of infantrymen.

Given that the most massive of raging fires would have found little purchase in progressing through this verdant tract where trees grew so close as to nearly touch and their branches intertwined, and where the undergrowth was a nearly solid wall, it was no wonder that mere men found it slow going there. If anything, it was even more difficult to traverse it on horseback than afoot.

As might be expected, collective sighs of relief and even the occasional vocal "Hallelujah" could be heard coming from the men who, after hours of hacking and stomping at grasping vegetation just to move forward a few miles, finally broke free of the trees into one of the treacherous forest's few clearings.

But the open ground ahead only made Mankiller more tense and suspicious, and he voiced his concerns to the officer in charge of the infantrymen.

"Why don't you hold your men back for just a few minutes, Captain

Hodges?" he suggested. "Let me and my men scout ahead first."

"I don't see the need for that, sergeant," the officer snapped imperiously. "We've had no sign of the Rebels all day, and this looks like a good place to let our own poor devils rest for awhile. They need it."

Bloody experience had taught Mankiller when it was pointless to argue a point with an officer, so he said no more to Hodges. He did, however, motion for his corporal, Theo Hutton, to come closer.

"Pass the word, corporal," he said. "Tell the men to remain mounted and to spread out; I want five feet between horses."

"Aye, sergeant," the laconic Hutton replied.

Like men dying from thirst who have come at last upon a river of fresh water, the foot soldiers pulled themselves free of the clinging forest and rushed out into the clearing. Some threw themselves on the ground even as others poured out behind them.

Only when they were all in the open did the shooting begin.

Highly disciplined Confederate soldiers had been lying in wait on the other side of the clearing, biding their time as the Union boys rushed into their carefully laid trap.

At a shouted command, the first volley from their muskets and rifles was fired in almost total unison. Like a sharpened piano wire, a thread of lead swept forward across the clearing, to deadly effect.

The screams of horses mingled with those of men, and Sergeant Mankiller saw three of his men go down.

"Return fire!" he yelled. His own pistol had been in his hand from the moment they entered the clearing, and he was firing with calm efficiency at every spot in the undergrowth where he saw the flash or smoke from a Reb muzzle. His men, as they knew well they should, followed his example.

There was no such sense of order among the infantrymen. Those who had not been cut down by the initial enemy volley were falling all over themselves. Captain Hodges was screaming at them at the top of his lungs.

"Fight back, you damned dogs!"

His next invective was cut short by a slug entering his head just below his left cheek. He toppled to one side like a felled tree.

Seeing their commanding officer go down before their very eyes shattered what little resolve his men had retained in the face of the Rebels' withering fire. They broke and ran, back the way they had come.

But a small contingent of Rebs had come up on their rear as well, and they now opened fire. Federal soldiers, dead and wounded, fell back against those crowding behind them, adding to the panic.

Caught in a crossfire, seeking nothing but life, they pushed off to one side and plunged into the underbrush. Many of them left their weapons behind as useless impediments to their attempt at flight.

Mankiller and his horsemen came up behind them; too small a force to take on the combined Confederate forces alone. The sergeant reined in his mount, assessing the odds. Slowed by the devilish vegetation, the retreating foot soldiers would be easy targets for any pursuing force. The slaughter that might follow would be wholesale. He saw only one option, one course of action that might prevent this.

"Dismount!" he shouted.

As he followed his own order, he saw that he was the only one who had done so. As bullets and minie balls whistled by like angry hornets, his own men simply stared at him with disbelief.

"You heard the man…dismount!"

This second command had come from Corporal Hutton. Rifle in hand, he swung down off his sorrel. The rest of the men exchanged questioning glances, then one by one obeyed the order.

All but a few.

Fearing too much for their own lives to worry about those of others, a handful of riders chose to disobey Mankiller and make a break for it.

They whipped their horses into a gallop that took them into the level ground of the clearing, but at an angle westward that would not lead them straight into the blazing guns of the Rebels. Their hope was to lose themselves in the treeline and eventually break out of this damnable Wilderness altogether.

Their plan might have had the dimmest hope of success; if the entire clearing was composed of solid ground. It wasn't.

The first of the deserters discovered this when the pounding front hooves of his mount suddenly sank so far into topsoil floating atop a brackish pool of swamp water that the horse pitched forward and plowed head first into the quagmire. Its rider went over its head, somersaulting before splashing down into the muck.

It was too late for any of the other deserters to halt or alter their course. Dirty water sprayed as all plowed into the swampy morass. The water was not deep, but the mud at its bottom was. Men and horses struggled to pull themselves from its sucking grip. One soldier, thrown from his horse, was killed when his steed's flailing front hooves struck him in the head, caving skull into brain.

Before any could make their way clear, a squad of Rebs, skirting the quagmire, came to the edge of the pool. At a shouted command, they began to fire at will.

Blazing death tore into both man and beast. The deserters and their mounts screamed and bled and died together. The comrades they had left behind could do nothing but watch their final moments on earth. The slaughter was total, and finished with quickly.

"That's what comes from disobeying my orders!" Mankiller bellowed, bringing his remaining men about. "I want two skirmish lines here, dammit. Front row kneeling, back row standing."

Horses were released and left to their own devices as the soldiers jumped to obey his command. Mankiller didn't hope to hold the opposing forces off for long with his paltry firepower, but he knew that even minutes might be all that was needed for the rest of their forces to make good their escape.

As he watched, both the force that had first opened fire on the Feds and the smaller unit that had come up behind them now came spilling out of the woods and into the clearing, careful to avoid that part of it in which dead men and horses were now floating.

The two gray tides flowed into one, milled about for a few seconds, then coalesced into a single line. A Confederate officer raised his saber, then brought it slashing down. With a roaring Rebel yell, the soldiers charged across the clearing toward the paltry Union line.

"Hold your fire," Mankiller said calmly. "Wait for my command. When you have it, front rank alone will fire, then step back. Rear rank will step forward, kneel and fire. Repeat on my command."

The Rebel horde drew closer. Many of them began to fire, but Mankiller simply stood and watched, even when slugs came so close he could feel the displacement of air caused by their passing.

One of his men, barely a boy really, who was seeing his first real action, jerked off a shot.

"Hold your fire, dammit!" Mankiller yelled before the premature shot could touch off more. "I said wait for my command!"

The boy hung his head in shame, until the soldier behind him leaned down and told him to change places. He did so, moving back and standing before hurriedly reloading his weapon.

Mankiller felt eyes on him, and looked to see that even the loyal Corporal Hutton was beginning to fidget nervously. He smiled.

"Just a little closer, corporal. Just a little."

The Rebel charge, unabated, picked up speed. Mankiller nodded in approval. Let them get in a rush; let the bloodlust carry them onward. And...

"*Fire!*" he screamed.

Flame leapt from the barrels of a dozen rifles. The front ranks of the charging Rebels faltered as lead cut the legs out from under them. So tightly packed had they become, so unmindfully were they running that many of the soldiers coming hard on the heels of those hit stumbled over their falling bodies. They in turn were struck by others coming behind them.

"First rank, step back," Mankiller called. "Second rank forward and kneel." Now, his men obeyed with crisp precision.

"Fire!"

He repeated this stratagem again and again. While the front row fired, those behind them reloaded. Again and yet again.

A thick and choking pall of gun smoke hung over the battleground, nearly blinding the combatants. The Feds were inflicting serious casualties on the enemy, but were paying a price. Standing behind the ranks, Mankiller saw several of his men go down, while the gray wall before them inexorably moved closer.

"On your feet, boys," he said at last, at a moment when he saw the Rebs needing to regroup before continuing their advance. "Pull back into the trees in an orderly fashion. Once we're there, stop every few feet and throw a little lead behind us."

The first private to turn at his command took off in a run, only to be blocked by Mankiller. He seemed almost to bounce back from the sergeant.

"I said orderly, private," he told the frightened soldier forcefully. "Not like scared rabbits."

The soldier's eyes were wide with fear; his heart threatened to burst free from his chest. Too scared to think straight, he jerked his rifle up to his shoulder, took aim at his own sergeant.

Mankiller brought him down with a single pistol shot to the head.

"We're all scared, boys," he said, sweeping his eyes over his remaining charges, seeking to calm them by the sheer force of his will.

"But do what I tell you and most of us'll make it outta here alive."

Corporal Hutton stepped up beside him, standing shoulder to shoulder with him.

"I aim ta do what he says, fellas, and I suggest you all do the same. This here's a man that Providence has laid a hand on. If anyone can get us outta this with our skins still on, it's him."

"The ground behind us slopes upward," Mankiller told them. "That'll give us the advantage of the high ground once we get a little ways up. Use the trees for cover. Now move out."

He extended both arms and moved them back in a sweeping motion. As he did, the remaining soldiers spread out and moved into the cover of the forest. Mankiller turned to his corporal, gripping his upper arm.

"Corporal, while the rest of us continue to fight a holding action, I want you to run up ahead and see if there's any sign of our infantrymen. Then come back and report."

Hutton nodded in acknowledgment and sprinted away. Mankiller began to move upward more slowly, calling out encouragement to his men, directing their fire as needed.

They did him proud that day, but the weight of numbers was still too great against them. Though now advancing more slowly and cautiously, ever more Rebs were coming up behind them, while boys in blue continued to fall.

Mankiller spared a glance at the sky, at a sun that was barely visible through the vaulted foliage. By its position, he judged they had been engaged in battle less than an hour. Funny how time seemed to slow when you were walking with death.

A hand on his shoulder caused him to spin. Corporal Hutton was there, now bending over with hands across his knees, gasping for breath.

"Good news, sergeant," he managed to wheeze. "Once ya get to the top o' this rise, the goin' gets easier. And then just beyond is a road.

"I shimmied up a tree and caught sight of our foot soldiers a good piece down that road, headin' north at a right furious pace. Ain't nobody gonna catch them."

"Good work, corporal," Mankiller commended. He raised his arms and his voice.

"Listen up, men!" he shouted, so as to be heard by all above the din of continuing gunfire. "You've done your job well, but now it's time to cut and run." He pointed up the slope of the ridge.

"Up there lies the road to home. Take it!"

The beleaguered soldiers needed no more prompting than this. As one they turned away from the fray and began to scramble upward as fast as their churning legs would carry them.

Having caught his second wind, Corporal Hutton followed hard on their heels, yelling at them to go north. He'd gone some distance upward himself before he realized Sergeant Mankiller was no longer with them.

Hutton stopped in his tracks, letting the others flee on without him. Fearing the worst, but determined at least to retrieve a body if possible, he retraced his steps back down the incline.

He shook his head in amazement as he drew near the spot where he had last seen the noncom. Mankiller was crouched behind a large tree, calmly and methodically reloading the two pistols he always carried with him: the same two pistols that had served him in good stead against the Rebs that day atop Wolf's Hill.

His men had loyally followed his orders here today, placing their lives on the line to cover the retreat of their foot soldier comrades. Now he meant to do the same for them by single-handedly buying them the time they needed to reach safety themselves.

Only now he was no longer alone. He scowled as he watched Hutton come sliding down to stand beside him.

"Get the hell outta here, corporal," he snarled. "That's an order."

The lanky Hutton simply smiled. "And what're you gonna do if I disobey, sergeant, shoot me before the Rebs can?"

Mankiller glared at him, then nodded curtly.

"We do have a couple of things in our favor," he said as his corporal knelt down beside him.

"We still hold the high ground. And since I'm sure they've seen the rest of our boys taking off, I hope we'll have the element of surprise; I doubt they'll expect anyone to linger behind."

Mankiller removed his slouch hat and tossed it to the ground, noting a quizzical look in his corporal's eyes.

"I want them to see my face," he said.

Hutton nodded his understanding. Below them, he heard the sounds of the approaching enemy. He blinked as sweat stung his eyes, wiped the palms of his hands on his trouser legs; wondering not for the first time how his sergeant stayed so placid in times such as this.

"I'll start this little shivaree," Mankiller whispered to him at last. "Then you can pick any partner you want and commence to dancing."

Hutton steeled himself, exhaling carefully to slow his breathing. Still Mankiller made no move, and the corporal could now hear dry vegetation crackling under many sets of feet.

He was as surprised and jolted as the Rebs were when Sergeant Mankiller stepped away from the cover of the tree and cut loose with a scream that would freeze a witch's blood in her veins; one that rivaled the vaunted Rebel Yell that was being trumpeted by the charging Confederates.

With stunning rapidity, Mankiller fired round after round into the body of soldiers massed below him. So tightly bunched were they that it was hardly necessary for him to take aim to be assured of hitting something.

Ever ready to follow his sergeant's example, Corporal Hutton screeched at the top of his own lungs as he swung into action, firing and reloading and firing again as quickly as his slightly trembling fingers could manage.

Mankiller could see in the eyes of the Rebels he had allowed to get so close to him both recognition and fear. In Confederate camps, horrid, gruesome tales of the man who cried blood ran as rampantly as did stories of the boogey man through nurseries.

Even those who were not hit by his flying lead fell back away from him, stumbling into those coming up behind them. Like bowling pins, many tumbled down the incline, cutting the legs out from under others as they did.

But this wasn't Gettysburg, and Mankiller knew his bravado and deadly gunfire would only carry him so far. When the hammers of both guns clicked on empty cylinders, he thrust the pistols back into his belt and grabbed his corporal by the collar of his tunic.

"C'mon, Theo," he hissed. "Let's head for the high cotton!"

This was not an order that had to be repeated. Both men were glad to turn tail and run, scratching and clawing their way up the ridge as quickly as possible.

Chaos reigned below them, as soldiers fought each other to get arms and legs untangled. Only a few had the chance to take hurried shots at the fleeing pair rapidly moving away above them.

Mankiller heard a loud grunt and turned his head to see that Corporal Hutton was on the ground. He allowed the slope of the hill to pull him backward in a slide that carried him to his fallen comrade.

Hutton was clutching at his right knee with both hands, rolling in obvious agony. Blood was flowing freely between his fingers.

"Go on, sergeant," he moaned. "Leave me here!"

"Would you leave me behind, Theo?"

"Quicker'n a shady butcher could skin a cat!"

"I believe you would," Mankiller replied easily. Hooking his fingers under the armpits of the wounded man, he lifted him up and off the ground almost effortlessly. Slinging him over his shoulder like a bag of flour, he resumed climbing toward the top of the ridge.

"Yer a damned idjit!" the corporal puffed.

"Shut up, corporal. That's an order, too."

Mankiller was as fit as any man in the army was and stronger than most. But climbing a hill under the weight of a full-grown man, even one as slight as Corporal Hutton, took his full measure.

Each step brought him closer to the top, but with each of those steps he expected to feel the burning thud of a Rebel slug entering his spine. But he never looked back; there was no point in doing so. He focused instead on his feet, on continuing to place one after the other.

He topped the ridge unscathed and thought, fervently hoped, that the cacophonous sounds of the Rebels behind him had not grown greatly louder or closer.

As Hutton had told him, the ground leveled out now, the foliage grew less densely. He picked up the pace, stepping more lively. And when he broke free of the last of the tenacious undergrowth and found himself standing on a beaten path, he turned northward and began to sprint.

Each pounding step sent a jolt of pain through his back and shoulders, but he refused to succumb to it. For over a quarter of a mile he never slowed.

Only after that did he at last come to a halt. He turned to look back the way he had come, sighing with relief. There was no sign of any pursuit.

Nor, he noted, was there any sign of his own men. He wondered if they needed horses at all, as fast as those boys must have churned their way toward safety as to be plumb out of sight already!

He gently set the corporal down on the ground before falling to his own knees beside the wounded man.

"Are you all right?" he asked.

"Me?" Hutton sputtered. "Hell, sergeant, *you're* the one carryin' the load!"

"Give me your belt," Mankiller ordered. Blood seemed to be still flowing freely from the corporal's leg and it needed to be stopped.

He strapped the belt as tightly as he could around the wounded man's thigh, ignoring his groans. Once he saw the flow of blood had begun to slow, he lifted Hutton and tossed him back over his shoulders.

Mankiller never set him back down until, some two hours later, staggering under the weight, he limped into a Union encampment.

As he neared the camp's field hospital, a pair of orderlies spotted him and came running to meet him with a stretcher. As they lifted what was now their burden and began to carry him away, Corporal Hutton reached out and desperately clutched at Mankiller's sleeve.

"Don't leave me, Sarge," he gasped.

Mankiller patted the hand clawing at him. "It's all right, corporal. You're gonna be fine."

"No," Hutton replied. "We both know what's gonna happen in there. They'll take the leg." His eyes bored into Mankiller's.

"Please. Don't let 'em take the saw to me," he pleaded. "I'd sooner die."

Mankiller stood silently, studying the wounded man's face.

"We've got to get him to a doctor, sergeant," one of the orderlies said. Mankiller nodded.

"Let's go."

Corporal Hutton fell back flat on the stretcher, relief etched in his features.

True to his word, Mankiller was standing right beside his corporal when they laid him out on an operating table.

Minutes later, an Army surgeon approached. The front of his smock was spattered in blood, as were both arms from elbows to fingertips.

With quick efficiency he cut away the right leg of Corporal Hutton's trousers. He took one look at the raw, gaping wound and turned to an orderly.

"Bring me a bone saw," he said in a dull voice.

"He wants to keep the leg, doc," Mankiller told him.

"What difference does it make?" the surgeon said bluntly. He leaned forward to look Hutton in the face. "That knee of yours is shattered, soldier. Beyond repair. Either way, you're going to end up a cripple."

Now in too much shock and pain to speak, Hutton simply turned his eyes toward Mankiller.

"At least he'll be a cripple on his own terms," Jason said. "And on his own two legs."

"I don't have time for this, sergeant," the surgeon growled. His orderly had returned with the requested bone saw, and his superior turned to take it. "I'm the doctor here, and I say the leg comes off."

He turned back toward his patient, bone saw in hand to find himself staring down the barrel of one of Mankiller's pistols.

"This is Mr. Colt, doctor...and he says the leg stays."

The surgeon's eyes flickered from the gun to the sergeant's face and knew in the instant there was no bluff in the man.

"Fine," he sniffed, handing the bone saw back to the orderly. "But I take no responsibility for what happens to him."

"Fine," Mankiller parroted sarcastically. "Let it be on me."

The surgeon glared at him. "You should also know that we've run out of laudanum. You'll have to hold him down."

"I've done it before," Mankiller declared. He didn't tell the sanctimonious bastard how many times he had done so. He cast his gaze about.

"Who's got whiskey?" he hollered.

Another orderly slapped a nearly full bottle into his hand.

"Drink this, corporal," he instructed, helping Hutton rise up as he pressed the neck of the bottle to the man's lips.

"Will this make it stop hurtin', Sarge?"

"Course it will." Mankiller figured being lied to was the least of the corporal's problems.

As the surgeon stood by, fidgeting impatiently, Mankiller poured more than half the bottle's contents down his man's throat. Once the combination of booze, shock and fear had him sufficiently woozy, Mankiller took the belt he'd used as a field tourniquet, doubled it over and shoved it between Hutton's teeth.

He then poured a liberal amount of the remaining whiskey over the wound.

The belt muffled Corporal Hutton's wail as his back arched off the table in fresh pain, but Mankiller threw himself atop the wriggling man to pin him down. Looking up, he nodded to the surgeon to begin his work.

Mercifully, the corporal passed out twenty minutes into the procedure.

Both Mankiller and the doctor were bathed in sweat when the surgeon finally stepped back from the table.

"Finished," he panted. "He should at least survive...if infection doesn't kill him." A possibility Mankiller knew verged on near certainty.

"I'll take care of that," the sergeant offered, when the surgeon reached out his bloody hand to take a roll of gauze wrappings an orderly was offering him.

The surgeon shrugged and left; there was no shortage of other patients awaiting his tender touch.

As the orderly looked on, Mankiller poured fresh whiskey over the patched and puffy skin around Corporal Hutton's closed incision. With the little that was left of the liquor, he doused his own hands.

Carefully, and with surprising gentleness, he wrapped the leg. He glanced over at the orderly, the same one who had given him the bottle of whiskey; he had stood and watched Mankiller with great interest.

"What's your name?" Mankiller asked.

"Homer Dalrimple, sergeant."

"Do you know who I am, Homer?"

Rather nervously, trying not to stare at the teardrop tattoo, the orderly nodded.

"Well, Homer, I'm putting you in charge of this man's care. I want you to keep that wound clean and put fresh bandages on it real regular." He locked his eyes with those of the orderly.

"...Mr.Colt...says the leg stays."

"I'd consider that a personal favor."

"Yes, sir," Homer gulped. "It'll be done."

Knowing there was nothing more he could do, Mankiller patted the still unconscious Corporal Hutton on the head, smoothing back his hair, and left the tent.

He wandered a short distance outside the perimeter of the camp. Spotting a fallen tree, he sat himself down, arms on his knees, head bowed.

"Mankiller!"

His head snapped up at the sound of his name being called. As it did, and his hands reflexively flew to the grips of his pistols, a flash of light made him wince.

As his normal vision quickly returned, he wasn't surprised to see the smiling face that popped out from behind the camera that had just snapped his photo.

It belonged to Leslie Bellows. The reporter had continued to make a habit of traveling with the army, camera always close at hand. Only the many photographers covering the battlefront on behalf of Matthew Brady cranked out more product than did the ambitious Bellows.

Mankiller had lost track of the number of times the newsman had made him the subject of such photos and the fanciful stories that went with them since that first fateful encounter at Gettysburg.

"Are you ever gonna get tired of taking my picture, Leslie?" he asked.

"Only when someone more bankable comes along, m'boy," Bellows answered candidly. "Or this damned war ends!"

Mankiller devoutly hoped both came soon.

"Mind if I take a seat?" Bellows asked, gesturing at the tree trunk.

Mankiller shrugged and patted a spot beside him. Despite the man's often pushy and obnoxious ways, Jason had actually rather grown to like the reporter though he'd never admit as much to the man.

"I hear it was pretty hairy out there," Bellows said.

Mankiller allowed as how it was, even deigning to give him a truncated version of what had transpired earlier that day. He downplayed his own part in the fray, knowing full well that Bellows would probably snowball it up to mythic proportions anyway.

"Damned dirty business," Bellows said.

He reached into an inside pocket of his linen coat and withdrew a small metal flask, offering it to Mankiller. Jason held up a hand and shook his head.

"You taught me the evils of alcohol," he said.

Bellows grinned and took a healthy swig for himself. The two men just sat in silence for a time.

"There's something I've been meaning to ask you, Jason," Bellows said at last.

"Ask away."

"It's about something that happened a few weeks ago, outside Washington. President Lincoln paid a surprise visit to your camp. You remember that?"

"Sure."

It had been a minor, almost comical and certainly inconsequential incident. While walking through the camp, Lincoln had notice Mankiller helping to unload a supply wagon, taking special note of his obvious height.

As he was wont to do on such occasions, Lincoln approached the sergeant, doffed his trademark stovepipe hat and challenged him to see which of them was the taller. Mankiller dutifully stood back to back with the president, who chuckled as an aide declared him to be the winner by virtue of the fact that he was a good three inches taller than the soldier.

Mankiller accepted his "defeat" graciously, grinning as he turned and shook hands with the victor.

"As I recall," he now said to Bellows, "you took a picture of that, too."

"Of course I did!" Bellows snorted. He then took another pull on his flask and grew more serious.

"What I didn't get was a picture of what happened next, and I really wish I had."

"What are you talking about? Nothing happened next."

"The two of you exchanged a few words, remember?" Bellows said. "And maybe more."

Mankiller did of course recall. As they had shaken hands, Lincoln had taken his first close look at the soldier. His arm stopped pumping, though he retained his grip on Jason's hand.

"That's a mighty queer tattoo you got there, son," the president drawled.

Mankiller made no response.

"I'm told you were quite the hero at Gettysburg, Mr. Mankiller."

"There may have been heroes there, Mr. President; I wouldn't know. Me? I was just a fella trying to stay alive."

Now it was Lincoln who remained silent. He and Mankiller stood like that, facing each other, for so long that some of those bearing witness began to shuffle back and forth uncomfortably.

The face of the man looking back at him reminded Mankiller of the cracked bottom of a long dry creek bed, so lined and deeply furrowed was it. The skin, pulled taut over jutting cheekbones, was sallow, almost yellow in complexion.

Blue eyes more inclined to gray than his own icy orbs were so deeply sunk into dark and cavernous sockets as to be barely visible. Yet he knew they were staring deeply into his.

The moment only ended when Lincoln's aide took the president's arm and led him away for another appointment.

"I've wondered ever since," Bellows said, intruding on Jason's thoughts. "When the two of you were looking into each other's eyes…what did you see?"

"I can't say what Mr. Lincoln saw," Mankiller replied, sighing. "That I don't know. But when I looked at him, I saw a fella who was sick…and tired…and very sad." He scuffed at the ground with the toe of one boot.

"I don't think the man is long for this world."

"Aw, hell, Jason," Bellows scoffed. "Ol' Abe's a rail-splitter from way back. He's still strong as an ox. He'll outlive the both of us!"

"Me, maybe," Jason said.

Unnoticed by Mankiller, Bellows closely examined his face. He'd forgotten just how young the soldier was.

"It's been a rough war for you, hasn't it?"

"No rougher than it's been for everybody else."

"Did I make it worse for you, my friend?"

"Do you care if you did?"

"Of course not!" Bellows declared ebulliently. "All I care about is the story!" Yet as he stood to take his leave, he gave Jason a squeeze on the shoulder.

"You take care now, y'hear?"

"You too, Leslie."

As the photographer walked away, lost in his thoughts, he made no note of the soldier who passed him and approached Mankiller.

"Sergeant Mankiller?" the soldier asked respectfully.

"Yeah?"

"I've been sent ta fetch ya. You're to report back to your unit on the double."

"What's up, private?"

"Hell if I know, sergeant. But rumor has it we're headed ta some damned place called Spotsylvania."

CHAPTER 17

That was the last time Mankiller had seen Corporal Hutton until today. He'd dismounted and taken a seat on the edge of the sidewalk with his fellow veteran.

"I'm sorry I wasn't able to make it back to visit you in the hospital, corporal," he said.

"Don't make no never-mind, sergeant," Hutton replied. "An orderly who took real good care of me told me what all ya did ta save my leg that day. I'm grateful."

Mankiller pointed at the leg in question, sticking out straight and immovable. "How is it?"

"Not too bad, most days." Hutton smiled wanly. "And it does a hell of a good job forecastin' changes in the weather."

Mankiller chuckled.

"They mustered me out of the service as soon as I was able to leave hospital," Hutton explained. "I went back home to Michigan; found work in a general store.

"I'd left a pretty little gal behind there when I went off ta war. But I avoided her when I got back. Figured she prob'ly wouldn't want damaged goods.

"Word got back ta her that I was in town, though, and she tracked me down." Now it was his turn to chuckle. "She gave me nine kinds o' hell for not comin' ta see her.

"Six months later, we got married. We're still together, with two fine children ta show for it."

"How'd you come to end up here in Texas?"

"When Sally—Sally, that's my missus—when Sally lost her mother a few years ago, that was the last kinfolk either of us had left in Michigan.

"I'd kept in touch with another veteran I'd met in hospital, and he invited me down. Offered me half share in a tobacco shop.

"Not long after, he decided ta move on ta greener pastures, so I bought out his share of the shop. Done well enough with her, too till about a year ago."

"What happened?"

"What didn't? There was the Depression, o' course. Then an army post close by was abandoned. Finally, the stage line that use ta bring people through regular went belly up, bankrupt.

"Businesses here began ta fail, people started movin' away. You've seen; there's little left. What there is will be gone soon."

"Sorry to hear that, Theo."

"Oh, it gets worse, Sarge. Just yesterday, some no-account drifter came into town. The saloon's been long gone, but he found some liquor at the general store and started soakin' it up like a sponge.

"The more the day progressed, the drunker he became. And more belligerent. Next thing ya know, he was firin' a pistol off real indiscriminate. Shot out the windows of several empty buildings and some that weren't empty.

"Fortunately, the town marshal, a decent fella by the name o' Tom Shannon, had agreed to stick around till the last of us had cleared out. He was able to come up behind this fella and disarm him.

"As he was marchin' him to the jail, though, that bastard spun 'round and got the jump on 'im. They wrestled in the street till the marshal's gun went off. Shot poor Tom right in the belly.

"It happened just outside my shop. I seen it all, I did. I don't know what I was thinkin', but I grabbed an old ax handle I keep behind the front counter, hobbled out to the street and laid it right across the back o' that drunk's thick head.

"I dragged him over to the jail, that's this building we're sittin' in front of, and locked his sorry ass up.

"Sally and some of the other women took care of the marshal as best they could; our only doctor pulled up stakes weeks ago. But he was gut shot: I don't have ta tell you what that means.

"Tom screamed through most of the night before finally passing out around dawn. He died just a few hours ago.

"Everybody was pretty much treating me like I was the new marshal, but I figured we needed the real law. This morning I sent a boy to ride over to the county seat and fetch the sheriff back ta deal with our prisoner."

"Sounds to me like you did everything right, Theo," Mankiller said. "Everything you could. So what's the problem?"

"It's the prisoner, sergeant. Last time I went to check on him, he'd sobered up just enough ta start getting' cocky and talkative.

"He's braggin' that there's a whole gang a'followin' after him. They know that Angelus is nearly dead and they mean to swoop down and pick clean whatever bones remain.

"He wouldn't tell me how many are comin' or when they'll be here. He won't even tell me his own name."

"It's probably just bluster, Theo."

"But what if it ain't?"

"Are there enough other men left in town to fight off a few outlaws?"

"Naw. There ain't but about a dozen of us left, and most of them are women. I'm the closest to a real fightin' man that we got.

"Even if there's time enough to pack up and move out, most of us got no place ta go. They're like me; they used to make enough money to keep food on the table, but little besides.

"The fact that I been tryin' every way I can to scrape together enough for a fresh start explains why me and my family are still here. Same for the others.

"But I ain't about ta stand by and let a pack o' human vultures just take what little I do have. I won't stand for it."

Mankiller closed his eyes. He'd regained much of his strength during his stay in San Ramon, but he was still far from fully fit. Nor did he relish the idea of taking on problems that weren't his, for people who were mostly strangers. He rose to his feet.

"Let's have another go at that mouthy prisoner of yours, corporal."

Hutton led the way into the jail, through the front office and back into the holding area, which contained three cells. As they neared the first of these, Mankiller could see an occupant stretched out on a cot.

At the sound of their approach, the man swung off the cot and rushed to the door of the cell. He had a grin on his face.

"You come ta let me outta here, gimp?" he asked. Then he saw Mankiller, and the smile became more of a sneer.

"Who the hell are you?"

Mankiller said nothing to him, turning instead to Hutton. "I gotta say, Theo, that there's about the scroungiest, sorriest excuse for an outlaw you got there that I ever did see."

The man in the cell gripped the bars tightly. "Let me outta here, mister, and I'll show you who's got the makin's and who don't."

Mankiller studied him: medium height and build, clothes that had seen better days, dark hair unkempt, face unshaven.

And eyes that said he'd kill a saint before he'd break an honest sweat. Jason had never seen him before, but he'd seen plenty of his kind.

"I might just take you up on your offer," he said to the man, "if you tell me who it is I'm gonna be stompin' into next Tuesday."

The man just grunted and looked away.

"Maybe you'd like to tell me the names of your partners, instead."

The sullen face swiveled back in Jason's direction, but still no reply came.

"What time do you expect 'em to be joining us?"

Again the cruel lips turned up on one side into a sneer.

Mankiller dropped his own head, exhaling loudly, standing silently with hands on hips as if lost in thought. When he looked back up, it was to address Theo Hutton.

"Here's the plan, Theo. You stay in here. I'm gonna go out on the street and wait for the others. When you hear the first sound of gunfire..." He wagged a finger at the man in the cell.

"*Kill him.*"

CHAPTER 18

The arrogant sneer on the lips of the prisoner disappeared.

"You cain't just gun me down!" he yelled. "That'd be murder!"

"Yeah. It would," Mankiller said, staring at him impassively. "What's your point?"

Stunned, the prisoner clutched the bars of his cell more tightly. His mouth dropped open, but no sound emerged. Jason turned and began to walk away.

"Blake Larimore!" the prisoner practically screamed. "My name's Blake Larimore!"

Mankiller halted, swiveled around and walked back closer to the cell.

"That's better," he declared. "But it's gonna take a lot more than that to save your sorry ass, Larimore.

"How many more of you are there? What are their names?"

"Four. There's four of 'em," Larimore quickly replied. As hoped, fear for his own life had loosened his tongue greatly. "Their names are Jim Parsons, Wesley Satz, Dave Cole and Glen Woodard."

Mankiller had never heard of any of them, but he had no doubt they were cut from the same dirty cloth as Larimore.

"What was the plan, before you flummoxed it up?"

Larimore glared at Jason, but continued talking. "We were supposed ta meet north o' town as close ta two o'clock this afternoon as we could manage, then all ride in together."

"Why'd you jump the gun?"

"I got here yesterday. Got bored, so I figgered I'd go ahead and take a look-see at what was waitin' for us."

"If you don't show up today, will the rest of 'em come in anyway?"

"You can count on it," Larimore snapped, a little of the braggadocio returning.

"And I don't suppose any of what you just told me is a lie, is it, Larimore?"

"It's the truth, you painted nancy boy," the outlaw said sullenly. "I swear."

"Good. 'Cause if it ain't…I'll still kill you."

With a jerk of his head, Mankiller led Theo Hutton out of the holding area and back into the jail's main office. A glance at his pocket watch told him it was one-two p.m.

"You're sure there's no one else in this town who could be of help to us, Theo?"

"No one we could really count on, Sarge."

"Then we'll make do with what we got. I got two things I need you to do. Tell the rest of your people to get under cover and stay there. Then see if you can rustle up, oh, about twenty feet of good, stout chain and two padlocks."

Hutton nodded, took a few steps toward the door, then turned back.

"What you told that fella back there, Sarge. About just killin' him, I mean. Would you have really done it?"

"Guess we'll never know, corporal. Now get moving; time's a'wastin'."

Within twenty minutes, Hutton was back, carrying a length of chain looped around one shoulder like it was a coil of rope. Mankiller, who had been sitting behind the late Marshal Shannon's desk, snatched up the keys to the jail cells and led the way back into the holding area. There he tossed the keys to Hutton and drew his pistol.

"Let 'im out, Theo."

Even when the door swung open, Larimore hesitated before inching his way out of the cell. Mankiller motioned for the outlaw to move out ahead of him, calling for him to stop when they reached the outer office.

"Leave that old piece of pipe you call a rifle here, Theo. There's a Winchester rifle and a Remington revolver I found in here while you was gone, sitting on the desk. They're yours now."

"You sure, Sarge?"

"You see anybody else laying claim to 'em?"

Hutton scratched his head and grinned, then moved to snatch up the weapons, thrusting the pistol into his belt.

The three of them stepped out onto the sidewalk before Mankiller again called a halt.

"Corporal," he directed, "I want you to loop one end of that chain around the upright of this awning here, and lock it into place." The corporal swiftly did so.

"Now put the other end around Larimore's middle and lock it nice 'n' snug."

Larimore's eyes flared fearfully, but under the threat of Mankiller's gun he remained still as Hutton chained him. Mankiller took the outlaw by one arm and led him out into the street, as far as the chain would allow.

"Theo," he said, "set yourself up in a doorway across the street, one that'll hide you from the view of anyone coming from the north.

"We're gonna work this just the way we did that day in the Wilderness. You just stay put till I fire the first shot. Then you jump in with both feet."

His corporal took off at a trot, or as close to a trot as his game leg would allow.

"What about me?" Larimore asked, his voice raspy from a suddenly dry throat.

"You got the easiest job of all," Mankiller told him. "Just stay right where you are." He holstered his pistol, but his hand stayed on its grip.

"And just so you know: you move too sudden like, you try to wriggle outta that chain, you give one word of warning to your cronies when they come in...you'll be the first to die."

Having already fetched his own rifle, Mankiller now stepped back into a concealing doorway on the jail's side of the street, directly across from Theo Hutton. Levering a live round into the rifle, and easing the hammer down, he leaned back against the doorframe and waited.

Minutes later, after casting a fearful look back at Mankiller, Larimore slowly dropped to the ground, sitting cross-legged in the dirt. Mankiller spared a glance across the street from time to time. He could tell that Theo was nervous, but he was also alert. He'd do what needed doing.

The rest of Larimore's gang was late in arriving, but an hour later Jason saw four horsemen slowly riding abreast into the north end of town. He straightened, used hand signals to alert his comrade across the street.

Blake Larimore saw them too, and leaped back up on his feet. They spotted him as he did and reined in their horses, now grown suspicious of trouble. The lead horseman, Jim Parsons, stood up in his stirrups.

"That you, Blake?" he called. "What the hell's goin' on?"

Larimore opened his mouth to shout out, but was given pause by the distinctive sound of a hammer being cocked, coming from behind him.

"Don't say a word, Larimore," Mankiller ordered, just loud enough for the chained man to hear. "Wave 'em on in."

Larimore did as he was told. The other four outlaws exchanged glances, talked among themselves. Parsons started his horse forward at a walk and the other three followed, casting their eyes back and forth, up and down.

When they were no more than ten feet away from their chained cohort, they again halted. Parsons leaned forward in the saddle, smiling.

"Boy, howdy, Blake," he drawled. "Looks like you got yourself in one *hell* of a predicament."

All four of the mounted outlaws commenced to laughing at Larimore's expense, while he merely glared at them in silence.

The last sound of their laughter had not yet faded away when Mankiller leaned out of the doorway and fired his first shot.

The slug entered the left side of Jim Parson's body, just below the breast. It continued upward at an angle, exiting from his right shoulder blade in a bloody spray.

Before the outlaw's body hit the dirt, Mankiller had cocked and fired three more times. He could tell from the sounds that Theo Hutton was doing the same from his cover across the street.

Horses squealed, men cursed and shouted. Blake Larimore was back down on the ground, curling into a ball and throwing his hands over his head.

Chips of wood flew from the doorframe where Mankiller stood as bullets flew wildly. With their horses pitching madly under them, it was nigh on impossible for the remaining three outlaws to draw a steady bead. It also made it damned hard for them to be hit. And with the fighting becoming general, a stray bullet could prove just as fatal as one carefully aimed.

A second outlaw pitched backwards out of his saddle, a bloody hole where his nose had been. He hit the ground at an awkward angle, his left foot still caught in the stirrup.

A bullet sizzled across the rump of his horse and it took off in a pained panic. The outlaw's lifeless body dragged behind it, bouncing up and down on the hard-packed dirt road.

A third gang member seemed to stand up in his saddle, lifted by the impact of a bullet. In that second while he seemed to hover in mid-air, Mankiller punched another slug into his chest. The man dropped back into the saddle, then fell to the street. The odds were now in favor of the town's two defenders.

Movement caught Mankiller's eye, and he turned his head in time to see his old friend across the street spinning from the impact of a slug.

As he fell to the sidewalk, Hutton triggered off another shot of his own. The bullet slapped into the forehead of the horse carrying the final outlaw, the man named Dave Cole.

With a keening screech, the dying horse pitched to its left. Cole managed to jump clear of its saddle as it did and he landed on his feet, running down the middle of the street in the opposite direction from where Mankiller stood.

The two frightened horses remaining were rearing and bucking about so as to block off any shot Mankiller might have of the fleeing outlaw.

Leaving the protective cover of the doorway in a low crouch, Jason headed off along the sidewalk in hope of getting an unobstructed angle on Cole.

As he did, one of the horses, bleeding profusely from a chest wound, hopped sideways up onto the sidewalk. Mankiller was unable to move out of its way quickly enough, and the animal's heaving flank slammed into him.

He heard the sound of breaking glass as the force of the blow picked him off his feet and sent him hurtling through a window.

CHAPTER 19

Mankiller lay flat on his back, staring at the ceiling while gasping for breath.

Able to inhale deeply at last, he pushed himself to a sitting position. Nothing seemed to be broken, but he did feel pain.

Looking down, he saw a jagged piece of glass, a good three inches long, protruding from the back of his left hand. Gripping it firmly, he slowly pulled it out.

Blood flowed freely from the wound, but he could still move his fingers. He retrieved his kerchief from his pocket and wrapped it around the hand.

He warily stepped back outside through the broken window. No more shots came, nor was Dave Cole anywhere in sight.

The horse that had knocked him through the window was now lying on the ground, its legs thrashing helplessly, blood pumping out of its mortal wound into a dusty pool.

Levering a round into his rifle and holding the barrel close to the desperate animal's head, Mankiller quickly put it out of its misery.

Across the street, he could see that Theo Hutton was still alive and had pulled himself to a sitting position in the doorway from which he had fought. The black of his vest was stained red with blood. Staying low, Mankiller sprinted to his side.

"You all right, Theo?" he asked.

"Better than I woulda been if you hadn't happened along, Sarge," the corporal answered gamely. Lifting his rifle with one hand, he pointed its barrel back across the street.

"I saw that last fella run into the saloon. If he didn't duck out a window or the back door, he's still in there."

Mankiller nodded, then glanced over to the spot where Blake Larimore had gone down. Almost miraculously, the chained man had come through the melee without a scratch. He still lay cowering on the ground.

"Are you fit to keep an eye on Larimore?" Mankiller asked. Theo nodded. "Good. I'll be back to see to your wound."

Without another word, he was on his feet and scurrying diagonally back across the street. No shots came his way as he did.

Reaching the sidewalk, he slowed so as to lessen any noise he might make. When he came to the saloon, he dropped to his hands and knees and crawled under its large front window, straightening then as he approached its entrance.

The day before, Larimore in his quest for liquor had kicked open the establishment's solid front door. The portal was still open, save for its batwings. Arching his neck, Mankiller could see over the top of them well enough to see that the bar stood to the left of the doorway as you entered.

A chair, left behind when the saloon's owner abandoned the property, stood near him out on the sidewalk. Grabbing it with his left hand, Mankiller slung it through the saloon's swinging doors.

The echo of the gunshot elicited by it had not faded before he threw himself through the batwings. Hitting the floor, he rolled behind the protective cover of the bar. A second bullet narrowly missed him, chewing a divot from the floor.

In those few seconds, Mankiller had caught a fleeting glimpse at the shooter. The outlaw was above him, on the saloon's second floor landing.

Mankiller scooted around behind the bar, crawling partway down its length so his intended target would not know from where he might pop up.

Picking his time and place, Jason sprang to his feet, rifle at the ready. The outlaw Cole had moved also, and it took both of them a crucial beat to home in on each other. Two shots were fired so closely together that they sounded as one.

The mirror behind Mankiller shattered, spraying fine bits of glass onto the back of his neck. His own shot had been truer, hitting Cole low on his right side. The outlaw sagged against the landing railing, then lurched away out of sight down the nearest hallway.

Mankiller set his rifle down on the bar and drew his pistol. In the narrow confines of the upstairs, the short gun would prove more effective. He cautiously made his way up the stairs, eyes never leaving the entrance to the hallway down which Cole had fled.

Reaching the second floor landing, he saw two hopeful signs. One was spatters of blood from Cole's wound. The other was the outlaw's pistol, dropped when he was shot.

That didn't necessarily mean his prey was unarmed; he could have a knife or second gun. Mankiller kept on his guard as he entered the hallway. There were rooms on either side of it, and Cole could be in any one of them.

As it turned out, he had ducked into the very first one. Standing with his ear to its closed door, he was able to faintly hear Jason's footfalls. Cole rammed the door open with his shoulder, so quickly and so hard that Mankiller was thrown back against the opposite wall. The impact caused his own pistol to fly from his hand.

Quickly, Cole was upon him, the man wounded but strengthened by desperation. He swung Mankiller around, slinging him back the way he had come. Jason hit the floor and rolled out onto the landing.

Cole leaped astraddle him and the two began to tumble back and forth, first one on top then the other. Fists flailed about, causing little real damage.

Finding himself momentarily on top again, Cole managed to grab Mankiller by the hair and bang his head against the floor. The cracking impact stunned Jason enough that he couldn't prevent the outlaw from then dropping his hands to Mankiller's throat.

At full strength, Jason could have given a better fight of it. But now he found himself unable to pull the outlaw's fingers away as they dug deeper into his neck and it quickly became hard for him to inhale.

He pushed at Cole's torso, managing to bring a knee up under the outlaw, but not enough to gain true leverage. His oxygen-deprived brain was growing muddled and his arms were losing their power. His left hand slipped away from Cole's chest, slid down his right side.

It came away from there wet with blood from the outlaw's wound.

Mankiller drew his left arm back, then thrust forward with his hand stiff and straight, driving the fingers into that wound.

Cole's eyes and mouth popped open wide, his lungs sucking in air as excruciating pain raced like lightning to his spine. He pulled back away from the source of the pain, releasing his grip on Mankiller's throat.

Giving himself no time to recover from his own agony, Mankiller drew his leg completely up and under the outlaw's body, planted a foot against his chest and shoved.

Cole was pushed up, off and away from Mankiller, landing on his feet but staggering backward. His lower back caught the top of the railing behind him; there was neither time nor chance to catch his balance before he flipped over the rail and fell to the floor below.

With one hand on his throat, struggling to draw air back into his body, Mankiller crawled on his belly to where the outlaw's pistol had fallen earlier. Snatching it in hand, he dragged himself up to peer down over the railing.

He relaxed and focused on breathing. One look had told him the outlaw posed no danger of either escaping or causing further trouble. Cole's neck and back were bent at sharp angles and there was no movement in him.

The rawness in his throat diminishing, Mankiller thrust the outlaw's pistol in his belt before retrieving his own. He didn't holster his weapon, though, as he made his way back down the stairs.

Approaching the downed outlaw, he saw that there was still life left in the man. Hearing Mankiller as he drew closer, Cole tried to twist his head around. It was a slow and clearly agonizing process; Jason could hear the scratchy sound of bone grinding on bone.

"I must be all busted up inside," Cole moaned, looking up at Jason. "I can't feel nothin'."

Mankiller stared down at him silently.

"...Please..." the outlaw begged.

Out on the street, Theo Hutton had limped over to stand guard over Larimore, who had resumed his seated position on the ground.

The corporal was getting apprehensive. He'd heard exchanges of gunfire after Mankiller entered the saloon, but no sound at all had carried out to him for the last several minutes.

Because of that, he jumped slightly when a single gunshot now rang out.

He lifted his rifle with his one good arm, thumbing back the hammer. He smiled and lowered its barrel as he saw the familiar figure of Jason Mankiller push through the saloon's bat wing doors and step outside.

As he holstered his gun, Mankiller saw that one of the horses ridden by the outlaws was standing nearby. It appeared to be unharmed and was calmly drinking from a water trough.

It raised its head as Jason drew near, but showed no fear of him. It was a bay mare that had belonged to Parsons, the first outlaw to be killed in the gun battle. Mankiller stroked its neck before gripping its bridle and leading it back toward the place where Hutton waited.

"That's a nice horse you've got, sergeant," Hutton said, smiling and tossing off a casual salute, which Mankiller returned in kind.

"Actually, corporal, I was thinking *you've* got a nice horse here, if you want her."

Theo's smile widened and he nodded.

"On your feet, Larimore," Mankiller snapped at their prisoner. He unlocked the chain from around the man's waist. "Now, back into the jail."

"You don't have ta do that, do ya?" the outlaw asked in a voice that had lost all trace of bravado. "After all, I sorta helped ya get the rest of 'em. You could just let me go!"

"I could," Mankiller agreed. "But I won't."

Once Larimore was safely back behind bars, Mankiller led Hutton back into the front office of the jail and seated him atop the marshal's desk. He gingerly removed his corporal's vest and shirt so he could examine the wound he had sustained to his shoulder.

The front door banged open, and a short woman with mousy brown hair, dark eyes wide and fearful, swept into the room. She was the first and only townsperson to have left hiding.

"Theo!" she cried, throwing herself across the room and into the sweep of Hutton's good right arm. He grunted with pain as she circled him in her arms and squeezed, but he made no protest.

"In case you haven't figured, Sarge," he said, "this here's my wife Sally. Sally, this is Sergeant Mankiller. You 'member me tellin' ya about 'im, don'tcha?"

In response, she released her husband and flung both arms around the nonplussed Mankiller. She buried her face in his chest so he couldn't see her tears.

"Thank you, sergeant," she wept. "Thank you."

"You're welcome, Mrs. Hutton," he said, awkwardly patting her on the back. He looked over her head at Theo, silently mouthing the words, "What do I do?"

The corporal merely smiled and shrugged.

Mankiller took hold of the woman's arms and gently but firmly pulled her back away from him.

"Your husband still needs some doctoring, ma'am," he told her.

One small fist flew to the "o" of her mouth. Her eyes darted to Theo's bloody wound, then back up at Jason.

"Is he going to be all right?"

"He should be fine, little lady. It looks to me like the bullet went clean through and out the back. No busted bones that I can tell. But there's a couple things you can do for him."

"What? Just tell me!"

"While I get him cleaned up a bit, I need you to find me some clean cloths we can use to bandage him. And if that lowlife Larimore didn't drink the town dry, some whiskey to clean the wound."

The tiny woman nodded and rushed back out of the office. Jason watched her leave, chuckling.

"Looks like you get yourself a keeper there, corporal," he declared.

"I've always thought so, Sarge."

"While we're waiting for her to come back, there's something you should know, Theo." Hutton's ears perked up.

"While you were out digging up that chain, I took a look through your marshal's desk drawers. I found a wanted poster on our friend Larimore and dodgers on at least two of the others we laid out.

"So here's what I want you to do. When that sheriff finally gets here, you show him those posters and you tell him you're laying claim to the rewards."

Hutton squirmed uncomfortably. "What about you?"

"I'll be gone by first light tomorrow. Far as I'm concerned, the money's all yours."

"That don't hardly seem right," Hutton protested. "You did most o' the killin'. You should have most of the money."

Mankiller shook his head. "At the moment, old son, I got money. And I got a place to go. You got neither.

"So you take the money, as much of it as you need to look out for you and your family. If there's any left over, maybe you can give it to some of the other folks hereabouts who are needin'."

Theo sat with his head bowed for just a minute. Now it was he who was hiding tears from Mankiller's sight.

"This is twice now you've proven ta be a godsend ta me, Jason." He lifted his head, his emotions now mostly under his control.

"If there's ever anything I can do to repay you, all you got to do is ask."

"I know, corporal." Mankiller smiled. "Maybe you could start by having me over to supper tonight."

Hutton brightened. "You bet, Sarge. It'll have ta be simple fare, but you'd be amazed what Sally can do with a scrawny rabbit and a pot fulla vegetables."

"Is he going to be alright?"

"I look forward to it. Meanwhile, here's something else for you to consider, if you haven't already made other plans for the future. Once the money for those outlaws comes across, you might think about relocating to a place I know of a ways north of here.

"All things considered, it's a pretty nice little town, with room to grow. And unless I'm mistaken, it don't currently have a bona fide tobacconist such as yourself.

"It's called Ft. Rogers."

CHAPTER 20

Jason Mankiller rode back into Ft. Rogers himself a few days later. He didn't enter on either of the main roads, instead circling and riding in from the northeast. Hat pulled low over his face, he rode his dun horse along the narrowest and least traveled streets of the town until pulling up behind the Last Stand saloon. Tying up his horse, he surreptitiously entered the establishment's back door.

He stood just inside the door, casting his gaze about. The place seemed empty; not terribly unusual for late afternoon. Behind the bar stood Sam Dobbins, busying himself by cleaning glasses.

"Place seems a mite quiet," Jason said.

Sam's head snapped up, his surprise at hearing a voice come from the back of the saloon evident. His face brightened and a broad smile came to his lips as he recognized its source.

"Jason!" he hollered, scurrying out from behind the bar. He pumped Mankiller's right hand with his own, gripped the drifter's upper arm with his left hand and used both to pull him over to the end of the bar.

As they pulled away from the dimmer light at the back of the saloon and Sam could see Mankiller more clearly, he thought his young friend looked a bit drawn and haggard. The bartender made no mention of it, though. The boy must be doing all right by himself, the bartender figured; he was even wearing obviously new pants and shirt.

"Good ta see ya, son," Dobbins said in heartfelt tones. "I was almost beginnin' ta believe you really *was* dead."

"And what made you think that was a possibility in the first place, Sam?" Mankiller asked, somewhat taken aback. The bartender hung his head slightly.

"Well, for one thing, you just upped and disappeared without so much as a fare-thee-well.

"Then, a couple days later…the McClures showed up here in town."

"All of 'em?"

"All that matters. There was old Squire himself, and his two oldest sons, Micah and Billy.

"Turns out that his youngest boy, Tyrone, was already here when they arrived; he claimed he had been since even *before* you come up missin'."

Dobbins exhaled deeply.

"Well, when the rest o' the clan come sniffin' 'round, damned if young Ty didn't puff up and start crowin' like a real cock o' the walk.

"He told his kin, and ever'body else who'd listen, how he'd done got rid o' the high and mighty Jason Mankiller. Right proud o' hisself he was, too."

"And his people believed him?"

"Guess they had no reason not to, Jason; you wasn't here to say otherwise. They hung around town for a day or two more anyhow, raisin' nine kinds o' hell."

"I don't suppose Marshal Russell tried to stop 'em?"

"'Course not. Fact is, he was outta town the whole time them McClures was here. Real convenient like."

"Real convenient."

"Oh, try not ta judge Clay too hard, son. In his day, he woulda stood toe ta toe with old Scratch hisself. He still does all right when it comes ta buffaloin' a drunk cowboy on the prod or roundin' up a chicken thief.

"But now he's old and tired, and just tryin' ta get by."

Mankiller shrugged then motioned toward where a large mirror had been hanging on the wall behind the bar. Large sections of it were now missing; most of the fragments that remained were laced with cracks.

"They do that?" he asked.

"The mirror? Oh, yeah. Someone told 'em this was where you hung your hat, so they felt the need to engage in a little hooliganism."

"And you?"

"Me? Why, hell, I'm just as old and tired as the marshal is. You know that. I didn't do a blessed thing ta stop 'em."

Mankiller's eyes narrowed. "You know what I meant, Sam. Did they hurt you?"

The barkeep coughed uncomfortably. "Oh, one of the boys, Micah, I think it was, mighta got rambunctious and slapped me around a little. Barely raised a bruise." He smiled crookedly.

"Hell, I was married once to a gal what threw a meaner punch."

"I'm sorry, Sam," Mankiller said. "This was my fault."

"Like hell it was!"

"It was, and we both know it. I brought 'em down on you." He shook his head.

"I'll find a way to see that you're reimbursed for the damages at least."

"You'll do nothin' of the kind, nor worry your head about it," Sam protested, then winked at him.

"Besides, just between you, me and the gatepost, I been makin' money hand over fist offa you ever since them McClures left and headed back to the tall uncut!"

"How's that?"

"Why, hell's fire, you done made this place famous, son, no longer than you was here." The bartender pointed to the back of the saloon, where sat the perch Mankiller had occupied each night.

"So I charge folks as wants twenty-five cents to sit in the great man's chair for two minutes and hold his shotgun. Unloaded, o' course."

Jason's eyebrows arched. "People actually *pay* you just to do that?"

"More of 'em than you'd imagine. And for an extra fifty cents, they can have their picture took a'sittin' there!" He smiled sheepishly.

"Hell, *I've* even become sort o' famous, just by association! I've even noticed gals givin' me the eye from time ta time and that's the first time in a coon's age that's happened."

Mankiller couldn't help but smile, even as he shook his head. Then he grew serious again.

"Any idea where the McClures went after they left town?"

"Hard ta say. Maybe raisin' hell somewheres else; maybe just holed up wherever it is they go between jobs."

"Where might that be?"

"No one but them knows." Sam chuckled softly. "Guess you could always ask young Tyrone McClure real nice."

"What do you mean?"

"Don't you know? No, o' course you don't; you wasn't here. When the rest o' the clan lit a shuck outta here, Ty stuck around. Seems he'd took a likin' ta some of the local talent."

"Any talent in particular?" Mankiller pressed.

"Yeah. You remember a little painted cat used to work here, name o' Dixie?"

Jason stiffened. "Yeah. I remember. You say she 'used' to work here?"

"That's right. She up and quit comin' in right after you disappeared." Sam paused.

"Where you been all this time, by the way?"

"Long story, Sam. I'll tell you all about it later. What about Dixie?"

"What about her? Oh. Yeah. Anyway, she told me she'd decided ta go work full-time for ol' Bucktooth Bertha Hanson in her cathouse over on Carson Street.

"Word is, though, that when Dixie ain't busy workin' she's busy entertainin' the baby McClure. Seems the boy's become a reg'lar Petticoat Pensioner, just livin' off her earnings."

"Interesting," Mankiller commented. Clearly, the treacherous soiled dove had been in league with young McClure when she set Jason up for the ambush in her crib.

He now turned sideways to the bar. The saloon was still otherwise empty, and he could hear nothing from upstairs.

"When the McClures were here," he said coldly. "Did they hurt anybody besides you, Sam?"

The older man smiled knowingly.

"If by 'anybody' you mean a certain little faro dealin' lady…no."

"I don't see her or Cash around," Jason continued, choosing to ignore the smirk on Sam's face.

"Nor will ya, I'm afraid. Gamblers is like gypsies, Jason; I don't have ta tell you that. The day after the McClures lit outta here, Cash pulled up stakes too. Bundled Jane up and caught a stage bound for Kansas."

Mankiller merely nodded in acknowledgment of this.

"Aw, hell!" Sam exclaimed. "That reminds me o' somethin'. Wait right here." He scrambled away from the bar, still muttering under his breath. "How could I have forgot that?"

Dobbins disappeared into his office back behind the bar proper, and Jason could hear him opening and closing desk drawers. When he reappeared a minute later, he was carrying two steaming cups of coffee.

"Figured you could use a good cup o' Arbuckle's," he said, sliding one of the cups across the bar to Mankiller.

"Always. Thanks."

Wiping his hands on his apron, Sam then reached into its pocket and withdrew a thin square of paper, folded in on itself and sealed with wax. Mankiller gave him a quizzical look as Dobbins likewise slid this across the bar.

"It's a letter for ya, Jason…from Jane. She gave it to me the day her and Cash left. Asked me ta give it to ya whenever you made your way back here."

Mankiller smiled drolly. "Am I to take it that at least *she* didn't believe I was dead?"

Sam snorted. "No such of a thing! I believe her exact words to me, when she gave me that there letter, was somethin' like: 'Ain't no way, on the best day God ever gave him, that a squirrelly little peckerwood like Tyrone McClure could take down a man like Jason Mankiller... not face to face, anyway'."

Jason nodded. He suspected Sam had paraphrased what Jane had actually said just a bit, but had accurately captured the sentiment.

He carefully lifted the letter from the bar, as if afraid it might fall apart in his hands and blow away.

"You can see it's still sealed," Sam hurried to assure him. "It ain't been tampered with a'tall."

"Thanks, Sam. I appreciate it."

Mankiller took the letter and his cup of coffee and walked away from the bar, moving to a far corner of the saloon. Unusual for him, he chose to sit at a table near a window: one that fully allowed in the rays of the sinking sun. From the bar, aflame with curiosity, Sam Dobbins watched him intently.

Jason took a small sip of his coffee, then set the cup down. For a moment, he simply examined the wax seal on the letter. The woman had apparently pressed a ring into the wax before it cooled; he recognized the pattern imprinted in the wax as matching that of an ornate ring Jane always wore on her right hand.

Finally, he carefully broke the seal on the letter, unfolded the paper and began to read.

It appeared to Sam as if Mankiller read the contents of the letter more than once. The drifter's face remained totally impassive, though, making it impossible for the barkeep to judge even the general tone of the missive.

Eventually, Mankiller set the letter down on the table and picked his coffee cup back up. Holding it in both hands, he took a sip as he stared out the window.

A few minutes later, he set the cup down and read the letter again. Over the course of nearly an hour, he repeated this pattern several times.

"What's he doin'?" Sam murmured. Memorizing the letter's contents? Or hoping that this time the words he read would be different in some way? The older man, much chagrined, just couldn't tell.

Finally, Mankiller slowly and carefully refolded the letter and slipped it into his shirt pocket.

By now, it was nearly full dark outside. The Last Stand had begun to fill up with its evening crowd, though no one had yet made note of his presence. Only now did he finally drain the last of the cup of coffee he had been nursing.

Rising from the table, he walked over to the bar and set his empty cup down in front of Dobbins.

"Thanks again, Sam," he said, then walked quickly out of the saloon, again using the back door.

He was totally oblivious to the state in which he had left Sam Dobbins.

Curiosity about the contents of the letter was about to make the slack-jawed bartender explode.

CHAPTER 21

Mankiller stayed in the shadows and moved along the side streets and back alleys, lest he be seen and word of his return to Ft. Rogers spread through town faster than he wanted.

He moved quickly to the east end of town, into the red light district known as the Tenderloin. Separated from the rest of Ft. Rogers by an imaginary border known as the Dragline, actually the north-south running of Fifth Street, it was there that all of man's baser needs could be met.

It was home to half a dozen brothels, including one where it was whispered that young men were the principal item on the menu. An opium den drew those who sought to leave this world for a time on a cloud of Asian delight. An underground arena was on hand for the staging of cock and dog fights and the occasional bare-knuckled boxing match between men. The saloons here were seedier; serving snake-head whiskey that would peel the paint off a boilerplate. The cheapest thing to be found in the Tenderloin, though, was life itself.

But as long as these dark trades, and those who plied them, remained east of the Dragline, they were left alone. The "decent" folk who lived in the west, many of whom spent their evenings in the Tenderloin, could thus pretend that there was no vice in their fair city.

Ft. Rogers, like human society as a whole, was largely fueled by hypocrisy.

Slightly more upscale establishments, such as the Last Stand and the other places like it in Tiger Town, were allowed in small numbers west of Fifth Street, but not many and not by far; and they were watched and regulated stringently. Above all, the illusion of propriety must be maintained.

If Marshal Russell's form of law enforcement was slightly lax in the west end, it was virtually non-existent in the eastern quarter of the town. You took your life into your own hands when you crossed the Dragline.

Tonight, that was just fine with Mankiller.

His earlier explorations of the city and all its environs served him well now; enabling him to set a straight course for the house owned and operated by the woman called Bucktooth Bertha.

In any other setting, the two-story Victorian structure would have been considered beautiful, fit to house the cream of society. Here, painted as it was in garish shades of yellow and purple, it looked more like a temple to decadence.

Mankiller boldly marched up the steps leading to its front porch, through the entranceway and into the parlor.

To his right was the drawing room, where the girls came to parade their charms and the men made their claims for the evening. A quick scan of the room revealed no sign of the girl Dixie, so Mankiller kept walking until he came to the foot of the stairs that led up to the second floor.

From the corner of his right eye he saw a short and rather plump woman scurrying toward him. Dressed in a too-tight beaded gown she truly believed made her look elegant, she was the madam herself, Bertha Hanson.

Assuming Jason to be just another prospective client, she approached him with hands fluttering, her smile amply revealing the overbite that gave the woman her nickname. She was probably far younger than she looked, but even heavy makeup was not able to turn back the clock on the ravages to her face that her profession had laid upon her.

"Won't you step into the drawing room, handsome?" she said by way of greeting, her voice bubbling. "I'm sure we have just the girl for you!"

Only when Mankiller turned to face her full on, when her eyes lit on the teardrop tattoo, did she realize who he was. Her smile faded, her words died in her throat and her blood ran cold.

"Tyrone McClure," Mankiller said in clipped tones. "Is he here?"

The madam could do nothing more than manage to shake her head.

"I'm not a man you want to lie to, Bertha."

Her eyes widened with fear. She swallowed hard to regain her voice.

"Upstairs," she squeaked. "Turn right at the landing. Second door on your left."

"Obliged."

He tipped his hat to her and set off up the staircase. Feeling her knees grow weak beneath her, the madam clutched at the banister of the stairs to keep from falling to the floor.

A man hurried over, placing a protective hand around her waist to support her. He was a large, muscular black man, sporting a moustache but with the top of his head shaved clean.

He was dressed in the fancy garb of a wealthy home's butler, but his massive size showed him for what he really was: one of three bouncers Bertha kept on hand at all times to maintain order in the house.

His eyes bored into the back of the man making his way up the stairs, then flicked back to Bertha. Those eyes looked at her with true concern.

"You want me to escort that gentleman out the house, Miz Hanson?" he asked, his voice low and rumbling.

"No, Caesar," she gasped, gripping his arm. "You leave him be, y'hear? But I do want you to round up all the girls and their callers down here and lead them outside." Her eyes were still focused on the ascending Mankiller.

"And send a boy to fetch the marshal. Do it now!"

Ignoring the mild commotion he could hear below him, Mankiller took his time climbing the stairs, eyes scanning to both sides, careful to step lightly and make no undo noise.

Reaching the second room on the left, the drifter pulled his pistol and cautiously placed an ear against the door. He could hear lustful giggles, both male and female, and his features twisted in disgust.

Rearing back, he knocked the door open with a single kick.

The couple inside the room, being otherwise occupied, was taken completely by surprise. Mankiller saw a man roll to the side, falling off the bed and onto the floor, taking the sheets with him.

The woman, screaming shrilly as she simultaneously scrambled to cower in a corner and pull a pillow up to cover her nakedness, he recognized instantly: Dixie.

The man on the floor rolled, kicked free of the tangling sheets and tried to lunge toward a nearby chair where his clothes and his holstered pistol hung.

Mankiller snapped off a single shot. The bullet drilled into the scrambling man's left calf and knocked his feet out from under him.

The wounded man writhed on the floor, clutching at his leg in an effort to staunch the flow of blood. Mankiller elbowed the door closed, then walked across the room, for the moment paying no mind to Dixie over on the bed. Still pressed into the corner, her screaming had subsided to a series of pitiful whimpers.

Mankiller pulled the shot man's pistol from its holster and flung it out the nearest window before holstering his own and stepping over to stand above his victim. Jason saw enough of a resemblance between this grimacing fellow and the late Zeb McClure to feel certain that this was young Tyrone McClure.

"Recognize me, boy?" he hissed, leaning down toward the fallen McClure.

"Oh, Jesus," McClure moaned as he looked up to find himself facing a man who appeared to be crying blood.

"What's the matter? Ain't you ever talked to a dead man before?" His only response was another groan.

"Where's your daddy and his other two whelps, McClure?"

"I don't know."

Sighing, Mankiller straightened. He planted his right foot atop the hand McClure was using to stop the bleeding from his leg and began to grind. McClure screamed in fresh pain.

"Where are they?" Mankiller repeated.

"I don't know, mister. I swear to God!"

"Like that means anything. What did they tell you when they left you here?"

The wounded man just glowered up at him, so Jason put the boot to his throbbing leg again, eliciting another scream.

"No more," McClure pleaded. "Please."

"Then say something I want to hear."

"They told me they were going back to the ranch, and that I could meet them there."

"That's more like it. Now, where might this ranch be?"

"I can't tell you that; they'd kill me!"

This time, Mankiller kicked McClure's leg viciously, bringing a high-pitched shriek.

"*Where is it?*"

"Oh, God," young McClure moaned. "Oh, God." Tears were rolling down his cheeks.

"Due north of here," he gasped at last. "Just this side of the Red River."

"A little tributary heads off to the southeast, into a box canyon. That creek and the trail next to it are the only ways in, and there's always a guard on lookout."

"You saying there might be more than just your daddy and brothers there?"

"Probably."

"How many?"

"No way to say. Usually no more than five or six."

Mankiller straightened, pondering this information.

A sudden rustling sound came from behind him, prompting him to spin around. Dixie, still naked, was out of bed and lunging at him with a knife she had somehow procured. The point of its blade was aimed right at his midsection.

As he twisted to the side, his right hand flashed across and closed on hers, the one holding the knife. His fingers clamped down on her hand like a vise, stopping her thrust and causing her to whimper in pain.

"My daddy always told me a woman would be the death of me someday, Dixie." His voice was harsh and cold.

"But it won't be today...and it won't be you."

The soiled dove's eyes widened, and not just from fear. Sensing new danger, Mankiller, keeping a tight grip on her knife hand, spun around again.

Behind him, Tyrone McClure had managed to rise to his feet and was throwing himself forward to attack from Mankiller's blind side.

Jason jerked Dixie's hand forward impaling McClure with her knife. Blood gushed as the blade slipped in just below his left ribcage.

McClure made a sickening, choking sound as Mankiller twisted Dixie's hand and the knife. Warm blood flowed thickly over her and Jason's hands, until he released his grip on her. Her stained hand jerked away from the knife as if she had been scalded.

Unmindful of the blade still protruding from his body, the youngest McClure stared blankly ahead. His mouth opened, but all that rolled out was his tongue.

He toppled backwards to the floor, twitching several times before all the life bled out of him.

Dixie had been plunged into a total state of shock, staring in horror at her own bloody hand that she held up before her disbelieving eyes. She trembled from head to toe.

Mankiller grabbed her by the jaw and jerked her around to face him, partly snapping her out of her daze; bringing her to the reality that she might be the next to die.

"I ought to kill you for what you've done," Mankiller said brutally, and her eyes grew even wider.

"If I ever lay eyes on you again…I will."

He gave her head a sharp twist.

"You understand me, girl?"

Numbly, she nodded.

"Good. Come morning, you'd better go fast and you'd better go far; far as you can go and still be this side of heaven or hell."

He then shoved her roughly backwards and she toppled onto the bed.

Using one of the sheets lying on the floor, Mankiller wiped the blood from his own hands before turning back to the dead man stretched out nearby.

Not bothering to try to cover the naked corpse in any way, Mankiller used his left hand to grab the body by one ankle and, dragging it along the floor behind him, exited the room.

With the dead McClure in tow, he descended the staircase. Each step brought the chinking sound of his spurs, followed the next moment by the hollow thump of McClure's head banging against successive steps.

As he neared the bottom of the stairs, Jason saw two men hurriedly pushing their way into the parlor of the brothel. One he recognized instantly as being Marshal Russell.

The other man was unfamiliar to him, though the badge he wore on his vest identified him as likely being a deputy. He was a smallish man, who frequently licked his lips nervously. His name was Newt Carpenter, and he fancied himself the eventual heir apparent to the marshal's job.

Mankiller saw their faces twist in dismay at the sight laid out before them as he callously dragged the body of Tyrone McClure behind him, leaving a wet and sticky trail of blood.

No one else appeared to be inside the brothel, at least on its lower level. But Mankiller saw other men, bystanders with their faces pressed against the windows, straining to catch even a fleeting glimpse of what was going on inside, awestruck by what they were witnessing.

This was a good thing, or so it seemed to Mankiller. When the stories of what had transpired this night spread and were doubtless embellished to mythic proportions, his reputation and legend would grow accordingly.

Not that he cared in the least about either, but such tales as would be told of his ruthless and deadly skills might dissuade others from trying their hand and their luck against him.

At least, this is what he hoped.

One man who did not care to see this killer's reputation rise from the ashes of his own was the marshal of Ft. Rogers.

"I'm getting mighty damned tired o' you turning my town into a slaughterhouse, Mankiller," Clay Russell snarled.

"And I'm getting mighty damned tired of doing your job for you," Mankiller snapped back.

For just an instant, the spark that used to burn brightly in the lawman's breast flared up anew, triggered by the insult and the implied accusation of cowardice.

Without conscious thought, Russell's right hand leaped to his gun, as did Mankiller's.

"Whoa, whoa, whoa!" Deputy Carpenter cried, inserting himself between the two men, hoping his move was not as suicidal as had been the marshal's.

"Let's not do somethin' we're all gonna regret, men," he said soothingly. "Let's just all take a breath."

Mankiller's eyes blazed with anger: anger at himself for coming so close to killing a man of the law.

In that frightfully long instant before, he had also recognized the look in Marshal Russell's eyes when he went for his gun. It was a look Jason had seen before, in the eyes of men who had killed and were prepared to kill again.

No doubt, had there been a mirror to hand…Jason would have seen the same look in his own eyes.

What Sam Dobbins had said earlier was true; in another time and place, Clay Russell had surely been a real hellion.

Now, bowed by age, responsibility and seemingly endless years of performing thankless duties, he was just a man doing his best to get by from day to day.

Unable to sustain rage against such a man as this, Jason relaxed, sliding his gun back into its holster.

Marshal Russell saw this and did likewise, exhaling softly. He knew that his own draw had been fatally slower than that of the drifter. If not for his deputy's intervention, he could easily be a dead man now.

Still, he maintained his icy glare as Mankiller resumed dragging Tyrone McClure's body the rest of the way down the stairs and across the richly carpeted floor before dropping it at the feet of the two lawmen.

"Forget what I said before," Mankiller softly said to Russell. "Not many men could do your job, marshal… including me."

Mollified, Russell's jaws softened their clench. In time to come, the exaggerated accounts of how he had faced down Jason Mankiller and lived to tell of it would do much to better his own reputation. Friends and supporters would make sure to retell it anew every time an election rolled around.

"I'll leave the paperwork and burial to you," Mankiller said of his latest victim. "I'll be back in a few days to collect the reward on him."

"And what if you don't come back?"

"Then you can keep it for yourself."

Without another word, Jason made his exit from the cathouse, pushing brusquely through the press of onlookers. Not caring who saw him now, he took the most direct path back to the Last Stand. As he entered the saloon, an anxious Sam Dobbins slid down the back of the bar to greet him.

"What happened, Jason?"

"I imagine you'll be hearing all about it in a few minutes, Sam." He ran a hand across his tired eyes.

"Do you have a room where I can spend the night?"

"O' course. Pick any one you like. No charge."

"*Gracias.*"

Mankiller started up the stairs to the second floor, stopping once when he heard a familiar pop and saw an equally familiar flash of light and puff of smoke.

Some local had just had his picture taken while sitting in the chair made famous by the notorious Jason Mankiller.

With a weary shake of his head, the drifter resumed his trek up the stairs.

CHAPTER 22

A day's ride north of Ft. Rogers found Mankiller sitting his horse atop a low grassy knoll, watching a disturbing scene unfolding on the flats below him.

Three horsemen were engaged under the spreading branches of a large elm tree. Two of them were dressed in garb typical of working cowhands. The third appeared to be an Indian. On the ground a few feet from them lay a dead steer.

As Mankiller watched, one of the cowhands dismounted, carrying a coil of rope. One end he looped and tied around the trunk of the tree. The other end he tossed up and over one of the lower branches: a very sturdy one.

"Oh, hell," Mankiller groused, gigging his mount and sending it cantering down the gentle slope of the knoll.

He slowed it to a walk as he drew closer, keeping both hands in plain sight so as not to unduly spook the interested parties. By the time he reined to a complete halt, the free end of the rope had been knotted into the familiar shape of a noose and dropped over the head of the Indian; the cowboy was back on his horse. The target of this planned lynching had both hands behind his back, presumably tied.

"Howdy, boys," Mankiller said as amiably as possible. "Planning a party are you?"

"What business is that of yours, stranger?" the older and larger of the cowboys snarled.

His younger companion's eyes lit on Mankiller's tattoo, and he blanched slightly. He leaned over and whispered something in the older herder's ear. The man's eyes widened slightly as he listened, then narrowed to little more than slits.

"I asked what business this was o' yours," he repeated.

"None at all," Jason assured him. "I was just curious, that's all."

"Well, I'll just tell ya what we're about," the older cowboy growled. "We caught this Injun red-handed, so ta speak." He smiled grimly at the play on words. "He was about ta butcher a steer he stole from our spread."

Only now did Mankiller turn his full attention to their captive. The Indian stared straight ahead with a stoic expression; but in a low voice he was chanting what Jason recognized as being a death song. He also recognized the language of the song.

"You're Kiowa?" he asked, using that native language. The Indian broke off his song and looked at Mankiller with mild surprise.

"You speak my tongue?"

"Well enough to get by. Are you all right?"

The Kiowa shrugged. "I've had better days."

"Do you know why these two are plannin' to string you up?"

"I'm an Indian and they're white men. What other reason do they need?"

The cowboys exchanged glances, puzzled by what to them was a string of gibberish passing between the other two men. Being totally ignored now, they simply sat and watched.

"They say you stole that steer," Mankiller explained, indicating with one hand the fallen animal.

"They say wrong," the Kiowa responded. "If I was on a raid, I wouldn't be alone. And I wouldn't have taken just one scrawny cow.

"I found it wandering out here alone, too, and I killed it...but I didn't steal it."

Jason nodded. "All right. Let's see if I can get us all outta here with our scalps still attached."

The Indian flinched slightly at the word "scalps."

"He says he didn't steal the steer, fellas," Mankiller said in English, speaking once again to the herders.

"Hell, mister," the older cowboy replied, "what do you expect him ta say, with a noose around his neck? You can't believe nothin' these savages tell ya." The other, younger rider grinned in agreement.

Mankiller sighed.

"I happened to notice that poor, mangy critter doesn't seem to have a brand or any other mark of ownership on it."

"So?"

"So, that makes it a maverick. And in Texas, that makes it fair game for anyone."

"Anyone *human*," the lead cowboy sneered.

While they had been talking, Mankiller had been slowly turning his horse to the right. That put it sideways to the cowboys, thus lining his cross-draw pistol on a straight line to them. The move was almost imperceptible, but it and its significance had not been lost on the older and more experienced of the two cowboys.

"I know who you are, mister," he said through gritted teeth, "and that don't cut no mustard with me. I've got a pistol too."

"Yeah?" Mankiller replied. "And what was the last thing you used if for, a hammer?"

Only now realizing what was going down, the younger cowboy stiffened, the smile vanishing from his lips.

"Me, on the other hand," Mankiller continued easily, "I only pull my gun out for two reasons: cleaning and killing." He paid no mind to the younger herder; his eyes were boring straight into the other.

"And right now, mister...it don't need cleaning."

A silent test of wills followed. The only question remaining was whether the cowboy would go for his gun.

"C'mon, Eldridge," the younger cowboy urged at last. "It ain't worth it for no cow. Let's get outta here!"

His comrade didn't look at him, didn't appear even to hear him. His right hand still hovered near his holstered pistol; his fingers twitched slightly.

Then he blinked.

He moved the hand, not to his pistol but to join the other on his reins. Jerking them hard to the left, he spurred his mount harder than necessary and took off at a gallop. His young friend wasted no time in following.

Mankiller sat and watched them, assuring himself they weren't intending merely to circle and come back. The Indian coughed softly.

"If it's not too much trouble, brother, do you think you could take this rope from around my neck?"

Jason smiled tightly and drew his horse alongside that of the Indian. After relieving him of the weight of the noose, the drifter pulled his skinning knife and cut the ropes binding the Kiowa's hands.

"We'd best get that beef butchered in a hurry, friend," he told the Indian, "before them two find more buddies and decide to come back.

"Then we need to get as far from here as we can."

The Kiowa nodded in agreement, threw one leg over the back of his pony and dropped lightly to the ground. Mankiller did likewise.

Using the noose end of the rope that was intended to be the means of executing the Indian, the two of them looped it around the slain steer's hind legs, stringing it up from the tree. They then set to work to field dress the animal.

When the internal organs spilled out onto the ground, the Indian scooped up the still-warm liver and began to eat it raw. From the way he attacked it, Mankiller suspected it may have been a spell since last he ate.

Catching himself and feeling guilty of bad manners, thinking that was why the white man was now gazing at him, the Kiowa offered the remainder of the liver to him.

Jason took it without question, hefted it as if making a toast to his host and ate it with gusto, wiping spilling blood from his chin with the back of one hand.

After performing a hasty but efficient job of butchering, the two men bundled as much of the meat as they could inside the skinned hide of the steer and took off at a gallop. The Kiowa had retrieved his battered rifle from the spot where he had dropped it when the cowhands surprised and captured him, and held it in one hand as he rode.

They didn't stop till night was falling and they had put a good fifteen miles behind them. Finding a rocky draw that was easily defensible and which would hide the glow of a fire, they decided to make camp.

As the Indian cooked steaks and the steer's tongue on sharpened sticks that dangled them over the fire, Mankiller prepared a pan of fried potatoes.

Not many words had passed between them as they rode, but as they sat near the fire and ate, Jason struck up a conversation.

"What's your name, friend?"

"I'm called Three Pony," the Kiowa replied.

"That's a good name. A strong name."

"I think I already know your name," Three Pony said. "You're the one the People call 'Kills Many,' aren't you? The one who weeps blood."

"I've been called that, yeah," Mankiller said, nodding.

"Do you really do that?" Three Pony asked. "Weep blood, I mean."

"What do you think?"

Three Pony pondered on it as he slowly chewed a succulent slice of tongue.

"I think that when I tell the story about how the two of us fought off *ten* bloodthirsty white men, I'll say that you do."

"Fair enough."

"You're not of the People," Three Pony observed again, meaning the Kiowas, "but you speak the language good."

"My grandmother was Kiowa. I've spent time among 'em, as a boy and as a man."

"Your grandmother: was her name Sparrow Wing Woman?"

"It was. You've heard of her?"

"Stories. I was told that the white man she married was big and hairy, like a bear. Kinda smelled like one, too, the old ones say."

Mankiller chuckled. "That sounds like grandpa, all right!" He took up a stick and stirred the embers of the fire.

"Why are you out here all alone, Three Pony? Where's your village?"

"It's about two day's ride west and north of here," the Indian replied. "On the banks of the river that runs red.

"These haven't been good times for us, Kills Many. There's not much buffalo any more; your people have seen to that.

"Hunters like me have to roam farther and farther to find game." He peered across the fire.

"You have my thanks, brother. Not only because you saved me from being strung up like a dog, but because you've helped to put some much-needed meat into the People's cooking pots."

"I did nothing," Mankiller professed. "The Kiowa are partly my people, too, so I should help them."

"You're mostly white, though, so I'd expect you to be mostly selfish."

"There's good in every tribe and bad."

Jason took it...and ate it with gusto...

"This is so." Three Pony wiped his greasy hands on his leggings.

"You'll always be welcomed in my lodge, Kills Many. And if I can ever return the good you did for me, I will."

"I don't doubt that, Three Pony. That's the way it is for men like you and me."

When they had prepared their beds, far enough away from the smoldering fire so as not to be lit by its lingering glow, Three Pony noticed that Mankiller drew his pistol and held it in his hand even as he spread out and rested his head on his saddle.

"I promise I won't try to kill you in your sleep, brother," he said, smiling.

"Never figured you would," Jason replied without bothering to open his eyes. "But that still leaves an awful lot of other people who might."

Thinking about that as he lay down on his own blanket, Three Pony pulled his rifle close to his side before nodding off.

The next morning, Jason insisted on feeding them both with bacon and biscuits from his own provisions, to leave all the rest of the butchered beef for Three Pony and his village.

"So long, Kills Many," Three Pony said afterwards, when he had mounted his pony. "Be well."

"You too, brother."

Nothing more was said. As Three Pony trotted away, Jason saddled and mounted his horse, knowing he had business of his own that still waited.

Business that might cause him to further earn his Kiowa name.

CHAPTER 23

A tough looking fellow by the name of Harry "Slope-Eye" Torborg stifled a yawn.

He squirmed uncomfortably astride the rock upon which he sat, shifted his grip on the rifle he held loosely in both hands. Keeping watch alone at the mouth of this box canyon was boring beyond description.

Probably pointless, too; its location was known to only a few and no one who knew of it but hadn't been ushered in by the McClures personally would dare try to enter it. Torborg wasn't inclined to argue that point with old man McClure, though. So he took his turn up in the rocks same as everybody else and kept his complaints to himself.

One look at this hard man's face told the story of how he had come by the moniker of "Slope-Eye." A raw, red scar running over his right eye caused it to droop perpetually. The scar was the result of a bar fight in which he was hit in the head with a beer mug.

He didn't care one bit about what the scar did to his looks; he had already been ugly as a mud fence, and he knew it. By the time the fight that left him with the scar had finished, Torborg's opponent had looked far worse.

An unexpected movement caught his attention, and he leaped to his feet. Something was floating toward him down the narrow creek that fed into the canyon.

There was no moon and only a few distant stars to light the night sky, so he had to squint his good eye to make out the object. He huffed out a blast of air and relaxed as it finally drifted close enough to his position for him to see it was nothing more than a tangle of tree branches.

If it had been daytime, he might have gone ahead and snapped off a shot at one of the branches, just for the target practice. But it was pointless to try to do so in the dark, and would unduly rouse those within the canyon proper.

He paid it no more heed as it floated past him and on into the canyon, instead focusing once more on the trail that ran alongside the creek, on its south side. It was on this trail that anyone trying to reach the canyon would be found. Of this he was sure.

In truth, the loose tangle of fallen branches was anything but. The foliage had in actuality been carefully arranged over and around a plank of wood hidden in its midst.

Jason Mankiller, his head only partly above water, rested his folded arms atop the floating plank. Also lying on it was an oilskin wrapped around his Winchester rifle and a bag of shells. His pistol was gripped in his right hand, ready to be used if the guard spotted him.

Below the water line, his legs quietly helped to guide him and his camouflaged raft. He pumped them slowly, so as not to appear as if the branches were moving even faster than the current would normally carry them.

He had been able to make out the silhouetted shape of the man standing guard, and held his breath as he drew near the man's position. He stopped paddling as well, letting the creek do all the work. As he passed the lookout, his muscles tensed as if anticipating a bullet in the back.

None came, and he allowed himself to breathe again. Still, he remained in the water until he felt sure he had floated well past the guard's post.

Only then did he paddle his makeshift raft to the bank of the creek and clamber ashore.

He removed his rifle and ammo from the oilskin, assured himself that they were still dry. His pistol had not gotten unduly wet either, but he now slipped it into its holster.

What needed to be done next, needed to be done as silently as possible. He had already removed his spurs earlier, leaving them back with his horse outside the canyon,

Keeping low to the ground, he made his way back to where Slope-Eye sat peering out in the opposite direction. Slowly, methodically, Mankiller made his way up a jumble of rocks toward the guard's position. In his right hand he now gripped the handle of his lethal skinning knife.

It probably would have been a clean kill if a loose pebble hadn't skittered out from under Jason's toes.

Alerted by the sound, Torborg began to rise and turn toward the noise. Reacting instinctively, Mankiller launched himself up and through the air, slamming into the guard before he could bring his rifle to bear.

The weapon flew out of Torborg's hands and he himself was bowled over by the impact of Mankiller's body. Both landed hard on the rock upon which Torborg had been seated: Jason atop the sentry. He slapped his left hand across the outlaw's mouth to stifle any outcry.

Flailing about, Torborg lashed upward with both hands, hoping to hit and claw his attacker's eyes, but Mankiller successfully twisted his head away. Frustrated in this effort, Torborg settled for grabbing Mankiller around his throat.

Torborg smiled wickedly as he felt his thick fingers sink into the soft flesh of his foe's neck, not realizing the fatal flaw in this plan of attack. With both of the outlaw's hands on his throat, Mankiller found his right hand totally free.

His current position didn't allow him to made a clean slash with the knife he clutched in that hand, but he was able to jab upward with it, driving the point of the blade into the outlaw's left armpit.

Torborg jerked and sucked in air painfully. With his opponent off-guard, Mankiller was able to push him up and partly over one side of the rock upon which they struggled.

Torborg's body was forced to bow up awkwardly. With his hand still clamped over the outlaw's mouth, Mankiller pushed Torborg's head back even farther, exposing the white flesh of his throat.

Torborg's eyes reflected his fear as he saw Mankiller scramble up and come forward with his knife.

The razor-sharp blade made a smooth cut, traversing the flesh from one ear to the other. Torborg's body jerked beneath Mankiller, who maintained his grip over the man's mouth so as to stifle even the faintest of death rattles.

It took less than a minute for the outlaw to bleed out.

Breathing heavily, Jason lay limply atop the body of the slain Torborg. He remained otherwise silent, listening for any sounds that might indicate anyone else had discovered his presence. Only the normal sounds of the night and the murmuring of the nearby creek came back to him.

Pulling his slain victim back up fully atop the rock, Mankiller examined his face as closely as the dim light would allow.

Before leaving Ft. Rogers two days earlier, Mankiller had paid a visit to Marshal Russell's office and politely asked if he could see any flyers the lawman might have on the members of the McClure clan.

There were dodgers on all of the immediate family: the patriarch and his three sons. Jason had been somewhat surprised by the size of the rewards offered for each; but of course, until a few weeks ago, he had not even been aware of their existence.

The hand-drawn portraits on the outlaws' posters were not of the highest quality, but he hoped they would be close enough to enable him to correctly identify his prey when he found them. Having seen Tyrone closely, he could tell all the McClures bore at least a passing resemblance to each other.

The scarred and ugly man he had just slain was clearly not a member of the family. He did, however, remember seeing a wanted poster among those he had studied of a man who closely resembled the outlaw lying dead before him. It seemed unlikely there would be two wanted men this distinctively ugly.

He had hoped to take the guard alive, that he might question him about how many others awaited him inside the canyon. The nature of their struggle had denied him that option.

Mankiller stealthily returned to the creek. He washed away the slippery blood staining his hands, drying them on the grass.

Retrieving his rifle from where he had left it, he cautiously moved deeper into the box of the canyon, using the well-beaten path beside the creek.

When he saw the sides of the canyon beginning to widen apart, he left the trail and started to climb up the near side of the sloping canyon wall before continuing forward, hoping to give himself the advantage of holding the high ground.

Reaching what appeared to be a good, defensible position, he closely surveyed the floor of the canyon now spread out before him in a great bowl.

Smack in the middle of the canyon floor squatted a large and seemingly well-constructed cabin, built of sturdy logs and stone. A hundred feet away from it stood a barn with a corral attached. He could also see a sizable pond, into which the lazy creek fed. The floor of the canyon was covered in sturdy prairie grass.

All and all, he noted, this would be a good place for an honest man to graze a few head of cattle or horses and make a modest living.

Too bad it hadn't been an honest man who had discovered it.

Mankiller paid especially close attention to the corral, where he was able to discern the shapes of seven horses. Assuming one mount per man and minus the slain guard, that still left six men for him to face.

It seemed foolish to try to breach the sturdy cabin alone, even under cover of darkness, but another plan of action quickly formed in his brain. It represented an enormous risk, but one he was willing to take.

Again leaving his rifle behind, Mankiller cautiously descended to the floor of the canyon. No light shone from the cabin, and he gambled on all those within being asleep. In a crouched run, he made his way to the corral and slipped inside.

He approached the nearest horse, speaking to it in soft, soothing tones. When he drew close enough, he looped one arm under its chin, stroking its neck. Its nostrils flared, familiarizing themselves with his scent. As they did, he blew his own breath gently into them.

He did this with each of the horses in turn, taking his time, calming them to his presence so they made no undue noise. There was an open-sided tack room attached to one side of the corral; entering it, he removed seven halters and a good length of coiled rope.

With all seven horses in tow, Mankiller left the corral, careful to keep one eye on the still darkened and silent cabin. Continuing to softly talk to the animals, he led them away to the spot below where he had killed the lone guard earlier.

Cutting the rope he had purloined into seven appropriate lengths, he hobbled the horses, knowing that with grass and water close at hand they would not be inclined to wander in any event.

Such action was a reflection of the drifter's confidence in his own abilities. His sole thought in pursuing this plan was to remove the outlaws' means of running away from *him*.

By the time Mankiller made it back to the strategic position he had staked claim to in the rocks, where he had left his rifle, the sky overhead was beginning to lighten. He knew full light was still some time away, in the moments when the sun would rise above the canyon walls.

A sound not from nature at last brought him fully alert. He knelt down so the barrel of his rifle rested atop a flat rock and homed his eyes on the cabin. Moments later, the door of the house opened.

A man, he couldn't tell whom from this distance, stepped out onto the front porch and stretched leisurely. The man had his pants and boots on, but no shirt on over his long johns.

Stepping down from the front porch, the man strolled over to the corral.

When he saw the gate was open and the horses were gone, he spun and crouched, pressed up against the corral fence, anxiously looking about in all directions.

Though he saw nothing, he sprang to his feet and set off running back toward the cabin, yelling at the top of his lungs.

Mankiller, taking careful aim with his rifle, allowed his target to get halfway home before he snapped off a shot.

The bullet hit the scurrying man in mid-stride, lifting and spinning him before slamming him to the ground.

The outlaw pushed himself back up to his hands and knees, swayed, then pitched forward face first into the dust. He would never move again.

The door of the cabin slammed open and a second man rushed out, intending to go to the aid of his fallen companion. Mankiller fired, but the bullet was deflected by one of the upright posts supporting the overhang of the porch.

The second outlaw slid to a halt, nearly falling down as he changed direction and dashed back toward the safety of the cabin. Bullets sprayed around him, sending splinters of wood flying, but he succeeded in diving through the doorway and out of sight.

Mankiller ceased firing, and no answering shots came from the cabin. Silence reigned for several minutes, and then a voice called out from the house.

"Is that you out there, Mankiller?"

Jason said nothing.

"It's bad enough you killed my brother," the voice from within continued, "but then you went and killed my boy Ty, too!"

Mankiller frowned. One or more of the men down there with the McClures must have ridden straight to them from Ft. Rogers for Squire to already know about Tyrone's fate.

Still, he said nothing to those he stalked.

"You can sit out there in them rocks till hell freezes over, Mankiller; you can't touch us in here!"

Now Jason did reply, after a fashion; by snapping off three quick shots that shattered one of the cabin's windows.

Then, after slipping fresh shells into his rifle, he just sat back to wait.

CHAPTER 24

An hour later, the front door of the cabin banged open and all five men inside rushed out at once.

To Mankiller's surprise, they weren't charging toward his position; rather, they were making a run for the barn.

Cursing himself for being taken off guard, he hurriedly adjusted his sights; but by then they had nearly reached their goal. Mankiller levered and fired his rifle as quickly as possible, hoping for a lucky shot.

One slug did clip the boot heel of the man farthest from the barn, hard enough to throw off his stride and send him tumbling to the ground.

By the time he scrambled back up on his feet, Mankiller had homed in on him. He put a bullet in the man's chest, followed by a second one before the outlaw had time to fall lifelessly back to the ground.

This sudden and unexpected move on the part of the outlaws had not only surprised Jason; it had left him puzzled as to the reason for it.

Why risk their lives just to reach the barn? Its walls were constructed of ordinary wood planks, undoubtedly thinner and of less protection than were the thick log walls of the cabin they had fled.

He decided it was possible more horses had been stabled within it; if so, they were probably saddling up now in order to make a break for freedom.

Whatever they planned, sooner or later it would require them to leave the barn. Wanting to insure the likelihood of getting off more accurate shots when they did finally emerge, Mankiller took up a new defensive position, moving down to a spot closer to the floor of the canyon.

The minutes slowly ticked by and even Mankiller's near limitless patience was beginning to wear thin. He removed his hat and used his sleeve to mop up the sweat beading on his forehead, waved a hand to shoo away an annoying fly.

All the while, he refused to let his imagination take the place of what his physical senses told him was happening. He maintained his position in the rocks and never allowed his eyes to stray from the barn.

Even so, his taut muscles jerked when the double doors of the structure were suddenly and loudly rammed open.

Rolling out of the darkness within came a buckboard wagon. Oddly, there was no sign of horses or men, and the wagon appeared to be coming out backwards.

Clearly someone, hidden from sight for the moment, was at the front of the buckboard, holding the tongue and using it to push the wagon out of the barn.

Mankiller's eyes narrowed. This was not a bad strategy on the part of the outlaws. His bullets couldn't pass through the wagon, nor would he have a clear target if they could. The buckboard would provide protection and cover, and allow them to close in on him. He braced himself, holding his fire.

A new movement caught his eye. From inside the bed of the buckboard, a man popped up into sight, a rifle at the ready. Scanning left and right, he spotted Jason in the rocks and opened fire. At the same time, he could be heard yelling directions to guide the men who were pushing the wagon.

The jolting and bouncing of the wagon prevented the outlaw from taking a steady shot, for which he tried to compensate by spraying as much lead as quickly as he possibly could.

One such bullet spanged off a rock to Mankiller's right, sending a splintered sliver of stone flying up and slicing along the ridge of his cheek. It stung and drew blood, but otherwise did no harm.

Mankiller wiped the blood away with the back of his left hand. Coolly, he brought his own rifle up to his shoulder, sighting along its barrel until he drew a bead on the shooting outlaw.

He squeezed the trigger, levered a fresh round into the chamber and fired again, levered and fired again, in less than three seconds.

The first bullet struck the kneeling outlaw in his left shoulder, twisting him and forcing him to lose his grip on his rifle. The second shot was a miss.

The third slug slapped into his head, making it snap back sharply. Seeing the man still remained upright, Mankiller took aim at his chest. Before he could pull the trigger, the stricken outlaw sagged to one side and fell down out of sight in the bed of the buckboard.

The odds still stood at three to one against the drifter, and the remaining outlaws were still hidden from his sight and shielded from his bullets.

He fired a few random shots at the ground beneath the wagon bed, in the slim hope a slug might ricochet up and hit flesh. It didn't work, and the wagon kept rolling closer.

To his amazement, all three outlaws suddenly came into open view. They had apparently let go of the wagon after giving it one final shove, and now stood exposed.

None of them was armed with a rifle, but each had a pistol in hand and began to fire them toward Jason's general location with blazing quickness.

Caught somewhat flat-footed, Mankiller threw himself flat on the ground behind the rock in front of him. The fearsome barrage unleashed by the outlaws kept him pinned down. He rolled onto his belly and covered the back of his head with both hands as bullets and stone splinters ricocheted all around him.

Then came his chance. Almost simultaneously, all three of the guns firing from below went silent. Assuming they were needing to reload, Mankiller jumped back up to his knees, rifle raised.

Only...he had no targets. The outlaws had dropped out of sight.

Mankiller's eyes rapidly scanned from side to side for any sign of them. He quickly focused on the buckboard; it had pitched over onto its side, spilling its grisly cargo out on the ground not more than twenty feet in front of him. The dead outlaw's body lay twisted at awkward angles, unmoving.

But while Mankiller saw nothing, he did at last *hear* something: a soft hissing, as might be emitted from a pit of vipers.

Only then were his eyes drawn straight down to see the small bundle lying just below his position in the rocks. It consisted of three sticks of *dynamite*; the hissing sound was coming from the rapidly burning fuse attached to them.

In the blink of an eye, it all became terrifyingly clear to him. That was why they had made their risky dash to the barn; it was there that the dynamite had been stored, doubtless for use in some of their illegal ventures.

The cover of the wagon, behind which the remaining three cutthroats were probably now cowering, had enabled them to get close enough to use the dynamite as a weapon against him.

All this registered on Mankiller's brain in the instant it took him to leap to his feet in an attempt to scramble away before the dynamite could detonate.

Too late.

An ear-shattering roar was followed by searing pain and a wave of pounding force that propelled him into the air and sent his body flying.

CHAPTER 25

Squire McClure cried out in pain, slapping both hands to his ears as if trying to keep his head from exploding.

The force of the dynamite detonation had been far greater than he had anticipated. The ground itself had bucked up beneath him like a steed gone mad; he curled in a ball as whistling shards of rock rained down upon him and his sons. Other rocks had been blasted with enough horizontal force to actually rip through the bed of the upturned wagon they had counted on for protection.

Dust and smaller bits of debris were still falling to earth when McClure was at last able to hear the sounds of his own screams. He could feel the pounding of his blood in his temples, willed his heartbeat to slow as he removed his hands from his ears.

Rolling over and blinking dust from his eyes, he spied his middle son, Billy. He was still curled in a ball inside the driver's box of the buckboard, coughing and spitting dirt from his mouth but seemingly unharmed. That left only the oldest boy, Micah.

He was not so fine.

He lay flat on his back, several feet away from the shadow of the wagon. His father saw blood spreading across his son's shirt, heard his breath wheezing like a broken train whistle.

"Billy!" McClure snapped at his middle son, who was trying to crawl toward his father. "You get up in them rocks, y'hear? If there's anything left o' that drifter ta bother with, you kill 'im. Kill 'im good."

Billy McClure nodded obediently. Pushing himself to his feet, he drew his pistol and made sure it was undamaged and fully loaded. Satisfied, he peeked around the corner of the buckboard before setting out at a crouched run toward the spot where the dynamite had detonated.

Squire McClure scurried over to see his fallen son. He sucked wind through clenched teeth as he saw what had laid the boy low.

One of the larger pieces of rock sent flying by the explosion had torn right through the bottom of the buckboard and struck Micah squarely in the chest. The impact had collapsed his ribcage inward, driving shards of bone into his lungs and possibly his heart.

The elder McClure knelt beside his firstborn and favored son, raising him upright with surprising gentleness.

"Pa," Micah gasped, before coughing up a dark stream of blood.

"Hush, boy. Don't try ta talk."

"Pa...I..."

The eyes were still open, still staring pleadingly up at his father, but the light had left them. Forever.

Hot, stinging tears making him blink, Squire McClure clutched his dead son to his bosom, sobbing as he rocked back and forth.

Up in the rocks, Billy McClure was moving slowly and carefully upward. His reason told him there was no way Mankiller could have survived the dynamite blast. That part of a man that generates fear, though, was not willing to assume that such was the case. Not after all he'd heard about this tattooed killer, all he'd seen with his own eyes.

McClure hopped over the rock behind which he had last seen Mankiller, but there was no sign of the man on its other side. To one side, however, he saw a Winchester rifle lying where it had fallen. Most of its stock was gone.

He moved off in that direction, senses screaming on high alert. Several feet past the damaged rifle, his eyes fell upon a small, dark puddle on the ground.

McClure knelt beside the puddle and dipped two fingers of his left hand into it. When he withdrew them, he could clearly see that their tips were coated with fresh blood. He smiled.

The clatter of dislodged rocks came from behind him and he spun, falling to one side and raising his gun to shoot.

"It's *me*, boy!" Squire McClure hissed. "Your pa!"

Barely in time, Billy stopped his finger from pulling the trigger. He dropped his head, panting, then pushed back up to his feet and motioned for his father to join him.

"He's hurt, Pa," Billy said, pointing down at the puddle of blood near his feet. "Hurt pretty bad, I think."

"Yeah. But hurt ain't dead." Squire cast his gaze about. "We still have to find 'im."

"That shouldn't be too hard," his son replied. "Look."

Just beyond the dark puddle could be seen a smaller stain, made by a single drop falling from a wounded man on the move. And more drops beyond that, close enough to tell that the man leaving them was bleeding freely.

"Keep your eyes on that blood trail, Billy, and follow it. I'll be right behind ya, keepin' a lookout in case the bastard's holed up somewhere he thinks he can jump us."

Billy did as he was told, though not without trepidation. As he'd said, the trail of black droplets was easy to follow. The larger puddle of blood must have marked the spot where Mankiller had landed after being caught in the initial blast of the dynamite.

After managing to rise back up, he had set off eastward, his path zigzagging to follow the natural pathways in the rocky face of the canyon.

It was quite possible that Mankiller would have bled out by the time they caught up with him, but McClure wasn't willing to bet on that. He remained cautious and moved slowly, stopping altogether when he saw the blood trail tapering out of sight behind the curved swell of a large boulder.

He turned and used his free hand to motion his father forward. When the older McClure did so, Billy silently pointed at the blood trail and where it went. Squire nodded.

The two of them pressed as tightly as they could against the side of the boulder and quietly slid forward till they reached the place where it curved away out of their line of sight. They moved away from the boulder, standing shoulder to shoulder.

"Now!" Squire snapped.

In unison, the two outlaws leaped around the swell of the boulder, pistols cocked and raised, expecting to be greeted by gunfire.

But there was none. Mankiller had stopped here, of that they were sure; they could see yet another, larger puddle where the blood dripping from him had formed another pool.

It seemed he'd only paused to catch his breath then, before taking off again. The droplets of blood that led away from the puddle now took a northward slant, heading back in the direction of the canyon floor.

The trail led them to a small ridge. In addition to the blood, they could see impressions in the dirt made by Mankiller: hands, feet and knees as he had struggled to climb upward. The two men following him did not have nearly so much trouble.

Thinking alike, each dropped down on hands and knees before their heads could top the ridge and present themselves as easy targets. They cautiously peered over the ridge; assured themselves the drifter was not lying in wait for them, then rose to their feet at the top of the ridge.

That's when a second explosion, stronger than the first, rocked the lonely canyon.

Before their very eyes, the McClures saw their barn lift upward and then burst outward at the seams like a smashed melon. A massive ball of flame erupted as the explosion sent the walls and roof of the barn flying in a hundred different directions.

"Mankiller!" Squire McClure snarled.

CHAPTER 26

Little of the McClure barn remained standing. An oily, dark, billowing cloud still squatted above the ruins. Small fires burned around the blast crater. Scorched planks of varying sizes littered the floor of the canyon for a hundred feet in every direction. A few were still floating lazily down from the sky.

"He must'a set off every stick o' dynamite we had left in there!" Billy exclaimed.

"A lot o' good that'll do 'im," Squire said grimly. "If we move now, we'll be between him and the only sure way outta this canyon.

"If he wants to leave…he'll have ta walk over us!"

Leading the way, Squire McClure descended to the floor of the canyon. Staying close to its wall, he moved westward, averting his eyes as they passed the still form of his dead son Micah.

Billy wished he'd done the same. His stomach knotted at the sight of his older brother's bloody corpse.

"I figure Mankiller's prob'ly took cover in the cabin," Squire said at last. "Let's take a little closer look. But not too close."

Billy nodded. He moved up abreast of his father, though keeping a few feet of distance between them as they slowly walked toward the cabin. When they were still a good two hundred yards away from it, Squire stopped. As always, Billy followed his lead.

The older McClure couldn't admit to his son that this was about as far as his thinking had taken him. It would be just as impossible for the two of them to successfully storm the stout cabin as it would have been for Mankiller to have done so earlier.

The need for any inventive strategy on McClure's part dissipated when the door of the cabin opened and the target of the old man's fury calmly walked out to stand on the edge of the front porch.

Even with aging eyes and from a distance, Squire could see the drifter was in a bad way. His shirt was shredded and his left arm hung uselessly at his side. It appeared that blood was still dripping off the fingertips of his left hand.

But his right arm seemed fine, and in its hand was firmly gripped a Colt pistol.

"You're a hard man ta kill, trail trash," Squire called out to him.

"Can you say the same?" Mankiller replied.

"How'd you get away from my boy, Tyrone?" There was no tactic behind

Squire's verbal engagement. He just wanted some answers to the mystery of this cold killer.

"I didn't have to get away from him," Mankiller said. "He didn't have the guts to come after me himself, so he hired others to do the job for him.

"They weren't good enough either."

Squire shook his head. "That boy always was lazy."

"Pa...look!" Billy whispered harshly.

The sound of breaking glass came faintly from somewhere behind where Mankiller stood. From one of the cabin's side windows, tentacles of smoke swirled.

"He's set the place on fire!" Billy exclaimed, starting to move forward. His father reached out and grabbed him by the arm.

"Forget it, boy. If he's stupid enough to burn down his only cover, let 'im. Then he'll *have* ta come ta us!"

For perhaps the first time in his young life, Billy McClure cast an angry look of defiance at his father. He'd always been the good son, the obedient son; trying in all ways to earn a fraction of the affection the old man seemed willing only to lavish on Micah, his firstborn.

But here stood the man who had virtually destroyed Billy's entire family single-handedly, who was now burning the closest thing he'd known to a home since the death of his mother. He had to pay!

But in the end, as always, Billy obeyed the old man.

Flames were beginning to appear at the edges of the cabin roof as Mankiller slowly, almost nonchalantly descended the steps leading off the front porch and began to walk toward the two outlaws.

When he had covered about half the distance separating them, he came to a halt. Without speaking a word, he sent them a message.

"Is he *smiling*?" Billy gasped.

Both McClures jumped as yet a third explosion rolled the floor of the canyon. Behind Mankiller, the cabin was propelled up off its foundation. Obviously, he had not used all the remaining dynamite when he had blown up the barn.

"Damn you!" Billy McClure screamed. A red fog enveloped him, invaded him and drove out all reason, and he rushed forward.

"No!" his father commanded, knowing even as he shouted that he would be disobeyed.

Mankiller stood unperturbed as the young outlaw raced toward him, yelling incoherently. As he came on, Billy began to fire wildly at the target of all his anger, all his hatred.

So far away was he, though, that he hit nothing but dirt. So unconcerned was Mankiller that he had not even bothered to raise his own gun yet, and that enraged Billy even further.

When at last one of Billy's slugs hit close enough to spray dirt over his boots, Jason made his move.

Assuming his usual sideways stance, Mankiller raised his pistol straight out before him. He calmly sighted down the barrel and fired.

Billy staggered; his rush forward brought to a jarring halt as the slug hit him high on the right side, passing clear through. His arm couldn't or wouldn't obey his mental demand that it lift and fire off another shot of his own.

He glared down at the appendage that was refusing him. He still had one live round in the chamber, he knew; he had not given in so completely to the red rage that he had not kept count of his shots. And one bullet, if it was the right bullet, was all it took.

But the arm wouldn't move, and Billy swung his gaze away from it. He blinked: as if through a cloudy haze he could see Mankiller slowly walking toward him.

Some distance behind Billy, the patriarch of the McClure clan took a step forward, stopped. His left fist clenched and unclenched. The boy, he knew, was now beyond help.

Without breaking stride, Mankiller fired a second shot.

The .44 caliber slug drilled into Billy McClure's chest before tearing out a piece of his heart.

The outlaw kept his feet for a few seconds, swaying like a willow in a stiff breeze. Then his knees buckled and he collapsed in a heap.

Impotent rage burning within him like a fire that threatened to consume his black soul, Squire McClure watched as the man he hated above all others stood over the fallen body of his final son.

As he looked on helplessly, Mankiller took the time to eject the two shells he had expended on the outlaw's son, replacing them with fresh shells plucked from his gunbelt.

Framing the figure of this heartless killer of men were the tongues of fire rising from the ruins of the demolished cabin behind him.

With his gun hand back down at his side, Jason stepped over the corpse at his feet and resumed slowly walking toward Squire McClure.

In the instant, an emotion the old man had never really felt before clutched at his heart.

Fear.

Even before the events of the past few weeks, McClure had on occasion heard stories about this man who was said to cry blood. He'd never paid much mind to them.

Most had been told in saloons, by men too drunk, too crazy or two lost among the dregs to be considered reliable sources.

Some of the stories were so fantastical as to be obviously nothing but tall tales. Some had bordered on being downright supernatural.

But now…now a small but growing part of him wondered if somehow, incredible as it may seem, all those stories had been true; wondered if this man coldly stalking him was unstoppable.

McClure licked his lips nervously; cast his eyes back and forth rapidly in search of an escape route that did not exist.

Though it shamed him to his core, he found himself wanting to simply drop his gun in the dust and beg for mercy. Beg for his life.

By now, though, the advancing gunman was close enough for his face to be clearly discerned and the old man could see there was no mercy to be found in those pale blue eyes.

"*Aaaaa!*" McClure screamed, whipping up his gun and firing.

Mankiller felt a burning sizzle along his left side, but merely used this as the impetus to spin sideways and fire off a round of his own.

McClure doubled over as if he'd been kicked in the stomach as the bullet ripped through his abdomen. Releasing his gun as if it was burning his fingers, he clutched the belly wound with both hands as he dropped to the ground in a sitting position.

The outlaw stared down in shock at the sight of his own innards trying to escape from between his fingers.

A shadow fell over him, and he looked up to see his killer standing above him.

"Looks like it's finished, Mankiller," he gasped through gritted teeth. "You done killed me and all my boys."

"Yeah," Jason said in a voice tinged with weariness, showing no sense of triumph.

"And, McClure, the saddest part of it is…this all started over a *sandwich*."

"What?" The older McClure squinted up at him in puzzlement, not knowing what he meant.

"Just something for you to think about for the rest of eternity, old man," Jason replied.

His right hand rose in a blur and he triggered a final shot that plowed into the middle of the outlaw's forehead, slapping him backwards to the ground.

Squire McClure died as he had lived: violently. And his whole family with him. In the end, so small a man was he that the only reason he'd be remembered at all was for his role in setting into motion the actions that launched what would become the bloody legend of Jason Mankiller.

At the moment, the drifter himself could not have foreseen what was to come. He could barely see at all, so drained of blood was he by the myriad holes in his hide.

He fell to his knees beside the body of Squire McClure, then pitched over sideways.

CHAPTER 27

Marshal Russell stood on the sidewalk outside his office in Ft. Rogers, gazing up and down the street.

The clomping sound of footsteps on the wood planks of the sidewalk caused him to turn. Sam Dobbins, owner and proprietor of the Last Stand saloon, was trotting his way.

"Newt said you wanted to see me, marshal," the bartender said, slightly breathless from even this mild exertion.

"Yeah, Sam, I did. I was just curious, really. Wonderin' if you've had any word of Jason Mankiller."

"Not a one. What made you think I might've?"

"Well, you seem to have gotten mighty tight with the killer, Sam. Taken a real shine to him."

"He's someone I'd ride the river with," Dobbins said tersely. He scrutinized the lawman's face in profile. Every crease, every deep and dark wrinkle had come the hard way.

"I think we both know there was a time when you'd have said the same thing about him, Clay."

The marshal scowled. "Maybe. But that day's gone." He exhaled. "So you've heard nothin'?"

"Nary a word."

"Maybe we never will," Russell replied. "Despite all the stories about 'im, he's still just a human man. If he's come up against the McClures, like as not he's layin' out there somewhere dead."

"I don't want to believe that, marshal."

"I know you don't, Sam. I don't either. Not really."

The bartender's eyes had been drawn to movement down the street, and he was now only half listening to Russell.

"But let's be honest," the marshal continued. "You'd need a small army ta take down a bunch like Squire McClure and his boys."

"Then just start callin' Jason a one-man army, Clay!" Sam declared, grinning broadly.

Marshal Russell gave the bartender a curious glance, saw that Sam was looking beyond him, and turned to see what had grabbed his attention.

People had begun to gather on the sidewalks along either side of the street, some even leaving their businesses unattended. Russell saw the barber he patronized among them; standing next to him was a customer with a barber cloth still tied around his neck, his face half shaved.

So many hushed tones were being whispered at once that it created a droning sound like that coming from an active beehive.

Russell noted the onlookers were on the move, too: heading in his direction. They seemed to be pulled in the wake of a lone horseback rider who was slowly making his way toward the jail.

Marshal Russell suppressed a smile as he recognized the rider as being Jason Mankiller.

All mirth left the veteran lawman's weathered face, though, and his eyes narrowed as he looked past Mankiller.

In his right hand, the drifter was holding the lead rein to a string of seven horses plodding along behind him. Lying belly down over the backs of the seven horses were the bodies of seven dead men.

From out of the pack of onlookers, Russell's deputy, Newt Carpenter, broke loose and came running up to his boss.

"It's the McClures, Marshal!" he proclaimed loudly. "Mankiller's brought in ever last one of 'em...and a few extra ta boot!"

Mankiller seemed oblivious to the stir he was causing. All he was thinking about was reaching the end of a long road.

He'd spent the rest of the day after his battle with the McClures inside the bowl of the box canyon. After painfully crawling to the creek that ran into it and bathing his many wounds as best he could, he had begun extracting by hand slivers of stone from his own flesh.

Some had penetrated too deeply for his fingers to reach. He had considered trying to pluck them out with his skinning knife, but thought better of it. Instead, he'd used the knife to cut strips from a saddle blanket and bandaged his torn torso and arm as best he could.

Given the extent of his injuries, it had taken him another half a day to load all the bodies onto the horses and tie them into place.

Since then, he'd ridden almost nonstop: sleeping in brief snatches and stopping more often for the sake of the horses than for himself.

As he reined to a stop now in front of the jail, neither he nor Marshal Russell spoke. But the lawman examined this enigma before him with close scrutiny.

Mankiller's face was drawn, his eyes a bit sunken; the resulting shadows made those pale blue orbs seem to blaze even more fiercely than usual. His shirt was in tatters and heavily stained with dried blood. Ragged strands of horse blanket could be seen around his chest and left arm, similarly stained. It was clear he was badly injured.

But he sat ramrod straight in the saddle as he grimly nodded at the marshal. Russell returned the gesture; in such a way did men of their kind communicate.

"Would you mind, deputy?" Mankiller said, holding out the lead rein of the horses trailed out behind him.

Deputy Carpenter looked to his boss, and Russell nodded.

"Take 'em down to the undertaker, Newt," he said. "And best be quick about it; they're gettin' a little ripe."

The lawman then returned his attention to Jason.

"What happened out there, Mankiller?" he asked.

"I'll give you a full accounting, marshal...later."

Jason then turned his horse away, motioning with a jerk of his head for Sam Dobbins to follow him. The bartender hopped off the sidewalk, taking hold of the bridle of the drifter's horse and walking alongside it.

"Those seven horses I brought back," Jason said. "I don't think anyone will argue that they belong to me now."

"Sure enough."

"I'm giving 'em to you, Sam."

"Huh? What for?"

"They're all good, sturdy animals. They'll fetch a decent price, especially if you play up who they originally belonged to." He gave Dobbins a brief, knowing smile.

"You can use the money to fix up the damage that was done to your place, and to you."

"You gotta be joshin' me, Jason," Sam said in amazement. "A broke mirror and a couple o' busted chairs don't cost near what that amount of horseflesh will bring!"

"Then just consider the rest to be interest on a debt, y'hear? Or recompense for your trouble." He leaned down closer to the saloon owner.

"And you might wanna let it be known: Any other ranny tries to take the wood to you or your place he'll answer to me."

"So you've heard nothing?"

"You can be sure I'll spread the word."

"You do that." Mankiller looked around to make sure no one else was within earshot.

"Refresh my memory, Sam. You got any doctors in this town?"

"Hell, we got us two or three of 'em, Jason."

"Any of 'em any good?"

"Good enough, I reckon."

Mankiller grunted. "Well, as you can prob'ly see, I got myself a mite buggered up." Only now did he allow his body to sag in the saddle.

"So if you could get me to one of 'em...I'd be much obliged."

CHAPTER 28

Bank clerk Byron Longfellow looked up to see Jason Mankiller walking toward him. Smiling, he jumped up to greet First Cattlemen's most famous client.

"You're looking well, sir," he said as they shook hands.

This was the first time Mankiller had been in the bank since his return to Ft. Rogers a few weeks ago.

It was not, however, the first time young Longfellow had conducted business with him. When the bank draft representing the reward money for the members of the McClure gang had arrived, Marshal Russell had brought it to the bank.

Longfellow had insisted on taking it to Mankiller in person. He hadn't wanted to presume on the drifter, but had wanted to check in on his convalescence; this gave him the excuse to do so. Mankiller was recuperating in a room provided him by Sam Dobbins, over the main floor of the Last Stand saloon.

By this time, it had been over a week since Mankiller had ridden into Ft. Rogers with his cargo of corpses. It was still the talk of the town, though. And while the drifter was no longer in danger of dying from his wounds, he was clearly far from well. Longfellow had visibly cringed at the sight of him in such a weakened state.

Mankiller had shrugged his concerns off, as was his way. He claimed he was only pretending to be an invalid. Said he was enjoying having his meals served to him in bed and being spoiled by the gentle ministrations of the soiled doves who seemed to be constantly hovering over his bedside.

Longfellow had offered to personally deposit in Mankiller's account the considerable amount of money represented by the bank draft, so as to keep if safe until such time as he needed or wanted it, if Jason would sign it over to him. Mankiller did so without hesitation, even though the multiple rewards tallied up to a rather princely and tempting sum of money.

Longfellow excused himself and left, returning promptly with the paperwork proving the total sum had been deposited in Mankiller's name. Jason nodded, convinced his assessment of the clerk's character had been correct from the very beginning.

That had been nearly three weeks ago. Now, looking the man up and down, Longfellow could see a world of difference. Mankiller's frame and countenance had filled out. His stride was sure, his handshake strong.

"It's good to see you back on your feet," Longfellow said sincerely.

"It's good to be there, Byron. Though I have to admit, them lovely ladies that work over to Sam's place sure made it pleasurable to be off 'em."

The clerk chuckled and nodded, turning and offering Mankiller a chair before taking one for himself. The drifter looked around a bit, patting the padded arms of his chair.

"Looks like you've done well for yourself, Byron," he observed. "You got a larger desk, nicer chairs and a better location in here than you had the first time we met."

Longfellow chuckled again. "I suspect I have you to thank for that."

"How do you figure?"

"I don't know what you said to my supervisor on your way out that day, but it wasn't long thereafter that I received a promotion. And a small but welcome raise in pay to go with it.

"It's even raised my standing in the community. A daughter of one of the bank officers has agreed to let me escort her to an ice cream social at the church next Sunday evening."

It seemed to the drifter that he was working wonders on *other* fellas' love lives. But all he did was shrug.

"I had nothing to do with any of that," he insisted.

"Of course not." Longfellow leaned forward, folding his hands on the desktop. "So what can I do for you today, Mr. Mankiller?"

"You can start by calling me Jason."

"Fair enough. How can I help you, Jason?"

"I guess it was no big secret that I was in a pretty bad way when I brought the McClures in. Besides the obvious, I'd spent a lot of time not sleeping or eating enough for a growed man before finally settling affairs with them no-goods.

"But I'm fully recovered now, and it's just pure laziness that's kept me laying about and taking advantage of the free room and board Sam's been giving me."

Longfellow said nothing, though he knew good and well that the Last Stand's owner had not suffered any real financial hardship from his undoubtedly genuine good-heartedness where Jason was concerned.

Having the increasingly famous man hunter under his roof had continued to result in increased business for his saloon. In addition, the enterprising saloonkeeper had managed to purchase one hundred copies of Leslie Bellows' renowned photograph of Mankiller and General Custer together on that final day at Gettysburg. Jason had graciously agreed to sign each and every one of them.

Dobbins was doing a brisk business selling the autographed pictures for two dollars apiece.

"Now that I'm fit," Mankiller continued, "I'm getting a little restless and ready to move on. I reckon I'll be riding outta here in a day or two."

"Ah," Longfellow said. "So, are you wanting to withdraw your money, then?"

"No. Not most of it, anyway."

"All right."

"You know better than most just how much I got in this bank, Byron. Every one of them McClures and the three that rode with 'em was worth a lot more dead than they ever was alive."

"Amen to that, brother."

"I like the idea of letting the bulk of my money stay right here where it's good and safe, and let it continue to grow."

He paused, gathered his thoughts.

"But I do have one concern; it came to me while I was laid up. Tell me true, now, Byron. What would happen to all that money if I was to up and die?"

"You're right to be concerned," Longfellow replied, taking the question as seriously as he knew it was intended. "You've told me you have no blood kin that you know of. So as things stand now, if that was to happen, all that money would simply remain untouched and unclaimed."

"Is there any way to prevent that from happening?"

"One way for sure."

"Are we talking about a will now?"

"Yes. You get one of those drafted and properly filed, and upon your death, and let's hope that's many, many years from now, all your assets will be dispersed in exactly the way you yourself want them to be."

Mankiller exhaled slowly.

"To be honest, I never really figured this would be something I had to think about. Most of the jobs I've held down didn't pay more than twenty dollars a month. All you had to worry about was making it last till the next payday." He leaned in closer toward the clerk.

"Is this something you can help me with, Byron?"

"Not directly, but I'll be glad to help you out in any way I can. I'm friends with a local attorney-at-law who's very good with that sort of thing. Very trustworthy.

"I can set up a meeting for the three of us right here in the bank if you'd like."

"I think I would, Byron."

That settled, Mankiller then made out a withdrawal slip in the amount of three hundred and fifty dollars. When Longfellow returned to his desk, Jason counted it out carefully.

Most of it went into his pocket. He'd kept a hundred dollars out, though, and now slid it across the desk toward Longfellow.

"What's this?" the clerk asked.

"Just a little something for your trouble."

"No," Longfellow said firmly, pushing the money away. "I can't take money from you for just doing what the bank already pays me to do. It's my job."

"And you do it right well, old son. But I'm asking you to be more than just my banker. I'm counting on you personal to make sure my business affairs are always kept in order. We can put that in writing, too, if you want.

"Think of it as a retainer," he said, again pushing the money toward the clerk. "I'd consider it a favor if you took it, Byron. Add it to your own savings." The corners of his mouth turned up slightly.

"Who knows? If that ice cream social turns out well, you might end up with an extra mouth to feed."

Longfellow looked at him intently. The smile on the drifter's lips was offset by the steely resolve in his eyes. The clerk knew he'd lost this battle. His hand closed over the small stack of bills.

"Are you sure you've left yourself enough for your own immediate needs?"

"More'n enough. This much money oughtta last me at least six months, long as I don't get too profligate with it."

He pushed his chair back and stood.

"You just send word to me at the Last Stand when you get that meeting with the lawyer fella set up."

"I'll do it, Jason," Longfellow said as he stood and extended his right hand. Mankiller gripped it tightly and pumped it.

As he turned to leave, he noticed the fat banker he'd spoken to the first time he'd done business here was staring at him nervously.

Mankiller gave him a tip of the hat before walking out of the bank.

CHAPTER 29

Marshal Russell was a bit surprised a few days later when the door to the jail opened and Jason Mankiller walked in.

"Let me guess," the lawman said gruffly. "You done killed someone again?"

"No one today, marshal," Jason replied dryly.

"What brings ya ta honor us with your presence, then?" Russell asked, casting a glance to one side to look at his deputy Newt Carpenter, who'd just come into the office after sweeping out the jail cells.

"I know the state don't owe ya any more money."

"Not so far," Jason agreed. "I'm on my way outta town."

Russell smiled. "Well, now, that's about the best news I've hear in a month o' Sundays.

"You didn't have ta come tell me that in person, though. The way this town likes ta gossip, I'd have got word of your going before you'd left the city limits."

Mankiller nodded. "I just had one little favor to ask before I go."

"What kinda favor?" The lawman felt the muscles in his neck tighten.

Mankiller pointed at the stack of papers sitting atop Russell's desk.

"I was wondering if I could take another look through your wanted posters."

"Is that all?"

"That's all."

"Why not? Help yourself."

Mankiller pulled a chair up alongside the marshal's desk and spent the next hour poring over each and every poster. Occasionally he would set one aside, forming a second, shorter stack.

When he was seemingly finished, he looked at Russell, who had been pretending to be engrossed in paperwork of his own, and tapped on the stack of posters he had selected.

"Would it be allowed for me to keep these, marshal?"

"I don't see why not. You're welcome to 'em."

"Thanks." Mankiller picked up the posters he wanted, straightened and folded them in half before standing.

"I take it this means you're plannin' ta take up bounty hunting full time," Russell observed.

Jason shrugged. "As somebody once told me, it seems to be what I'm good at."

"Isn't that damned tattoo o' yours target enough, boy? Now, besides disgruntled Johnny Rebs who still want to re-fight the war and young toughs who think you're their quick ticket ta glory…you'll have every misfit, malcontent and cold-blooded killer west of the Mississippi lookin' ta put you under."

"They're welcome to try." Mankiller's voice was so icy it almost caused the veteran lawman to shudder.

"One more thing," Russell said, just as Jason was about to open the door on his way out of the jail.

"I wasn't tryin' ta be nosey or nothin', but I couldn't help noticing that the only flyers you're takin' with ya are the ones for fellas who are wanted alive or *dead*."

Mankiller fixed him with a cool stare.

"I'm sure I don't have to tell a lawman like you how many things can go wrong while you're trying to bring a prisoner back alive."

An almost sad look clouded Russell's craggy features.

"There's plenty can go wrong tryin' ta bring him back dead, too, son."

"That's true enough, Marshal."

The small room fell silent. There being nothing more to be said by either man, Jason simply nodded farewell and exited from the office.

CHAPTER 30

Mankiller strode to where his horse was hitched, preparing to mount, when he heard whispered voices coming from behind him.

He snapped around fast enough to see a pair of small heads quickly pulling back out of sight around the corner of the marshal's office.

A smile tugged at the corners of his mouth. In the time he'd been here in Ft. Rogers, he'd come to realize what an apparent object of fascination he was to children.

"Can I help you boys?"

He could hear a whispered argument, then one of the boys shoved the other out into the open. A cotton-headed little fella, he stared awkwardly at Mankiller, looking like he was about to wet his britches.

"It's all right," Jason said in soothing tones. "I won't hurt you. Or your buddy, either."

The exposed boy looked angrily at his unseen cohort, motioning him out of hiding. Finally, tentatively, the second lad also stepped out into view. He was a redhead, with the freckles to prove it.

Each boy was barefoot and shirtless, dressed only in a pair of patched overalls. They appeared to be about nine or ten years old.

"What can I do for you, men?" Jason prompted.

Using an elbow, the redhead nudged his pal forward. As the little blond boy nervously edged toward Mankiller, he extended a magazine gripped in one hand.

"Is this you, Mr. Mankiller?"

Curious, Jason reached out and took the tabloid from the boy's hand, which was promptly withdrawn. To the drifter's surprise, a familiar named leaped out at him from the cover of what he now saw to be a dime novel.

The Life and Bloody Times Of
Jason Mankiller
Texas Terror
-or-
Cowboy Cavalier

Dominating the front cover of the magazine was a lurid, brightly colored illustration of a man who more closely resembled Wild Bill Hickok than Jason: flowing hair, clothed in an Easterner's garish idea of a cowboy's garb. Only the red teardrop visible on the character's left cheek was accurate.

The dashing figure was blazing away with a pistol in each hand. Two men facing him were reeling from the impact of the flying lead, while two others were already sprawled out dead on the floor.

At the bottom of the cover of this literary gem, in bold letters, was printed the name of the book's author.

Jay Starr.

The two little bare-footed boys didn't know what to think when they saw a broad smile crease the lips of the stone cold killer they had dared to face unarmed, heard him chuckle out loud.

"So?" the redhead asked impatiently. "Is that you?"

"I reckon it's supposed to be, boy," Jason said, reaching out to hand the dime novel back to the blond youngster. Instead of taking it, though, the cotton-head held a pencil out to him.

"Would you sign it for me, Mr. Mankiller?" he asked with quivering voice.

"What for?"

The boy was obviously puzzled by the very question. "Why, 'cause yer famous, that's why. I never met no one famous before."

"'Sides," the redhead added, "We'll be the only kids who got one. They'll be envious fer sure."

"Sounds like good reasons to me," Jason allowed.

He accepted the stubby pencil, noticing the boy didn't snatch his hand back quite so quickly this time. He started to sign his name on the cover of the book, then stopped.

"I got a better idea," he said.

On one wall of the jail, just to the side of the doorway, was nailed up a cork board that served as a sort of community message center. Mankiller walked over to it, spotted a notice about a barn raising; the date on it had already come and gone.

He took down the sheet, folded it in half sharply, then tore it down the crease so it was now in two equal halves.

"What are you boys' names?" he asked.

They looked nervously at each other. It was again the redhead who spoke up.

"I'm Ethan," he said, then hooked a thumb toward his pal. "This here's Mark."

Mankiller turned the half sheets of paper over to their blank sides and, using the dime novel as a writing surface, scratched out a brief note and handed the first one to the blond. It read:

"To my friend, Mark. (Signed) Jason Mankiller."

He gave the other sheet, bearing the same message, to Ethan. The awestruck boys stared at the sheets of paper as if they had been hundred dollar bills.

"How's that, instead?" Jason said. "You each get one of them. *Plus...*"

He fished inside a shirt pocket and retrieved a silver dollar. He held the coin up for them to see. It shone dully in the sunlight.

"Plus, I give you this dollar...if you let me keep the book. What do ya say?"

Mark hesitated, as if suspicious that there might be some sort of catch behind this offer. Ethan again elbowed him in the ribs, then cupped a hand over Mark's ear and began to whisper earnestly to him.

As is common with the very young and the very old, his "whisper" carried far enough for Mankiller to clearly hear. He stifled a smile, kept a blank look on his face as he heard the eminently practical redhead remind his partner of just how much they could buy with a whole dollar, including a replacement copy of the dime novel if they so chose.

Mark stepped forward, spit in the palm of his right hand and extended it toward Jason. The drifter did likewise, then took the boy's hand.

The deal was struck.

As the two boys took off running, probably heading straight for the candy counter of the nearest dry goods store, Jason again examined the book, flipping gently through its pages as he headed back to his mount.

"Good for you, Jane," he said softly, carefully slipping this already prized possession into one of his saddlebags.

He had no doubt it was going to make for fascinating reading.

CHAPTER 31

Mounting the dun, Mankiller turned its head to the west and set off down the street.

He hadn't gone far when yet another boy came running toward him. He reined in the horse, recognizing this youngster. It was the newsboy who had sold him a paper the first week he was in Ft. Rogers. And in every week of his recent convalescent stay.

"Newspaper 'fore ya leave town, mister?" the boy asked. "Hot off the presses."

"Sure." As always, Jason flipped the newsie a nickel for his paper and for himself. He turned in the saddle to slip the paper into his bags for later consumption on the trail. When he looked back, the boy had already turned in his tracks and was running off to sell more papers.

"Hey!" Jason called after him. The boy slid to a halt and took a few steps back toward the drifter.

"You got a name, boy?"

"'Course I do," the lad said suspiciously. The two of them then stared silently at each other, till Jason let out an impatient sigh.

"You mind tellin' me what it is?"

"Toby."

"Toby, you got any family? Ma and pa?"

"Got me a ma. No pa. He went and got hisself kilt."

"That's too bad. Brothers, sisters?"

"No brothers. Two sisters."

"Hmm." Jason looked down, then back up. "Come here."

"How come?"

"'Cause I told ya to, that's why."

The boy did as he was ordered, though it was obvious he was prepared to take off at the slightest sign of trouble.

Mankiller reached into a pants pocket and withdrew some coins. He extracted four and shoved the rest back into the pocket. He held his hand out toward the boy.

"Here," he said. "This is for you."

Still suspicious, the newsboy stood as far away from the gunman as he could while reaching out with his left hand, palm up.

Jason dropped four large coins into it.

"That there's four dollars," he said. "One for every member of your family."

Toby scowled and shook his head.

"Don't want it."

"Huh? Why not?"

"'Cause I ain't no beggar, mister. I don't take charity; I work for a livin'."

"So do I," Jason said. He admired the boy's stubborn pride, perhaps because he shared it.

"But that ain't charity, Toby. I expect something in return."

"Like what?"

"Well, I'll tell ya what. I plan on coming back to Ft. Rogers from time to time. Can't say for sure when.

"But whenever I do, I'll expect you to bring me every edition of the *Diligence*, soon as it comes out."

"I'd do that anyway," Toby insisted. "Sellin' papers what I do."

"I'm sure you would, boy. Sure. But that money's to guarantee I get it quick. This is what you call a gentlemen's agreement, between two men."

The truth was that, in actual years, Toby was probably no older than the two other boys he'd just sent on their way. But in life years, he knew the lad was much older. In his mind, and in reality, he was the man of his house.

As for now, the boy's resistance to Jason's gesture was clearly weakening.

"When I bring you yer paper...will I still get my nickel?"

"Absolutely!"

The child stared longingly at the coins in his hand. In his hardscrabble life, they represented a veritable fortune. His eyes rolled up to look at Jason.

"You say this is the kinda deal *men* make with each other?"

"I wouldn't do it with no child, Toby. That's a fact."

Toby shoved the money into the pocket of his threadbare but clean trousers, turned without another word and ran away. Reaching the nearest sidewalk, though, he swiveled and looked back.

"Thanks!" he shouted.

Mankiller gave him a wave, then urged his horse forward with a light tap of the spurs.

He'd already said his good-byes to Byron Longfellow and Sam Dobbins, but there was yet one other person he wanted to see before going on his way.

One of his final chores in preparing to leave had been to have his clothes washed. He still didn't have many, but his recent windfall of cash had enabled him to buy a second pair of pants, fresh socks and a couple of extra shirts.

For this job, he had enlisted the services of the old Mexican laundress he'd helped and been helped by on his first day in Ft. Rogers. He still didn't know her name; for some reason, it didn't seem important to either of them that he did.

When he'd picked up his clothes from her yesterday, he'd mentioned when he planned to be leaving town, and she'd asked that he stop by the open-air laundry on his way.

As he approached the locale now, he could see the little woman waiting expectantly. She was holding a small pail in her hands.

When Mankiller reined in his horse, she stepped up to him and held up the pail, which he took.

"For you," she said. "To take on the road. Tamales. I made them myself."

He slipped the handle of the pail (its surface still warm, he noted) around the horn of his saddle.

"I look forward to tasting them," he said honestly.

He leaned down from the saddle and threw his right arm around her narrow shoulders, even as she embraced him, hugging him tightly. They kissed each other on the cheek.

"Pray for me, mother," he whispered in her ear.

"Every day," she promised.

As he straightened, he squeezed her left hand. He gave her a warm smile, which she returned.

Then his gaze turned back to the west. He tapped his horse's flanks a little harder this time, and set off at a trot. He would not look back.

After watching his back for a time, the old woman looked down at her left hand, which had been clenched since the man's hand had left it. Warm tears welled up in her ancient eyes.

He'd left fifty dollars in bills nestled in its palm.

Other eyes continued to follow Mankiller as he rode toward the edge of town. In the jail, Deputy Newt Carpenter had been watching the drifter from the front window. He let out a sigh of relief.

"I don't know if that young Mankiller has sense enough to know it or not, marshal," he observed, "but he's a walkin' dead man for sure."

"I 'spect you're right, Newt," Marshal Russell replied sadly. He walked over to stand beside his deputy.

"But you mark my words. By the time he's done…he'll have left a trail of corpses behind him all the way from here to the gates of Hell."

THE END

ABOUT OUR CREATORS

WRITER –

R. A. Jones is a native of Oklahoma (originally Indian Territory) where he still resides. R. A. has been a freelance writer and editor for the past thirty years.

His credits include newspaper and magazine columns, articles and short stories. He has been a movie reviewer and commentator in newspapers and on radio. He assisted actor Gary Lockwood (Star Trek; 2001: A Space Odyssey) in the writing of Lockwood's autobiography, *2001 Memories: An Actor's Odyssey*. With Michael Vance, R. A. co-wrote the syndicated comic book and comic strip review column *Suspended Animation* for five years.

The readers of *Comic Buyer's Guide* magazine voted him "Favorite Writer About Comics" in 1985, and in 2006 he was inducted into the Oklahoma Cartoonists Collection Hall of Fame.

He has scripted more than 100 different issues of various comic book titles in his career. Among the more noteworthy are Wolverine and Captain America for Marvel Comics; *Harlan Ellison's Dream Corridor* for Dark Horse Comics; and Star Trek: Deep Space Nine for Malibu Comics. He also co-wrote, for Image Comics, *Bulletproof Monk*, which served as the basis for the 2003 movie of the same title.

His comic book stories, "Cold Hard Facts" and "Three On A Match" which originally appeared in the magazine *Metal Hurlant*, were short films in France.

His novels include *Deathwalker*, *Global Star* (written with Michael Vance and Mel Fox), *The Equation* (co-written with Michael Vance), *The Steel Ring*, a superhero book based on characters from one of the earliest publishers of comic books, Centaur.

ARTIST –

Neil T. Foster studied art at Bolton Art College in England before moving to Australia in 1980. Neil contributed interior art and painted covers for the underground comic *Captain Koala* as well as various CD and video game covers before bringing *Planet of the Apes* back into comic form for fans with the web published *Beware the Beast*. Neil has provided illustrations and covers for various horror and fantasy magazines including 10 years worth of pictures for sci-fi/fantasy magazine *Tales of the Talisman*. He currently lives in sunny Queensland.

COVER ARTIST –
Graham Hill is a sometime Comic-book cover artist for small press publishing companies. He recently completed covers for *Bluewater Comics* on their Freddie Mercury (Queen front man), David Bowie and other graphic novels. (Brain May from the band Queen apparently liked the Freddie one...not sure what the "Thin White Duke" thought of his ...) Covers for magazines such as *Simian Scrolls, Ape Chronicles, Blokes Terrible Tomb of Terror*. Graham earned a first class BA (Hons) degree in fine art many years ago when he had more hair. Graham can be found on Facebook where he sometimes goes under the Pseudonym of "Cover Monkey" https://www.facebook.com/CoverMonkeyGrahamHill

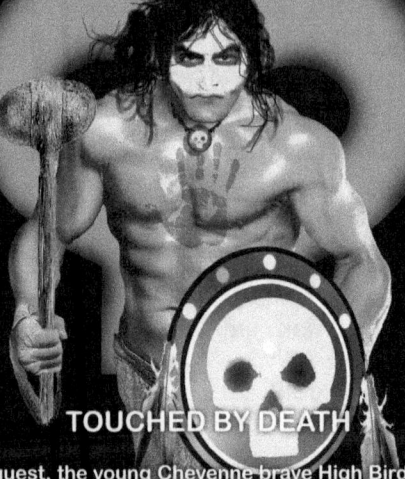

WATSON'S AMERICAN TALE

When Sherlock Holmes, who was presumed dead at the hands of his arch nemesis, Professor Moriarty, returned in the story Dr.Watson chronicles as "The Adventure of the Empty House," we were told how the Great Detective had spent the intervening years abroad in disguise as a secret agent for England. For the devoted Holmes fan, that seemed sufficient to close this chapter of the duo's life and move on to new adventure. But when a heavy locker box arrives at 221 B Baker St. from the United States addressed to Dr. Watson, it is Holmes who finds his curiosity piqued.

What is in the mysterious box? Who sent it and why? Holmes summons his loyal companion who in turn sets about telling Holmes of his own unique adventure abroad during his hiatus. What follows is an amazing mystery involving Watson's lovely wife, Mary, and her family history. The answer to the puzzle rests in the foothills of the Adirondacks of upper New York State and the couple soon set sail for America, Mary hoping the trip will pull her husband's mood from the gloom in which it was mired since the supposed death of Holmes. Once in New York, they encounter the vibrant, colorful civil servant, Teddy Roosevelt, who provides the vital clue that triggers the Watsons' quest.

From the majestic peaks of the Adirondacks to open plains of the wild west, Erwin K. Roberts spins a fantastic, rip-roaring yarn that will have Holmes and Watson fans cheering from the first page to the last.

PULP FICTION FOR A NEW GENERATION

CHECK FOR AVAILABILITY OF THIS AND OTHER FINE READING AT:
AIRSHIP27HANGAR.COM

www.ingramcontent.com/pod-product-compliance
Lightning Source LLC
Chambersburg PA
CBHW071239250626
47163CB00001B/243